Either Side of the Lotus

Side of the Lotus Eith
he Lotus Either Side
Either Side of the Lot

Either Side

he Lotus Either Side
Either Side of the Lot
Side of the Lotus Eith
he Lotus Either Side

of the **Lotus**

by Raymond Belli

iUniverse, Inc.
New York Bloomington

iUniverse books may be ordered through booksellers or by contacting:

iUniverse
1663 Liberty Drive
Bloomington, IN 47403
www.iuniverse.com
1-800-Authors (1-800-288-4677)

ISBN: 978-1-4401-4035-8 (sc)
ISBN: 978-1-4401-4036-5 (dj)
ISBN: 978-1-4401-4037-2 (ebook)

Printed in the United States of America

iUniverse rev. date: 05/05/2009

To my mother, father, and aunt, whose combined efforts to raise a
well-rounded young man have succeeded;
to Paul Green, whose musical (and non-musical) wisdom never
fails to humble me;
to the "real life" Cage Breakers, whose initial influence upon this
novel is immeasurable;
to Max, Paco, Sean, Zach Miller, Zach Goldstein, and Elijah,
whose company has shaped me into a better person;
to Darek Palczek and Andy Lucibello, whose combined efforts
helped catalyze my musical passion at a young age;
to my class peers, especially M.S. and D.R—as of late, you two
manage to keep me sane;
and to Chanel, simply for remaining close to me for so long and
always putting up with my bullshit;

I truly love you all.

"As a lotus flower is born in water, grows in water, and rises out of water to stand above it unsoiled, so I, born in the world, raised in the world having overcome the world, live unsoiled by the world."

—Buddha

"We reached the land of the Lotus-eaters, who live on a food that comes from a kind of flower. Here we landed to take in fresh water, and our crews got their mid-day meal on the shore near the ships. When they had eaten and drunk, I sent two of my company to see what manner of men the people of the place might be, and they had a third man under them. They started at once, and went about among the Lotus-Eaters, who did them no hurt, but gave them to eat of the lotus, which was so delicious that those who ate of it left off caring about home, and did not even want to go back and say what had happened to them, but were for staying and munching lotus with the Lotus-eaters without thinking further of their return ..."

—Homer's The Odyssey

Preface

As the author of this work, I feel the need to give you, the reader, a bit of insight regarding the origin of *Either Side of the Lotus*. Sometime during early 2007, I leisurely began writing two distinctly different stories. One of these followed the curious adventures of a totally whacked-out mental patient at an old-fashioned asylum, and the other dealt with the ups and downs of modern teen life—in a way, *my* life. There was never an intention of publishing (or even finishing) either of them, though one day, I randomly was possessed by the idea of combining the two. I had no steady direction, and this new story lacked a premeditated plotline. I just felt like writing for the hell of it. Both of my former projects were completely scrapped, and this new, untitled, likely-to-be-abandoned prospect was begun. This ambition of mine coincided with the coming of a brief (though tragic) phase of depression. My misery persisted for six or seven months, and most of this novel was scripted during that time. I'd just begun my sophomore year of high school.

The human subconscious is a miraculous thing. Though unbeknownst to me at the time, I was writing an interpretation of my life. My own problems and quirks unintentionally manifested themselves in the likes of the story's protagonist, Sid. His beloved ward and its functions morphed into a satire of my own qualms with life. In some ways, it's hard for me to believe that I actually was brave enough to bring Sid's story to an end, but the novel's completion overlapped with the receding of my depression. During those months, writing this story acted as my last hope, my one purpose, my crutch. With that said, I can't candidly admit to having written this novel alone—guiding every step of the way was undoubtedly a higher power. All of those nights spent awake and heavily caffeinated until two in the morning were not solitary in any way. Some kind of god was with me. Not the *God* sort of god, but the mortal god that lives within all of us, the mortal god that enables us to make a difference to humanity. This is the god that allows one to make something of one's self. Despite its rebellious undertones, the main message of *Either Side of the Lotus* is neither pessimistic nor nihilistic, as any keen reader will observe. *Either Side of the Lotus* is, in fact, a celebration of life.

I'd like to depart on that note, but I'm compelled to add a single bit of advice to this already-too-wordy preface. To all young, distraught, fearful, and emotionally tormented readers out there: just let your freak flag fly.

part 1

Greetings. My name is Sid Tate, and my life is a hell of a good one. Don't believe what anyone may tell you about me and my sucker verve—I live in a mental ward in the middle of nowhere, but I get by just fine. I have all the attention anyone in the world can ask for, and in the end, I guess that's all that really matters.

Before I begin, I suppose I should warn you with regard to my storytelling—don't forget that I am in fact "*crazy*," so my perceptions of reality are (presumably) quite disturbed and sometimes unreal.

I am immersed in a life of love and dedication, in a life where everything is always okay; I know of nothing less than perfection.

*   *   *

The black of sleep slowly wanes away.

Each and every morning, I wake up to the same rickety croak of some distant machinery. I hear these garbled sounds quite regularly, but haven't an idea what any of them might in fact be; sometimes I wish I had enough guts to ask the nurses about this deafening nonsense, but in the end, I just can't. (I think it comes from deep within the surgery wing, though I'm not absolutely sure.) I'm not very much of a risk taker, or anything *at all* for that matter; I do what I'm *told*, and once I'm done with whatever *that* may be, I just wait for *more* people to come and tell me *more* things to do. It's a bit of clockwork, I suppose you might say, but this never really manages to bother me. My memory of a past life is very dim and spacey, so it's kind of like I know no better—it's good like that, I guess. I don't get in anyone's way or take place in nasty sorts of affairs like my friends do. There's Gary, Butch, and of course ol' Paulie … they're just so wild! *Always starting up trouble and all.* It's very well known that I'm the nurses' favorite, and it's easy to see why.

I wouldn't mind being their favorite *forever*.

I love everything about this place; in fact, I don't think I'd ever want to change a *thing*. Because of how dear I am to the people that operate this ward, I'm treated absolutely *wonderfully*. The food's great too—especially breakfast—and as you might have already guessed, the staff is *truly* incredible. They care, see, you must understand that much, that *they care*. That's very important to me, 'cause in case you didn't know, I'm sensitive. *Really* sensitive.

It's been years since I've transferred out of that *other* ward. I don't remember it very clearly. Now that I think about it, it seems like it's getting harder just to remember things in general. Every tomorrow makes every yesterday seem further and further away. Ah, it doesn't really matter—there's not much 'bout my life that needs remembering anyhow. The name's Sid—I know that much—and I'm about fifty years of age. I think I'm from northern Maine or something, but don't take my word for it. I can't tell you anything about my home *firsthand*—all those memories are now far gone. I just know what the doctors and nurses tell me. Recalling my childhood is like imagining a sound or a color or a taste that I've never experienced before. Maybe that's why I'm here in the first place, because of this wretched memory of mine … well, that amongst other things, too.

I know it's quite embarrassing, but I can't read, not even a *little* bit, and that's of course a *huge* problem. I've tried teaching myself many times, but it just doesn't … click. Every time I've ever taken two steps forward, it's always been three back as well. Maybe that's just the way this good-for-nothin' brain of mine works. My actual *vocabulary* has remained intact (and is somewhat literate, if I may say so myself), though I can't begin to imagine why it's like that! Well, I am *crazy*, that's for sure. I've asked Mrs. Hanson—my personal assistant for as long as I've been here—to help me with my learning many times, but her response is always the same. She says there are more pressing things that I need to be worrying about, that there are other parts of my sick and twisted brain that need curing … mm, she's right, she's right. She's *always* right. Other notable quirks of mine are overreacting to nonsensical things (a tendency that quite frequently causes me to black out) and occasional mind-numbing delusions. They talk about the "cure," "getting cured," the "curing *process*" and all *kinds* of things like that, but it seems that nothing ever manages to work on me!

This *really* proves how crazy I am: I've been here for the twofold of eternity, and despite the countless number of tests and examinations I've been through, I'm *still* the way I was when I first came in—or at least I *think* I am. I certainly don't *feel* any differently.

The head surgeon tells me I've improved greatly, but it's difficult for me to fully understand this. I still have much to learn and much to be mended, but really, there's no rush. In fact, it's not *me* that's worried about all this curing nonsense! I'm quite happy the way I am; I could stay like this for the rest of my *life*! I'm insane (there's no doubting that), but like I've already said, I try my best to stay out of everyone's way. I'm not a troublemaker, and that's one of the things that the nurses love about me. *That's* why I'm so special. *That's* why I get all the attention. What has always set me apart from the other patients here is my strict cooperation—oh, how many stories are there to tell of nasty riots and outbreaks here on the ward? Of absolute chaos before "testings"? The others just can't accept their own tragic fates. What I think is that they're just *weak*. Can't take anything like *real* men! They're all in *denial* of the fact that they're crazy—isn't that funniest of all? If we weren't crazy, what would we be doing here in the first place, hmm? Can't everyone else see that Dr. Cohen just wants the best for us all? He truthfully does. I wouldn't lie—*he* wouldn't lie! He is a kind, genuine man!

Ah ... his name alone brings joy to my aging bones; people like the wonderful Dr. Cohen come about every couple hundred years or so. It's thanks to him that this wonderful facility is kept up and running.

Still, I cannot talk *directly* to the great doctor (or anyone else, for that matter) about the things that *really* go through my head. That, too, I suppose, is one of my many problems that needs to be "fixed." I'm *terribly* insecure—doing just about anything is so difficult and traumatizing.

But what am *I* complaining for? With a life like my own, I've got it made!

Things could be worse, *way* worse: just *look* at some of the No-Brainers, as they've come to be known. They're about deeper into the hole of lunacy than I know *I'll* ever be; ol' Frankie the Fish can't even move a couple of feet from his bed without one of the nurses' help, and even when he does, he gets all high-strung and nervous. I hate to say it, but it's actually rather funny! You see, he's about sixty or seventy years old, long-faced and scaly (hence his ever-so-appropriate nickname)—to see his ancient, wobbling legs carry that frail body around as he bawls like a newborn child is something of a hilarious sideshow!

To be honest, Frankie's the only patient I ever got to actually *know.* I said there were Butch, Gary, and Paulie, but I only sit with 'em at lunchtime. That's about it. My bunk is next to Frankie's, so we talk now and then before we go to bed. I know a little about him and he knows a little about me … the little that there is to know, that is.

I'm not so sure why all the docs like to have me secluded and away from everyone else all the time, but that's just the way it's always been. At all costs, they've tried arranging my schedule so I interact as *least* as possible with the other patients; it's because they don't want my mind to get ruined like everyone else's.

Mine is *special.*

So that clanking sound which has inconsiderately woken me comes to a stop. It usually does after a while. I lift up from my bed and look around; seems like I'm the only one awake. I never understood that—don't the others hear it too? The sound is something like a great, metallic knife scraping against the innermost curves of your eardrum!

I glance at the clock beside my bed. The digital face of its stout body tells me that it's still early, seven o'clock, so I wonder now just what in the world I might be doing up at such an hour! My "day" doesn't start until 10:30, so I've still got plenty of time to rest.

In hopes of finding a clue as to where these grinding noises are coming from, I sit up erectly for a moment and peer down a long corridor. As usual, my efforts are met with no avail.

Sigh. There's really no point. I know that I'll never find out anyway—or at least not *yet*. Once I get enough confidence to ask Mrs. Hanson, I *will* ... ah, just the thought of such a thing can wreck me with tears of joy! Soon—when I'm *cured.*

And you know what?

I have a feeling that it's all not so far away. I have a feeling that soon, real, real, *real* soon, I'll be as good as new, ten times better than I've ever been in my entire life. I always try to convince myself that I remain unbothered, but my heart knows otherwise.

Just as I'm ready to fall asleep, as if on cue, the sound kicks in mockingly once again, more obstreperously than before. It ruthlessly gnaws away at my brain—I just *hate* it!

I take my pillows and shove my head beneath them ... *useless.*

I better get cured soon. It's been impossible for me to get any good shuteye lately. Not only does that *clanking-clanking-clanking* keep me from my intentions, but it fuels a primeval curiosity within me that's just so hard to ignore. Sometimes I feel like I go to bed incomplete, as a puzzle that loses one more piece with each new day.

But not anymore, 'cause hell, do I *feel ready.*

Ah ... regardless of what my premeditated thoughts may try to convince me of, I am (and always have been) determined to get *cured*—whatever "getting cured" might in fact mean.

*   *   *

I wake up yet again, this time for real. I stretch a bit, yawn, moan, and once I feel that my body is well and ready to go, I roll over and touch my feet to the ground. The clock reads 10:15, so I still have a few minutes before I must check in at Mrs. Rory's desk. (Mrs. Rory is the head of everything here; my personal assistant, Mrs. Hanson, is the co-executive.)

I see that some of the others have already begun their daily routines. As I'm getting out of bed, I slip my legs into a pair of sweatpants and button up my nightshirt. Frankie the Fish is still sleeping; the older fellas don't have to wake up 'til a bit later (the staff makes sure we all get our appropriate amounts of rest). As usual, the bunk to my left is empty. If I remember correctly, it used to be occupied by another patient some time ago. I think after a few months he was sent off to another ward. We used to talk, though I'm not so sure about what. Ugh, already you must begin to see how frustrating this condition of mine is. Remembering just the *simplest* of things is quite a task, a relentless *heartache!*

I put on my slippers and head over toward the desk. When I arrive, Mrs. Rory is deep into a phone conversation. I can't really hear what she's saying (there's a big sliding-glass window that separates the two of us), but I suspect it's important; she's getting real into it. Her brow is ruffled, and she seems a bit confused—I can't read her. I'm bad at that sort of thing.

After a few minutes, she finishes up and acknowledges my presence. Mrs. Rory slides the window aside, accompanied by a grand smile. Her simple delight always fills me up with a sense of reciprocal happiness. The others think she's "fake," nothing more than a mere puppet of Dr. Cohen's, but I know this can't be true. As I look into her pristine blue eyes, I can feel her sincerity cascade throughout my body.

"Morning, Sid," she says, handing me a clipboard.

"Oh, hello Mrs. Rory!" I take it from her and delightfully sign in. I feel something confident welling up in me. Should I ask her? You know, about those … *sounds?*

Well, I'm contemplating it now, but I suppose the time is not right. She hands over some pills for me to take with a small cup of water. Confusedly, I look at the capsules in my hand. I've never seen this kind before; they're undesirably orangey and obtuse. I never bother to ask what any of the medication I take is prescribed for, but these particular pills, I must say, are perhaps the fishiest looking of any that I've ever been given!

It takes me awhile to decide whether or not I should inquire (and an equal amount of time to muster up the courage to do so), but after astutely staring them down for several moments, I ask: "Mrs. Rory, these are *new* pills, aren't they? Do you have any idea what they're for? What's happened to the old ones?" *Phew.* That took a lot. It feels as if I've just been walloped in the gut by a boxer's raging fist.

She says they're just like the ones I always take, but wafting these curious capsules leads me to believe that she's mistaken. "These are awfully smelly … are you *sure* they're the right ones?"

Mrs. Rory's smile continues to radiate brightly. "Why *of course* I'm sure, Mr. *Tate*," she says, turning away for a moment. Well that's that—there's no reason to argue any further. *Of course* she knows what's best. I ignore my previous judgments and shove these nasty looking pills down my throat with a nice flow of water.

Mrs. Rory is facing the other way, so she doesn't get to see the wretched look upon my face; I swallow hard and quick, as fast as I can to get rid of this excruciating taste. *Yuck!* What on earth are these things *made* of? I wonder whether or not I should bring this to her attention, but the main phone is ringing; when she picks it up, I just forget about the matter. It's not worth the trouble. From behind the sliding-glass window, I can see she's talking again, this time more anxiously than before. *Strange*, real, real strange … it's a rarity that that phone should ever ring at all; its beckoning twice in just minutes is *unthinkable*.

But maybe it's just in my head.

I am *crazy*, you know.

*   *   *

After my few chores for the day are done, I attend a group therapy session. My work schedule is quite lax compared to most of the others' here. I take care of trivial day-to-day sorts of things, but that's about it. My therapy group is small in contrast to most others, as well. There's just me (inevitably), Lil' Jimmy (because he indeed is quite little), and Hank Hank (because just one Hank never seemed right). Other groups consist of ten, eleven, and sometimes even *twelve* members, but mine is made up of only three. We—the *other* two, that is (ha; *I have no pact with inquiry*)—have asked many times why it's like this. All the different therapists we've had always say the same things. *That they know what's best. That there is a reason behind everything.* Lil' Jimmy and Hank Hank argue with them constantly—they always propose that they're treated "differently," unfairly and unjustly. I'm not in favor of their challenging the nurses, though it's hard to disagree with them on this one … I mean, it'd be *nice* to have larger group sessions, don't you think? Ah, but whatever; the matter never manages to bother me to the point of complaint—things always work best for me when my mouth is kept shut.

The "leader" of our session begins talking to us, going on and on about "personality," "individuality," and each of our own "unique identities." I usually listen intently to what they have to say—(I'm the only one that ever does; everyone else is so darn rude!)—but I'm having somewhat of a hard time right now. You see, I'm trying to focus—*I'm trying real hard*—but for some reason, I can't. I'm catching a few sparse words here and there, but it's difficult to remain in the heart of this discussion. Things grow blurry and the ground sways like the waves of a turbulent sea. My stomach begins inching into uneasiness, but I try to retain a hold of things—I feel sick, very, *very* sick.

To my surprise, our leader doesn't really notice; she's too busy talking up a storm with Hank Hank. He's uninterested (if my very fuzzy perceptions are at all correct) and quite discourteous.

"You know, Hank, that—"

"*Hank Hank*," he rapidly corrects her. He does this a lot, especially with the staff; Hank Hank takes it quite personally when you don't include the second of his two names.

He quarrels with her nonstop for a while longer. She's secretly frustrated, I think, but goes on determinedly, *so* determinedly, in fact, that she still fails to realize that I am just about ready to collapse!

"*Hank Hank*, you openly admit your confusion regarding "who you really are." I've taken a look at your past records from other psychiatrists that you've dealt with, and they all seem to indicate the same thing. In the week or so that we've been together, you've asked to come to me in private and discuss the matter, though you mention it constantly in these group meetings as well. I'm terribly sorry that we haven't had time alone, it's just that my schedule is awfully ... *busy*." She chuckles softly to herself. "Would you be opposed to sharing your thoughts openly with your fellow patients? I think now would be just a *fine* time to elaborate on this."

He shivers and looks around anxiously. At a speed just short of inaudibility, he mumbles, "*Yesthatsfine.*"

"Okay ..." She lifts up a clipboard and briefly skims through some notes she's taken. Her finger rides along the top page until she stumbles upon a point of interest. "You said yesterday that you've actually 'ceased to know exactly what—or *who*—is inside of you,' didn't you Hank?"

"*Hank Hank.*"

Cautiously: "Hank Hank. Did you not?"

"Yes ... *yesIdid.*"

"I, surely along with Mr. Tate and Jimmy here, cannot understand *precisely* what you mean; you're being vague and unclear. Can you explain this in more detail to us?"

She speaks sweetly, but her tone does naught for the aches in my head and belly. Lil' Jimmy looks at me and laughs scornfully—*how rude can one possibly be?*

Hank Hank and the shrink delve deeply into a conversation of their own. I tune them out for a while, trying to make comfort with myself in effort to end the kinetic warfare raging within. This goes on for what seems like a very long time before I begin to feel any better—still uneasy (*very uneasy!*), but nonetheless better.

Next, she begins inquiring about Hank Hank's psyche. It's obvious at this point that Lil Jimmy's attention has been completely lost; he's too preoccupied making funny faces and throwing obscene hand gestures in my face.

"… and what of this … 'new heart' you seek, hmm? This 'soul' that you're searching for?"

Hank Hank suffers a muscle spasm and jerks in his seat. "Imnotreallysure," he sputters. "It's just, you know, like … *you know!*"

The leader crosses her legs, folding her delicate hands as she cranes forward. "Oh, but I *don't!*" she says. "It is apparent that you have trouble expressing how you feel, Hank. Am I right?"

Subsequent an irate grumble: "Hank … *Hank!*"

The leader eyes him down patiently for a few moments before continuing on, unfazed.

For the next few minutes, they talk of personal business that doesn't really concern me. What's next to catch my attention, however, is a transplant of sorts that she suggests to him. I shift in my seat to face them directly. This causes a furious whirlwind in my gut; I rattle and shake and quiver all 'round, but it's only for a moment. I'm tempted to open my mouth and tell the shrink about this bizarre condition that's possessed me, but it'd be rude to disrupt her speech. Maybe once we move on to a topic of different nature, I'll ask to be excused. (Ha! What am I saying? I don't have the guts *for that!*)

"I think what you are looking for … is not unity with a mere 'notion', with something immaterial like the *soul*." Reassuringly she nods her head and curls her lips. "Yes, yes … I think you seek, *quite literally*, a new, tangible heart, Hank *Hank*." She stresses the second of his names condescendingly. "You feel so *incomplete* on your own, so *empty* and lost, that the implantation of something new and foreign, I believe, would reinvigorate and help your search for meaning. Is it so far flung to imagine that this new, vital organ introduced to your years-old body would help fill some missing link, this so called 'gap' of which you speak?"

To my disbelief, she's absolutely serious; I eye her peculiarly, wondering what she *possibly* could hope to achieve by this! Lil' Jimmy is laughing, and Hank Hank is shooting off words like a furiously sped-up record player.

"That's, like, ridiculous, that's like … the most ridiculous thing I've ever heard! You must be kidding, this is a joke, it's like, just *gotta* be! You can't *touch* a soul, you know, you can't just *find* it in like a box or something and then try to *shove* it into my body! You can *see* a heart and *feel* a heart and stuff like *that*, and what I'm looking for is the … the … OPPOSITE!" Stumblingly, he comes to an awkward halt. "D-d-don't you *see* what I mean? There's nothing on the face of this whole damned earth that you can put into me that will, like, change the way I feel on the … the *inside!*" He's all riled up and ready to jump out of his seat. Our leader stares him down calmly as she scribbles something down in that clipboard of hers.

Firmly: "No, *Hank Hank*, I think we've finally found the solution to your problem."

Right now, I'm a bit confused—this is absurdity! I mean, the nurses here *do* know what they're doing, but I can't *begin* to imagine how this could ever help poor Hank Hank's dilemma!

"I've been meaning to bring this up since we first were introduced, but just hadn't had the chance." She nods to herself, confidently. "I'm going to schedule the transplant for you sometime next week. We will remove your heart and physically replace it with a brand new one."

I want to open my mouth and say something, but some mighty inner force holds me back. She doesn't go over anything else with him or offer a compromise; she just keeps scribbling and scribbling away!

This gets Hank Hank furious. He roars, begins flailing wildly, and stomps the ground with infuriated heels. The leader watches him bounce around like a raging child until he actually lunges for her. She's knocked mercilessly off her seat, and you see, it's things like *this* that get me real upset; I'm ultra-sensitive around ultra-violence. My sickness wells up again in a sudden burst of nausea.

Oh, I can feel it, I can feel it like a cat or dog feels small fleas scurry amidst its fur; it's under my skin and is quickly spreading, *mmf, mmf, mmf,* all along my spine. I hear the parading of a few security guards coming to cease the havoc, but still no one seems concerned with me! Lil' Jimmy's laughing again, even harder than before—he doesn't know when to stop! (. . . just goes ahead and makes everything worse . . .) Now it feels like I'm falling, face numbed by thousands of needles ruthlessly dug into it. My mouth dries up like a sandy desert and it becomes difficult to breathe. It's in this mindless tornado that I will fall—I'm falling *now,* off the edge of a miles-high cliff!

Here's the drop,

the drop,

the drop!! the drop and the crash!!!

I can hear countless voices bickering indecipherably, but eventually, reality shuts down. All the pulsating pains have stopped. I try to open my eyes, but there's just blackness everywhere—up, down, to the left, to the right. Even my vague awareness soon melts away.

I crumble, deteriorate, and drop all the little fragments of my body into a deep abyss.

And then there is nothing.

*   *   *

I'm sprawled out in the middle of the medical wing upon a comfy bed, though I'm not exactly sure *why*. You see, I have a real bad memory and can't remember very much of anything. I sift through my brain for a clue as to why I'm here, but can only draw a blank. I sit up and look for one of the many nurses that work here—I'm sure they'll be able to answer my questions. They know *everything*.

Mrs. Hanson is my personal assistant, in case you didn't already know. She's just arrived at my bedside with a warm greeting, so I ask her what in the world I might be doing here in the medical wing.

She puts her petite, maternal hand gently on my shoulder and lightly chuckles. "Oh, you should be *very* grateful, Sid," she says. "If not for Mrs. Weir, you might have gotten pretty badly hurt!"

I have trouble recalling the knowledge of any Mrs. Weir. "You know about this memory of mine, Mrs. Hanson," I tell her. "Mrs. Weir, Mrs. Weir ... the name's not ringing a bell."

She reveals that "Mrs. Weir" is the leader of my therapy group. I call upon the power of each and every of my brain cells to help recreate a coherent picture—very vaguely do I remember attending her last session, but why she has served as an importance regarding my current whereabouts is beyond me. Mrs. Hanson explains the facts.

"Don't you remember? That mischievous Hank Hank is always getting himself and others into trouble!"

"*Hmm.*" She urges me to think as *haaard* as I can. Locked in a deep gaze with Mrs. Hanson, I slowly begin to recall what happened. "He ... he *attacked* me, didn't he? Hank Hank attacked me!"

She nods satisfactorily. "Oh yes, and much more than that! He tried to *kill* you!"

I shudder. Yes, I *do* remember now: it was me, Lil' Jimmy, and of course ol' Hank Hank. We'd just been engaged in a normal therapy session, and suddenly, he decided to go berserk for no apparent reason at all. He tried *strangling* me to death! You heard Mrs. Hanson—if it wasn't for the group leader's bravery, I'd probably have been crushed alive! She butted in, broke up the fight, and ordered the security guards to take him away.

And what is to become of him now? If I properly recall, he was being taken away for some very extensive brain test, some sort of "psycho surgery." That ought to set him straight—thank goodness for the blessings of science and technology!

"That is correct. Ol' Hank will be *juuuust* fine. Our top surgeons are going to be working with him for the next few weeks, so you might not see him around for a while." She takes her hand off my shoulder and poses playfully like a muscular athlete. "He'll be in better shape than ever before!"

She hovers over me like a guardian angel. In some ways, I am like her own child—I am unashamedly in *love* with her.

It's not before long that she urges me to head back down to the main ward and get on with my daily schedule. First, however, Mrs. Hanson administers my mandatory medication. She withdraws a cylindrical container of pills from her breast pocket. She fetches me some water, and I down two capsules quickly.

"Very good, Sid!"

I'm glad that I'm able to please her … I'd do just about *anything* in the world she asks of me. I suppose that's what love is all about. I'd be a fool not to put my faith in her—she knows the "cure" and *so* much more!

I bid Mrs. Hanson farewell. She says I should check in with Mrs. Rory at the main desk, just to be sure that she knows I'm okay; for my own caution, she orders a nurse-in-training to assist me.

I know the way, but safety *always* comes first.

*   *   *

DR. COHEN: Mrs. Burr, my dear, *what* are you trying to say?

MRS. BURR: *(reluctantly)* Nothing that I haven't already said before. You know I believe in moving forward, it's just that … it's just that I've got this feeling that sooner or later, things are going to start smelling … fishy. We're stepping into boundaries that I'm not so sure are ready to be *stepped into.*

C: Oh, let's not be ridiculous here! Do you know the sheer power we've got in this facility? We're a division of the *government,* for Chrissakes, the *government!* If there's ever been a right time to completely expand our experimental focuses, it's *now;* we've got the funding of unions and sponsors flooding in through that front door like mad! Our methods are *foolproof,* in case you haven't already noticed. Nearly forty years in this sort of business and not *once* has anything gone wrong.

C: I'm starting to believe that you doubt my genius ability to run things smoothly here on the ward—is that it, Missus Mrs. Burr, is *that* what it is? Is it because I'm growing *old?* Ha—I am *ageless!*

B: Not at all Doc, that's not it at all … *honestly.* It's just—

C: *(belittlingly)* Sweetie … *sweetie.* For someone who's been at my side here for nearly ten whole years now, I imagine you'd have a better understanding of the way things are done.

B: *(frustrated)* It seems that I'm not getting *through* to you; have I once criticized our actual functions or the way we run our programs? Listen to me, Doc, just *listen* to me … there's a fine line between good and evil, and I think you're beginning to cross it!

C: *(following a burst of condescending laughter)* Nonsense—what the hell's gotten into you? You're starting to sound like a *real* human being! What's such a fine *experiment* as yourself dabbling with—dare I utter such a word?—*emotions* for?

B: Oh, it's not *that*—it's just … some of your ideas are so … so *huge*, so crazy!

C: But isn't that what makes them so magnificent?

B: I suppose, but … *come on*, an underwater colony of humans? Of all things! Where would we get the space, the materials?—hell, what would even be the purpose?

C: Purpose? Why, the mere notion of a fully *aquatic human being* is just mind-blowing!

B: Yes … I guess you're right—that'd be quite a sight indeed … **(unsure; waveringly)** … there are no reasons to hold ourselves back, I suppose.

C: Nor is there anyone here to hold us back in the *first place*; the great pleasures of a brilliant sadistic mind can't really be explained, can they?

[LONG PENSIVE SILENCE; THE DOCTOR SPEAKS AGAIN.]

C: Have I ever told you about my first big success in the lab? About how *great* I felt once the realization had come that I'd done everything right?

B: No, I don't think you have.

C: **(grinning lustfully)** Well, I think it's finally about time I told you, then, hmm?

B: *(honored that the great Doctor would bother to waste such time on her)* Why of course, Doc! Please, please … share your story!

C: *(seductively)* Okay then … let's get *comfortable* first.

[MRS. BURR MOUNTS HERSELF ON A LAB BENCH AND SLIPS OFF HER SKIRT, THEN THE PANTIES: DR. COHEN UNBUTTONS HIS SHIRT, LOOSENS HIS BELT— CARESSINGLY, HE INSERTS HIS FINGERS INTO THE NURSE'S WET VAGINA. SHE EMITS A GRATIFYING MOAN AND IS SOOTHED.]

C: I was young and had just graduated from my studies. The apartment I lived in had an empty room that wasn't being used, so I decided to turn it into a full-blown laboratory, or at least as "full-blown" as I was able to at the time. In the beginning, I just fooled around in there with experiments and equations of which I already knew; I enjoyed myself and what I did, but nothing was ever very *productive*, partially because of my overall lack of motivation. Nothing in particular seemed to *force* me into the new and daring biological territories I mourned to seek … until my girlfriend at the time moved in with her goddamned *kitty cats*, that is.

B: *(beginning to feel aroused)* And what ever became of her?

C: My girlfriend? *(A laugh.)* Hmm, that's a good question. I believe I skinned her alive, boiled her remains, and then indulged in a nice cannibalistic dinner—*if* I'm thinking of the right girl.

B: For no reason at all? Even for *you*, that's a bit harsh.

[THE DOCTOR CROUCHES; STARTS POKING AROUND WITH HIS TONGUE. HE IMMEDIATELY HITS A SWEET SPOT AND MRS. BURR YELPS.]

C: I just found out she'd been a *bad girl*, that's all. (Condescendingly) Something about women, *real* women, unlike yourself … something so *useless* about them …

RAYMOND

[AN EXTENDED SILENCE. SEXUALITY IS WROUGHT IN THE AIR.]

B: What ... did ... her ... *uhrr* ... cats ... have to do with your success-s-s-s-s-s?

C: Well, one of them—the mother, I think—started wailing like crazy at four in the morning one night, and of course her bitching had begun to drive me *insane*. I picked her up in my two hands (you can't say I didn't give her a chance) and said, "Hey, you better calm the fuck down, kitty, or I'm going to *chop off your head*," and *of course* she didn't listen, so *of course* I was forced to carry out my threat. Now, just as I'm about to do it, one of her kittens comes jolting from out of nowhere to save the fucking day. They both start screeching and eventually what I've got around me is a cacophony of disgusting meows—I was just about to lose my *mind*! I thought to myself for a moment, and then realized how much more fun I'd have cutting their heads *open* rather than *off*.

C: I took them into the lab, and the rest is history.

B: *(softly, extremely stimulated)* What did you do ... *mmf, mmf* ... Doctor?

C: If you really want to know ...

[COHEN DROPS HIS PANTS, GRABS HIS ERECT PENIS. BURR GROANS AND EAGERLY SLIPS IT IN.]

C: I switched their brains around, of *course*! What more could you expect from a guy *like me*?

B: *(after shared laughter)* Was that your first attempt at such a thing?

C: It was. In fact, I'm quite fortunate that things went as smoothly as they did. That crazy girlfriend of mine went totally berserk when she woke up and starting wrecking the lab—luckily I was able to *kill* her before things got *too* messy. For such an amateurish experiment, the results were superb. I was sure that I'd have screwed up *somewhere* with *something*, but the outcome was nothing short of magnificent!

B: What ... *mmf, mmf* ... happened to the cats?

C: The changes in either of them did not come so immediately. It was a few weeks before I noticed anything significant, but by the end of two months—(get a load of this!)—the mother had nearly doubled in size!

B: *Doubled?*

C: Oh *yes*, Mrs. Burr. I was quite shocked with the effects as well. You see, the infant kitten brain that had been implanted in its mother obviously needed to grow; it still needed to go forth with the functions of the animal life cycle. She was now rendered ignorant of her instincts and all of which had previously been stored in her brain—all the knowledge she once possessed now sat in the hands of her child. Therefore, the kitten, whose body was only a few weeks old, contained a mind that had already witnessed a lifetime come and go. The mother then resorted to her own child for guidance, and believe it or not, the kitten (whose growth had permanently been stunted) actually wound up raising its own *mother*! At the end of two months, the mother had grown *tremendously* due to the sped up reactions of her new brain's hormones; because of its foreign environment, the brain which she now possessed had run amuck, and the life cycle had entered a time machine into the future. The kitten's mind also lost control of itself, and to make a long story short ... *oh ... oh, yeah ... that's the spot ... mmm ...* both cats were driven to *insanity.* They waged an all-out war against each other and themselves. The kitten died first because the size of its tiny heart could not handle its physical and mental stress, whereas the mother (who continued to grow and grow and grow!) resorted to self-cannibalism and began eating away at her own limbs. Died of an infection, I think—can't be sure—

B: (*dreamily, sexually*) Oh Doc, where *do* you get your wild ideas?

C: (*pushing harder now*) I ...don't ... *grunt* ... know.

B: Is there any morphine leftover from last night?

C: Oh, we'll worry about that later, sweetheart.

B: Not even one shot? Not even—

C: Not now darling. Not right now.

[THEIR CONVERSING CEASES MONETARILY, FOR THE SEX IS SO GREAT]

[CASUAL CHANGE OF SUBJECT FROM THE DOCTOR; THE POWER HE HOLDS OVER HIS INFERIOR IS QUITE OBVIOUS.]

C: So, what do you have to say about the notion of an underwater society *now*, Mrs. Burr? Really, how *bad* of an idea can it be—I've already sown the seeds to a protocol specimen for you to tend to. His codename is *Poseidon*.

B: Oh ... *mmf* ... I'm ... *ugh* ... sure it will be ... *ahhhhh* ... just *great-t-t* ...

C: (**With a harsh thrust of the hips that shoves himself in farther than before**) Now you're talking some sense, my dear. Now you're talking sense.

*   *   *

The main ward (where pretty much everything goes down) is not far from here, but I suppose it's worth mentioning how *huge* this place is! I wonder what the bulk of this hospital is even used for; I don't think I could say that I've ever been through but a *half* of it all!

As I'm walking with this young nurse-of-an-escort, I eye her up and down inquisitively. She's ever so pretty. Her hair is a light shade of brown and is complemented nicely by her defined olive skin. It's almost laughable, but to be honest, I'm a little intimidated. I want to tell her how nice she looks or even just offer a hello, but I wisely hold myself back. (Mrs. Rory and Mrs. Hanson try to keep those kinds of things in line, or at least while they're not supervising—oh, *you know* what I mean ... *those* kinds of things.) When we arrive together, she wordlessly drifts back down the corridor from which we've come.

I head over to Mrs. Rory. Terribly busied by the mountain of files piled upon her desk, she glances up and asks if I could wait just a few minutes. Obediently, I nod and relocate to my favorite green couch over in the lounge.

Across from me, three fellow patients socialize mindlessly. One of them—a tall, lanky-looking fella—is strumming away on an acoustic guitar of his. My ear is not greatly keen toward music, but I'm for certain that he's not very good. The strings grumble loosely as he not-so-rhythmically picks away at his instrument. Beside him, the two others robotically sing along to some tune; they seem to be in a daze, disjointed and unconnected. It's obvious that they are unaware of their sour and boisterous voices. Hell, it's hard for me to even hear myself *think*!

I notice that one of them is terribly spaced out, even more so than the others—ah, yes, the *Magic Lamp*, he's just returned from a session with the Magic Lamp!

The Lamp is a wonderful thing when used properly, though It's got the potential to really mess up your head. Because of my great behavior, I've never been forced into the evil powers that It possesses; I've only witnessed Its *beauty*. Like the name states, It's *magical*—really! There's no other explanation. Though It looks just like any ordinary lamp, when the lights are out and the room is rendered black, It has the power to transport you to a completely new world. After you've swallowed and digested the *Magic Tablet* that works hand and hand with the Lamp, you are fully prepared to set out on your journey. You become magnetized to It, you fall in love with It, you never want to stop the onslaught of beauty that It forces upon you; It creates the most wonderful geometric shapes and allows them to float around freely in your mind.

Mrs. Rory has made it well known around here that overexposure to the Lamp and all Its Magic can damage your brain in the long run, so we're not allowed to abuse Its thrill—(yes, the Lamp is actually a reward for properly behaved patients, too). From the stories I've heard, the Lamp is capable of creating quite disastrous episodes. The procedures are the same, though I think it's the Tablet digested prior to the journey that's different. Ol' Frankie the Fish (the No-Brainer whose bunk is next to mine) told me of a story once where he imagined his whole body was set ablaze! Though they love us immensely here, the staff sure has plenty of creative ways to keep us in line. Luckily, I'm smart enough to manage my own discipline (I can't be *that* crazy then, can I?), so I am kept from these horrific cruelties. Whether it's used for insightful pleasures or as a devilish punishment, the Magic Lamp leaves you dazed for hours, sometimes even days.

Just as I close my eyes and try to recreate my last experience with the Lamp, Rory summons me back to the desk. She slides aside the window that separates the two of us and sticks out her head, ordering those couch-ridden songbirds to bring their tune to a halt.

"My dear Sid, are you feeling any better? I heard about what happened last night. Terrible, just *terrible!*"

I shrug humbly. "Oh, I'm all right; everything's fine. You know, sometimes the other patients just lose control of themselves."

"That Hank Hank's *really* been something of a *troublemaker* lately, hasn't he? Oh, if every patient here were as good as you!" she exclaims. I am charmed and acquire gooseflesh along my neck.

I sign in and turn away to go about with my day. Before I get very far, however, Rory calls me back urgently. Followed by cackling laughter, the fellow with the guitar plays a mockingly sour chord upon my arrival back at the desk. Mrs. Rory shakes her head in disgust.

"See what I mean? If *only they were as good as you.*"

She starts talking to me, and for a while it seems as though she's beating around the bush. That's strange—it's almost like she's trying to avoid what she has to say. I try not to make it obvious that I may have … "caught on" to something; it's quite blasphemous to question anyone around here. A sin, a wretched, disgraceful sin!

After a long while, she gets to her point. Her tone is sketchy; *worried.*

"There is someone who wants to *see* you," she manages to say at last. "I have spoken with him; he will be visiting around this time tomorrow."

Her narrowed eyes have me wondering; she makes me feel like I've done something terribly, terribly wrong! Is it because I'd questioned her motives for just a split second? I meant no harm— really! So she's read my mind … *once again.* Not only have I disrespectfully dared to reckon her nobility, but I'm almost *positive* that she's aware of my lustful desires with the girl down the hall, too! Mrs. Rory's always telling me not to disappoint her. She says my lack of curiosity is my greatest asset as a patient, a quality of which I'm very proud.

Have I let her down for the very first time? Have I totally blown all that I live for?

But *wait*, there's *more* to this sudden puzzlement—even more shocking than her dull and sullen tone is the news that she's just delivered to me: a *visitor?*

As you might have guessed, I'm lost for words. A million different things scurry through my mind in a matter of seconds. Mrs. Rory senses my confusion and demands that I confess to her what's on my mind—oh, there's no use to lie! She'll just use her psychic abilities in the end to find out on her own, anyway.

I ask her, *just for clarification*, if I've heard correctly. "To see *me*, Mrs. Rory? You mean that someone wants to see … *me*? I can't even *remember* the last time I had a visitor … heck, I don't think I've *ever* had a visitor! Wait a second … I don't think *any* of us ever have!" I become anxious, I become childish, but I cannot contain this … this … this *joy*!

"Yes, Mr. Tate, someone desires to see *you*." In a knife-sharp tone (which sends my gut cascading downward like a waterfall) she adds: "*Greatly* desires to see you."

She's under my skin now, I can feel her crawling; the blood in my veins has been exchanged with her consciousness. My sudden delight is shattered like fragile glass. I am on the awful verge of explosion, just seconds away from becoming a bawling fool.

"What have I done, Mrs. Rory, what has been my transgression? Oh, tell me now so I can repent! Please, accept my forgiveness! Just get out, just get out of my *head*!!" From behind the desk, she watches me crumble to the ground.

I no longer can see her, but Mrs. Rory's voice resonates from above me. "Get ahold of yourself, Sid," she says reassuringly. "You've done nothing wrong."

It takes me a few moments, but I manage to help myself back up. She looks into my desperate eyes with compassion—there is a chance, perhaps there is still a chance for redemption! She claims that I've not provoked her, but I'm *smarter* than that. I know otherwise; she is merely *sparing* my tainted soul from its own stupidity.

"Remember," she says, "that I *know* what you're thinking. *All of the time*. We're in this *together*."

Ugh, it's happened once again. Just *when* will I learn? Any instance that I've ever proposed wild assumptions to myself about the intentions of Rory, Hanson, or *anyone else* that operates this ward, I'm always left feeling like a fool. Can I be so ignorant not to realize their *guaranteed* validity, their round-the-clock affection? They love me, they love me more than anything else in the world. I'm their one and only, their *favorite!*

Once I'm feeling better (and she convincingly confirms that I am forgiven), I ask for the name of my visitor. She tells me not to worry about it. I am to meet him in person tomorrow.

I turn away, pondering how to spend this next twenty-four hours of mine recreationally. Mrs. Rory says I don't need to worry about my schedule today, so I can do just about whatever I want.

Aye! What a thrill! That's right—an *Outsider!*

Not a single memory of The Other World has managed to remain with me; for all I know, it may not even exist! We, the patients, know this world as *"The Outside."* My visitor's arrival here at the ward is going to be like an alien landing on Earth! What a radically historic event! Boy, I sure hope he's intelligent—maybe he can teach me how to *read!* We can talk of all different things, many things, anything, whatever he wants!

As I head off, I hear Mrs. Rory slam her window shut with suspicious aggression; I don't dare look back or question it. There's a *reason* for everything, just like she says there is. She *loves* me, and that's that.

With nothing better to do, I decide to relax here in the main lounge. I sit myself down directly across from those three unruly songsters. As I listen to them rant and rave, their music suddenly doesn't seem so bad; if a songbird were to flutter by cheerfully chirping away, I wouldn't be able to tell the difference.

Ah—the future is near, the future is good. I can feel it in the air, I can feel it in my blood, I am on my way to being *cured!*

*   *   *

The rest of the day zooms by and I excitedly awaken in the morning. As usual, it is the clanking of distant machinery that's dragged me out of sleep and ejected me from my dreams. Hurriedly, I sign in with Rory. She says that when my visitor arrives, she'll send a message throughout the building.

For some reason, she appears anxious, *distraught*, as if a horde of busy ants wriggles beneath her skin; I don't muster enough courage to ask why she seems this way, but it's none of my business, anyhow …

Let me tell you about my dream last night. It was a nightmare of pain, excruciating pain, but throughout it all, my body refused to wake up; I dreamt there were things poking about the realms of my brain, encroaching the privacy my mind is rightfully allowed— how *weird*. I recall quite vaguely the sounds of voices above me, discussing all sorts of matters, though I was unable to make any sense of the chitchat being thrown around … *not like it makes a difference anyway*, for the hour which I've been anxiously awaiting draws near!

*   *   *

To kill the spare time I've got, I decide to have sex. Not many patients here are allowed this lustful privilege, but you see, I'm very special. As long as I go about with it while Mrs. Hanson is "supervising," it's all okay. I'm not supposed to imagine anything *dirty* when she's not around—I can exploit these luxuries only while she's in the Game Room with me. I really love the way it feels once I get it going with a woman. I like fair skin, soft lips, flowing black hair—I'll even go as far as saying that sex (apart from the very essence of my life here at the ward) is my favorite thing in the whole wide world! Once it's all done, though, it feels like it's never happened in the first place. That's the strange part. I wonder if it's like that for everyone *else* too, like on the *Outside*; from what I hear, *everything's* different in the real world.

I'm not sure if it's just a tall tale, but rumor has it that on the Outside, many men wear a rubber sheath of sorts for "protection" before they sexually engage themselves. Protection? Protection from *what*? I mean, it may or may not be true, but to someone like me (who's immersed in such a technologically advanced world), that just seems so ridiculous! Maybe it's some outdated system that's only used *out there*. How can I relate to something so primitive when we've got *brain electrodes* here on the ward that regulate our sexual pleasures? Outsiders may be unfamiliar with and wary about such technology, but believe me, it's all really not that much of a hassle! The electrodes are planted, a switch is flicked, and there!—you're good to go! I'm not sure why this method isn't used on the Outside; how *old fashioned* their ways seem to me! Really, they've got it down to a *science* here—the whole preparation takes just minutes!

I inform Mrs. Hanson of my perverted fantasies, so she happily directs me over to the *Game Room*. It's initially dark and lifeless, but she quickly turns on the lights and everything is illuminated. There's not very much of anything in here, or at least anything out of the ordinary; just some computers, a rack of vials hanging on the wall, and intricate machinery with levers, buttons, and switches. She advises me to hastily get on with it—Mrs. Hanson says it's mandatory that I meet up with this visitor of mine on time. Indeed, I agree … I must be sure to leave a great first impression!

The procedure is always the same: I lie, face-down, upon a small lab table and orient myself comfortably. As usual, Mrs. Hanson straps me down for safety. I try to sneak a look at what she's doing, but I'm tied down so securely that it's impossible to move! I hear her sorting through and picking up and putting down a countless number of things. She uses much caution—this *is* dangerous stuff, after all! I have faith in Mrs. Hanson, though. She knows *exactly* what she's doing. I've lost track of just how many times she's aided me through fantasies like this—not once has something gone awry. She performs the miracle of science upon me, and before I have time to make sense of what's happened, she's already finished up.

I can feel my brain tingling uncomfortably—it's a good thing Mrs. Hanson works as quickly as she does! Wires are attached and some substance that lathers is rubbed along my scalp.

"Sid, would you mind just closing your eyes for a moment while I unbuckle you and bring out your fine lady?" she requests. It's always the same thing. She says my body reacts better to surprises, that that's *just the kind of guy* I am. I suppose she's right—she knows more about me than you'd ever believe.

I, as you might have guessed (like the automaton I take such pride in being), shut my eyes obediently and await the arrival of my woman. I remain shrouded in blackness for a short while—a minute, perhaps two. It is amidst this nothingness that I feel my body surge with electricity. This sensation warms my bosom instantly on its downward route from my brain. I begin shaking a bit, but that's just what happens to *everyone*. The brain naturally releases electricity when you're getting ready for some play in the Game. I've always wondered how that works and why it happens in the first place. The whole phenomenon is strange, if you ask me, but Mother Nature has her ways—it's always best not to mess around with Her.

After my brief euphoric stint, Mrs. Hanson undoes my many straps. I free myself as she orders me to stand up.

My eyes burst open and behold the magnificent stature of woman before me. Oh *yes*, she is perfect, perfection brought to the flesh; she comes to me just as she always does, *silently*, soft and youthful, curving in all the right, provocative spots. Her skin glistens like gold—so supple are those legs upon which she strides, her breasts gallop more frantically with each step she takes! I cannot marvel at her too long, though, and why should I, hmm? I should be on the ground now, filling up the volume of her sacred gash!

I tear my clothes off just about as fast as I can. She watches me, wordlessly as usual.

No longer is there any use for my sporadic thoughts—I've got her pure and tender body wrapped in my arms sensually on the floor. Hard, energetic thrusts cause my woman to howl with joy. Electricity courses madly throughout my body; I can feel my brain rumbling within the framework of my skull. My vision blurs, blinded by blue flurries of light ... oh, she *knows* how to get me, she *knows* all the right moves. She pulsates beneath me, shocking my body even more; I am glorified. The inners of my cranium grow warm (I can nearly *taste* the burning static force), but that's just how intense our love is—I cascade down a rushing waterfall of endless rapture.

We go on for some time, but for all I know, I am trapped in the ecstatic forever of eternity. Out of nowhere, my climax approaches; like a rumbling tremor of the earth, I complete our glorious journey.

Amidst the silence of our stark naked bodies, I can hear the fleshy exterior of my brain sizzle. Phew! She always manages to give me a workout!

I shut my eyes to regain full consciousness; when I reopen them, she is gone. As usual, she's vanished as if she'd never been there at all.

"All right, Sid, you've had your fun—now get up and ready. Look sharp—remember, you want to leave a good impression on this visitor of yours." I eagerly nod my head in agreement. "You not only represent yourself; you are a spokesperson for this institution as well." Rhetorically: "You want us to have a good name, now, don't you?"

Quick as a flash of light and still thoroughly numbed from my intense round of the Game, I gather up my clothes and redress.

*　　　*　　　*

It's not long before I find myself (in what feels like a medically inebriated daze) wandering off alone through the puzzling corridors of the ward; everything always manages to look somewhat different when I'm feeling a bit ... *off* like this. Both Hanson and Rory become infuriated when I drift around by myself, but there's no sense in fighting the will of the medicinal molecules whirling through my blood. Faces are distant, *blurry*, while the walls and floors and everything else seem thick and milky.

The euphoric bursts that spontaneously possess me are beyond comprehension. I'm too *crazy*, you know, too "strange" and "disconnected" to *fully* appreciate the way these drugs I'm fed make me feel. I'm all tingly, that's for sure, and everything contains this sort of dream-like quality. At times, my limbs are unresponsive like a motherboard whose controls have been disrupted, yet on occasion there are these sudden ecstatic urges that make me want to run around and ... and SCREAM! Because my brain is so dysfunctional, I'm assigned these really potent substances that sometimes affect my perception of things, you see. Like right now. I'm staring at something, something vague and distorted—a face? A clock? A vase? It's just a messy disarray of colors that swirls in constant perpetual motion.

I. Am. Hypnotized.

I stumble upon the hazy face of Dr. Cohen, the head of our facility, in the heart of the deformed cloud before me. As I move closer to it, the dimensions of his emerging countenance become clearer and clearer.

I am pleased to see him, for the Doctor always has something nice to say about me. I sit down robotically, transfixed upon this tricky miasma, and converse with him emptily. I am unsure of what I say or how he answers back, but the actual content of our little chat seems meaningless. I feel spacey—lost, especially—but am comfortably hidden amidst the swirling, mysterious shroud that binds me.

Before I know it, there is a draining feeling that compels me, and everything turns grey. Sounds become more garbled than before, though more intriguing than my disconnection from reality is the floating sensation that has begun to carry me around. My legs become weightless, and I am seized by the feeling of being possessed.

The hazy image of Dr. Cohen reappears doubly now (against the dreary backdrop of the pure pleasures of nothingness) and our communication is reestablished. This time, I feel like he tries to frighten me with strangely silent insinuations; we talk through the circuit of an invisible phone line rooted in our brains. His face becomes slowly more and more indistinct, and before I can even make sense of the haunting presages he's offered, the Doctor has melted away into the silky haze from which he's come.

And then the light returns, along with the real world, and I find myself physically distorted like a fool in the corner of one of our many restrooms. The muscles in my legs are tired and numb—it takes all the might I can muster to lift my body up from the ground. There's a distant hum, a discomforting buzz that lingers in my head. I turn around dizzily to see where it's coming from, but it appears to be generated from inside of me. Though I can make out the watery image of myself reflected in the face of a mirror, the room is still muddled.

As I gaze more intently into the sympathetic eyes of my reflection, its colors begin to intensify. Slowly yet surely, the pale shades of my face and clothes hurriedly grow brighter and brighter, eventually bright enough to force my aching eyelids shut. A riveting sensation groggily sweeps my weak and trembling gut; it begins tossing, turning. The screws that weakly hold my sanity in place become loose and all sense is lost.

My mental anguish persists until I realize someone else is approaching. My eyes jerk open, and reality mockingly returns—I jolt over to a stall just about as fast I can in order to create a purposeful illusion for this oncoming patient. I hope I can make it seem like I'm preoccupied and actually *doing something*!

My body is riddled with the shakes ... hell, I can't contain myself!

Thump, thump. Thump, thump.

He's approaching, he's approaching, whoever he is, he's *approaching*! I, of course, look away nervously and pretend to mind my own business. My heart races like the rhythm of a frantic drum roll. By now, you know how uncomfortable and anxious I get while mingling with the others here, especially when in such a state of mind as *this*—oh, what am I? What kind of miserable mistake *can I be?*

The flesh of my brain melts and turns to mush; I'm possessed by a cold sweat. He's right next to me—Godammit, he's come to the stall *right beside mine*! My jaw tightens fiercely, so fiercely that it pushes another pound of nervous fluids oozing up and out of my pores. Despite my efforts to keep my line of sight away from him, I am forced to take a look.

The face is hideous and disheveled, the skin is bloodied and bruised! I try to turn away in disgust, but the whimsical control of this drunken force is too powerful.

I am confronted by my very self!

This is no trick: I can see *Him*—(Me!), I can smell the odor of his rotting flesh—MY rotting flesh! Helplessly, I roar in animalistic confusion and frustration.

Before long, I completely black out—the sight of this walking corpse's messy detonation sends me clumsily to the ground.

*   *   *

"It's all right, *gracious Sid*, just put your head down and go back to sleep," Mrs. Hanson whispers.

I look at her blankly.

"It's all a *dream*, just a bad *dream*. Shut your eyes and get some rest. It will make you feel better."

I stare confusedly into her sincere eyes.

"Shh," she advises, "*just pretend that nothing's happened at all.* When you wake up later, everything will be fine."

I'm puzzled, but the nurse's cloudy image leaves me at ease. She sprinkles some of her magic powder upon me, and I doze off.

*   *   *

Not much later, I go over to the lobby, invigorated. I sit down to find that trio of sour songbirds howling away like wolves (once again) over some old-fashioned tune. The three of them are always moping around, doing nothing more than singing their rusty ol' hearts away. I truly pity them.

Over in the corner, there's a TV we're allowed to watch when we've got leisure time to spare. The staff commonly leaves the news on (we patients have a right to know what's going on the Outside too, no?), but something seems to have gone wrong with the screen. I want to go over and tell Mrs. Rory about it, though some part of my better judgment warns against doing so. Instead, I go over to a rack of magazines mounted on a nearby wall. I skim through dozens of different volumes, settling on the most recent publication of some worldly periodical. Just so you know, the staff keeps track of what they leave out for us to access—they're really concerned with our intelligence, you see. As I've already said, I can't read very much at all, so I just enjoy looking at the pictures. I can understand a few words here and there, but not enough to piece anything coherent together. Thanks to Mrs. Hanson and Mrs. Rory, I actually know lots about the current state of the world. I've even begun to develop some political views. However, I keep these to myself. You know how politics can be a controversial thing, especially in the current year of 2067.

I'm intently scanning the cover of my selected periodical now, looking into the dark, abyss-like eyes of Mr. Josef Stalin.

His mustache is fixed atop his upper lip, curving in the most proper of ways. The power he suggests is immense—I've seen him before, many, many times, and in each picture he seems to consume me wholly. I'm not sure exactly why—maybe it's because of that greenish suit he's always wearing, or maybe it's just his icy glare. His presence surely has been popping up a lot lately, and I don't mean just here on magazine covers; in the news, on posters, and I could imagine even within the conversations of the staff, too. Thanks to that Hitler fellow as well, there seems to be lots of confusing stuff going on across the world over in Europe. Maybe it all has to do with this crazy war that's raging; it's a mess, it really is. I've been told not too long ago that our own beloved America is even participating in all of this chaos.

All of these global troubles get you wondering 'bout the goodness of humanity. I mean, I, for one, have faith in it, but I can be so naive and foolish sometimes.

In case you don't already know, these wartime leaders have been gaining some notoriety lately. I've asked different nurses and docs for their own opinions, and they've all basically told me the same thing: it may take many years for the world to realize it, but in the future, we'll look back at these disreputable dictators with total respect—once the dust from the war settles, the dictatorial ways of the East are sure to migrate over here to America, or so Mrs. Rory thinks. She says these things optimistically—according to her, these are the ways of the future. Her theory is that all the limbs of our government are so extraneous and cumbersome; leadership should be something singular, something more *passionate*. Mm, it's quite easy to understand what she means!

As I'm skimming through the pages now, the squeaky voices of the others come to a halt. One of them eyes me up and down curiously with a very crooked, stained-toothed grin. His head always shakes rapidly thanks to a pitiful condition of his. He utters a parched cackle for no apparent reason and blankly asks: "Whatcha reading?"

I become uneasy. You're well aware of my overly nervous nature, so I won't even bother explaining how sick I instantly begin to feel. Stumbling over my words, I utter clumsily: "The *war*."

"The *war*, huh?" he echoes giggly. The other two beside him join in for a raucous fit of pointless laughter. "And whatcha think about it, hmm?"

My tongue becomes tied, frozen in my mouth like a rigid block of ice. I try to form some sort of response, but it takes my brain a while to set this all into motion. "It's—it's just—fine!" I mutter quickly without very much thought.

Fine? Oh, what have I just said? I've made a fool of myself!

Their hooting grows louder. A metal clamp closes down upon my brain and numbs it. Ugh, things like this happen a *lot*; I must learn to *think* before I speak. Quickly, I try to distract them with another question; perhaps maybe if I redeem my intelligence, they'll *forget* about my dopey reply. So many things race through my head, but the one thing that makes its way out is: "And ... and what do *you* think of the war?"

Their laughing recedes as the one with the guitar in hand begins to stare me down. He tries to hold a straight face, but I can tell he's having trouble. After a seemingly intense wracking of his brain, with every ounce of seriousness in him, he says, "Well I don't know very much 'bout nothin', but I will tell ya *this*—we all ain't been born *equal* or *perfect* or none o' that *bullshit*. Some people just *have* to suffer—some people are *meant* to suffer. We all know that. The world can never move forward without sacrifices; *you know* ... "

He looks over to his cronies. "Victims!" one adds in. "Society needs its victims!"

The third of these chums chimes in too, but I don't manage to catch what he says. They quickly lose themselves in strange, distorted worlds of their own. Still, I get a feeling that this episode is likely to elevate, and that's the *last thing* I want to happen.

Mindlessly, they dive deep into another song. I take the opportunity; I toss the magazine aside and casually walk away. As I leave, I think about what the guitar player's just said. He's right— despite all his emptiness, *he is right*. We *aren't* all created equal, and some people *do* have to suffer. I mean, look at me! Is it fair to other patients that I am treated so grandly, that I am so special and they are *not*? It's comp*le*tely true: to how many here is this restriction at the ward a punishment? For me, it's like a *privilege*, like something of a *reward*.

My attention is drawn to Mrs. Rory. She calls me over from behind the main desk. Can it be? Has the time finally come? You can imagine how excited I am—I can barely contain my joy!

To my disappointment, however, it is *not* because of my anxiously awaited visitor that I've been called upon; earlier this morning, when I first signed in, Mrs. Rory informed me of a mix-up with one of my most important pills, so thus far today, I have not taken this particular medication. She tells me now that the problem's been solved and a trainee will escort me over to the pharmacy to retrieve the correct dosage. It's really not that far from here, but the staff always likes to send someone along with me, just *in case* of anything.

Once this apprentice of Mrs. Rory's arrives, we quickly shuffle away to pick up my drugs.

*   *   *

I'm told to wait outside the pharmaceutical office while this trainee sorts things out.

With nothing more interesting to engage in, I stretch open my hands and begin counting the wrinkles and creases etched upon them. I do this a lot; quite often, I'm recreationally lost (*bored out of my mind* is a better way to put it!), so I throw myself into such pointless activities. Out of the lot of them, counting things has become my favorite—it never fails to deliver some sort of kick. True, I cannot count very *far* (up to about a hundred), so I'm always having to switch from one subject to the next. Perhaps that's what makes counting the things around me so interesting, the fact that after I've reached a certain point, I always must move on to something else. When your life is consumed by redundancy, you learn to amuse yourself with simple, mindless feats such as this. Oh, you mustn't get the wrong impression, though—I'm not speaking lowly of my beloved home. It's just that sometimes it's a little … *dull*. Ha; I suppose that's where this wretched memory of mine comes in handy—with each passing day, I'm likely to forget the events of the last, so I'm always discovering brand new things around me which in fact I've seen a million times before! In a way, I'm like an infant, a child reborn again and again each and every day!

Right behind me, there's a window that peers directly into the pharmacy. I'm curious to see what goes on beyond it, but I've specifically been told to remain glued to my seat.

I guess I'm just going to have to sit here and wait patiently—I would never break the rules. That'd just be *low*.

*   *   *

Five or so minutes pass by, and still the trainee has not returned with my pills. I wonder what's taking so long. She told me that'd she'd only be a matter of seconds …

An office door slightly farther down the hall opens. Out comes a stout man no more than five feet tall. He's decked out in the latest white uniform the ward has got to offer, so he must be a patient here. Hmm. He's new, I suppose. That's funny—there hasn't been a new patient drafted in *ages*! This is quite an unusual surprise!

He's assisted by a trainee just like the one currently fetching my pills. Boy, is he *tiny*, perhaps the *tiniest* grown man that I've ever seen! He sports a thick, black beard that covers his entire face and

RAYMOND

has got a gleaming bald spot on the rear of his head. Something about the way he carries himself instantly strikes a strange chord within me ... his semi-pompous swagger speaks an undecipherable language of its own.

He catches sight of me and stops in his tracks. Though his disposition is friendly, there's something frighteningly unique about him. His gait is that of a living *troll-creature*! Is he even human?

His jet-black eyebrows arch highly as he greets me. "Well *hello there*!" he declares, erupting with a surplus of energy.

In all my time here, not once have I ever set eyes upon such a fellow! He is nearly jumping out of his socks; the excitement of all the world oozes out of every one of his pores. I cannot summon any particular set of words that can give justice to this little scene. Even as the nurse shoves him forward, his eyes are still glued upon me. This tiny man just can't contain himself!

"And who are *you*?" he sings gracefully. The pitch of his voice is not quite low, not quite high, and not quite in the middle, either—it is a strange conglomeration of all three.

Annoyed, the nurse pushes him along more intently. "That's just Sid, Sid Tate."

His plentiful rump jiggles as he fixes a miles-wide grin across his face. "*Well how do you do, Mr. Tate?*" A few meters past me now, not an ounce of his enthusiasm has been lost. Against his aide's restraint, he turns anxiously in my direction. "Aw, nurse, come on, just for a few seconds! I wanna get *acquainted*, I want to get to *know my way around*!" he pleads.

"There will be plenty of time for meeting and greeting later, but we must get your papers and history over to Mrs. Rory. *She* will do the showing around. Come on, Mr. Fandango, we must be on our way."

His marvelous barking persists, though he is forced to proceed onward. Soon they are out of sight and this strange man's oddly pitched squeal becomes inaudible.

Wow! He vanishes out of sight just as quickly as he's appeared. How strange and peculiar! Mr. *Fandango*. What a wacky character indeed! To my own surprise, I want to *meet* him, I want to get to know *him* just as he wants to get to know *me*—what can I say? I've been charmed! I've never had such an itching desire to "socialize" with anyone ever before, but it's *useless* to fight this impulse of mine, *especially* since he seems to yearn likewise! I hope I'm brave enough to tell Mrs. Rory about this little situation. You know how much she hates when I want to "mix in" with the others, but maybe she'll allow for an exception this time.

My thoughts are broken by the bickering of two voices coming from farther down the hall. There's a man of my age, it sounds like, and Mrs. Friedman, the grumpiest and stockiest of all the nurses here. Though they're out of sight, their words are very clear and easy to understand, so I can't help but zone in.

"*That wasn't part of the deal*," the man resolutely declares. There seems to be a heavy debate underway. It's obvious that they've been at it for a while. Due in part to Mr. Fandango's grand entrance, I've missed the beginning of this argument—I have trouble making any sense of what they're talking about.

"*You cannot let him in on anything he doesn't know*," the nurse urges. "That is *not* what you've come here to do."

"I know *precisely* what I've come to do, and what you're saying now is likely to ruin the whole goddamned thing!"

"We have policies here, *strict* policies, and if you think that for your sake we haven't bent them *enough*, then you're a fool, a selfish, greedy *fool*." It's obvious that Mrs. Friedman is greatly offended. "You seem to have a tendency to push your luck. I'm sure old man Cohen wouldn't deal with this—you wouldn't dare argue with *him*."

"I'll push my luck off the edge of the *earth* before I fall into your bullshit! I think you've begun to confuse me with one of your own brainwashed scapegoats!"

"You can take the standards we enforce here in any way you

like, but once you meet up with Dr. Cohen, I assure you, all of your childish whining will come to an end. You will either shut up or *be* shut up. Be wise—you know there's no alternative. We struck a deal, and that's *that*."

"You ... you know only of what you've been told! You make it sound like you're something *more* than just an expendable messenger!"

The nurse's anger elevates. "Toss around whatever insults you like; you shall be put in your place shortly. Don't forget that any one screw-up on your part can be rigged and fixed on our behalf. You're at a disadvantage and *you know it*. There's nothing you can possibly do that we can't foresee or play some intercepting part in!"

The man rages on about the inequality of "this"—whatever *this* might in fact be. I wish I had some clue as to what they are talking about. It's pretty intense—I'm nearly falling off the edge of my seat by just listening in!

After a long while of trivial bickering, the woman brings a close to their quarrel. "You're free to do as you choose—you are capable of decisions, *bad* ones, too. Break some of our rules, complain to whomever you must. *No one* will believe you! We've got the entire *country* in our favor, for Christ's sake! You'll become your own victim! If your aim is an upheaval or the *great unveiling* of whatever you seem to imagine is going on here, then you might as well stop now and call it quits. There's simply *no way* for you to win this fight." There is an extended silence; I can nearly feel the tension wrought in the air grasp my neck. Mrs. Friedman's next words are as piercing as a supercharged thunderbolt. "If it's a *war* you want, then it's a *war* you'll get."

It's at this point that the mystery man decides to give up. Tiredly, he declares his departure and begins gathering his belongings. Before he leaves, he desperately pleads with the nurse, "Even if it's at the cost of my life, just let me *read* it to him—that's all that I ask of you."

He angrily stomps down the hall. Once this man reveals himself to me, as expected, I conclude that I've no idea who he is. He's got shoulder-length grey hair and a colorless, worn-into face—it's inevitable that this guy's made his way 'round the block and back. Overflowing with luggage, he grasps multiple suitcases and duffel bags in either hand. I can't imagine why he would bring all of this here onto the ward! I suppose it's not of my concern anyway, but there's no fathoming what he has in mind!

At first he doesn't notice me, but once our glances meet, he abruptly halts and seems … *dumbfounded.*

Is there something profoundly interesting that I exhibit—what the heck is going on? He's completely *motionless*! Like a possessed doll, he remains inert; his rock-hard glare frightens the life out of me! I can't help but mimic him and render myself immobile as well.

The stocky nurse comes barging out from around the same bend. Mrs. Friedman babbles to him about something until she, too, finds me sitting here on this chair. Likewise, she becomes transfixed.

My emotions soar, and suddenly, I feel sick. Up from my gut and throughout the rest of my innocence, guilt consumes me, just as it always does. I've become nothing more than a three-dimensional mess of colors and textures scribbled upon the miasma of actuality—my consciousness has boiled and turned to steam. The weight of their eyes comes crushing down; I cannot escape the stranglehold of their vice-like sights. The nurse mumbles something to the mystery man ("What's *he* doing here?!"), though she, too, doesn't budge an inch.

Another door opens from behind me. A tremendous force throws me upward and off of my seat. As I nastily collide with the ground, a burning sensation instantly arises in my hip.

The assistant sent out to retrieve my pills has finally emerged, only to find me twisted into a distraught heap on the ground before her. She rapidly barks a command to Mrs. Friedman, but I have trouble making out any of her words.

A deadly whirlwind is summoned from out of nowhere; it lifts me up, as usual, and hurls me off into endless darkness.

*   *   *

Though my memory seems to have been emptied, I feel greatly at ease—for all I know, I have not woken up once yet today!

I glance at the clock mounted on the wall. It reads a quarter to twelve. I can't quite recall how I've wound up here in this isolated room ... no, *this isn't where I'd fallen asleep last night*, that's for sure, and I don't remember participating in any trouble of sorts. I try thinking back to a time, any time I can, a time from the not-so-distant past, but nothing from this morning or the previous night seems to make very much sense. I'm absolutely *positive* that Mrs. Rory told me about a "visitor," but that's about it. As I lie here, gazing into what seems like blank space, I notice that I'm fully adorned with my day clothes. *So I had to have already awoken today.* I'm thinking and thinking and thinking, but *nothing* is revealing enough to solve my puzzles ... ugh, *curse* this crazy mind of mine!

Something peculiar greatly *nags* me—not something concrete, though not something of a charade either. I can only believe that the brewing of some significance had earlier been underway—if only I could put my finger on it, if I only I could ... ah, *that's it, now* I remember it perfectly: Mr. *Fandango!* Yes, yes, Mr. Fandango— that mad troll of a man! It seems like a million years ago that I'd witnessed his bizarrely enthusiastic swagger, but I'm *positive* he's only checked in this morning. More perplexing than his persona is his very presence here at all. Don't you find him a tad mysterious as well?

For just a moment, everything around me distorts. Not only am I for some unknown reason thrown into this lonesome room, but I can recollect an earlier event with no problem whatsoever—*weird*, all of this is just so *weird*!

Piecing up a mental timeline of the day's early hours, however, meets no avail. I imagine myself, I imagine the whole scene again just perfectly—it starts over in the main hall. I'd been waiting outside the pharmaceutical wing, though I'm not so sure why, and out of nowhere comes this Mr. Fandango fellow, bustling with the energy of a supercharged war machine. Yes, he wanted to *meet* me, he wanted to *get to know* me! I can recite his words verbatim: "*Just a few seconds, nurse? Come on, I just want to get acquainted!*" What *is* this lunacy? Am I slowly transforming into the human I once was?

I sit up and find that my hip aches as if I've fallen. Hmm, perhaps *that's* why I'm here. I'll just ask Mrs. Hanson about it when I see her ... or, on second thought, maybe I *won't*. It's just a pinch; I'm sure it'll go away in a day or two. It's not worth worrying about, anyhow.

As if my contemplating has summoned her presence, Mrs. Hanson strides into the room excitedly.

"Well, hello, Sid!" she says, brightly as always. She drops beside me and begins stroking my back sensually. Before I have the chance to pry her for reasons of my whereabouts, she offers the story.

"It's that new medicine of yours!" she informs. "Don't you remember taking it just earlier this morning?" Mrs. Hanson chuckles gently and taps my forehead with a single finger. "Sometimes your memory even manages to boggle me. Sid, it was just a *few minutes ago*!

"We've been trying to seal a deal with the company that regularly distributed your old pills. regularly distributes your old pills. They've raised their stock prices, so we ordered a similar drug from a sister company. It's cheaper, but obviously your body doesn't respond to it very well."

My spacey daze speaks for itself.

"You were a bit off schedule with your medicine taking, anyway.

There was some quantitative mistake that needed fixing. If you recall, you took your dosage two hours later than usual. It's almost as if you're a robot that can't escape its own programming! Here we are trying to *help* you, and look what we get: we've taken flesh and blood and transformed it into machine! This is worthy of reward, the *Nobel Prize*—wouldn't you say? What a monumental leap forward in science!" She sends a shiver down my spine—it's a frightening thought, it really is, but I know she's just kidding. I can't imagine being taken advantage of like that! She exploits her dark sense of humor with me sometimes, but it's all right. I know what Mrs. Hanson *really* wants for me, and that's only the best.

"If you're up for it, we can try this new drug out again once more tomorrow morning, but this time *on schedule*—we'll see if you respond any differently."

I tell her that sounds like a good idea. She stands up, ready to leave, and informs me that my visitor is on his way; he'll be here shortly. An electric pleasure surges within my veins.

"You're real excited about this, aren't you?" she asks.

The most genuine of smiles finds its way across my face; words need not speak for the brewing of this bliss. The mysterious vibe surrounding the nature of this visitor makes things all the more exhilarating!

Before she departs, I notice Mrs. Hanson scanning me suspiciously for no apparent reason.

"Is there something on your mind, Sid?" she asks curiously.

I try not to let the gnarled teeth of some tricky emotion sink into me, so I answer shakily—what does she foresee? Am I reacting in some way that I shouldn't? Am I guilty of an unsaid crime? Nervously, I utter, "Well … it's the *visitor*, Mrs. Hanson, it's the *visitor*! I'm just … very, very … excited!"

"No … something *else*. I feel that there's something *else* that's troubling you …"

Oh, she *knows* me—she knows everything about me that there

is to know! I really don't understand where these nurses extract their powers from! I suppose they've spent enough time around me to have learned my little whims and quirks, but it's like they've got built-in *radars* that can read my thoughts! Fandango! It's *Mr. Fandango* she's talking about, and *yes*, he's on my mind, and *yes*, he's made me very happy indeed! My nerves become fried in anxiety … I'm not so sure what to do! I had not planned to bring him into the picture just *yet*—I'm certain that's not a good idea. Oh, who am I kidding, anyhow? With Mrs. Rory's elusive psychic powers, without doubt I've already been convicted of my felony. (Sometimes it's so hard for me to ever get a sense of privacy. I mean, the attention is of course *great*, but sometimes I wish I could just have this little part of my mind reserved for *myself*, where *no one* can interfere with what I want to think. That damned Mrs. Rory knows it *all*! Hell, I'm sure she knows I'm thinking about her right now! Oh, geez, now there's *no* way I'll get to meet Mr. Fandango any time soon!)

A knife stabs my heart as the lie eases its way out. "I'm telling you, Mrs. Hanson, it's nothing, nothing at all! The thought of an Outsider wanting to get to know me is … is simply a thrilling thought!" I try to throw her off with some light-hearted facial gestures, but I'm a *horrible* faker—I can nearly feel her eyes ripping right through me.

She seems unsure, but finally concludes with belief. "If that's what you say, then I suppose I've no reason not to trust you. Someone as respected as yourself would never bother to lie about something silly like *this*."

I can nearly regurgitate the lump growing in my throat. "*Of course not.*"

Mrs. Hanson leaves, *betrayed*, naively lied to. I'm going to pay for this, oh I know it! Damn it, Mr. Fandango! If you'd only not have seemed so incredibly *obsessed with me*, then maybe I would have spared her the truth!

Halfway through the door she says, "Just remember: *you represent* us. Give the facility a good name. Talk smart, think smart. Just *be* smart." She winks. "Don't believe any nonsense, either. The Outsiders have some belief that all mental patients are dumb and idiotic, susceptible to *anything*. Excuse my language, but really, don't buy any *bullshit*—you know what I'm talking about. They always seem to love lying to our *'victims'* because they're so 'easy' to get to." She growls. "Prove 'em wrong! Show 'em that you're intelligent, show 'em that you're strong! Let 'em know that no one's going to ever take advantage of you! *Believe* what your heart *wants* you to believe."

I have no chance to offer her any gratitude. Hurriedly, she drifts away.

*   *   *

DR. COHEN: Morphine, my dear?

MRS. BURR: Morphine, indeed.

C: Morphine, my dear?

B: Morphine, indeed.

C: Morphine, my dear?

B: Morphine … *indeed.*

C: Then morphine it *is.*

*   *   *

Here at last—my *visitor!* We've only just met, and already I can barely contain myself. Mrs. Rory took me to the back of her office and had us introduced; I can't believe the time has finally come! He seemed glad to meet me as well, but in a *different* sort of way—he seemed *relieved*, as if my presence has brought an end to a long, tiring journey. We haven't spoken much yet—he's still dumping off his luggage somewhere. (To my understanding, he'll be staying for a while. I'm not sure of any details, but those are the least of my concerns right now!) I've repeated his name to myself at least one hundred times in the past minute alone, determined not to forget it—*Darren*. His name is Darren. I hope my crazy mind doesn't act up and start weirding out. If I only were a *normal* man. *If only*. My wishes are carried away in a hopeful yet unlikely prayer.

To my surprise, he says he'll be meeting with me *a lot* from now on. I'm so very anxious to find out more, especially *why* this Darren is so interested in *me*. He wants us to be alone, so we're going to engage in a nice stroll together. There's a track just outside in the recreational field, over at the other end of the facility. I suppose we'll circle it a few times and then stop back in for something to eat. Boy, I haven't stepped foot outdoors in months—*years*! A gleeful, childish energy takes me into its hands.

When he returns, Darren is free of all his clumsy baggage. He tells the nurse I've been waiting with that he's ready to bring me outside; we'll be back in an hour or so. The nurse's expression is one of much disapproval, but she allows us to proceed.

"Come on, buddy, let's go," Darren says.

Enchanted, I follow him down the hall. Along the way, he is rudely confronted by several nurses, all of whom he seems to totally ignore

As you know, simple conflicts like these can get me feeling a bit queasy. He notices this phenomenon immediately and stops to ask of my condition.

"You feelin' all right?"

I am compelled toward the truth; already, something about this man just seems so *right* in so many different ways. If I can get myself to lie to Mrs. Hanson but not to this *Darren*, something *must* be special about him. I tell him how I always get uneasy around troublemaking and go into a little account of how it makes me feel.

"You'll be *fine*, I promise," he assures. "When you know how to deal with them properly, stress and conflict can turn into *great things*, my friend."

Stress and conflict—*great things*? "I'm not so sure what you mean, Mr. Darren."

He is seized by a storm of great laughter. "Oh, please—it's *Darren*, just Darren." He strides like a triumphant man-angel. "Come on. Let's get over to that track so we can talk. *About whatever you want.* Today we'll just get to know each other a bit. I'll tell you a little about me, and you can tell me a little about yourself. Is that all right?"

I nod my head excitedly—this puts a special smile upon his face. There's something about it, something *unique*. It's like I've seen it *before*, though I know that can't possibly be.

As he opens the door that leads us outside, there arises an immense sensation all throughout me. I'm confronted by a blazing light that I've not faced in *years*.

*   *   *

Darren initiates a casual stroll 'round the perimeter of the track. Thus far, he's begun to explain why he's come to meet with me, and I am fascinated by every word he's spoken.

"It's a *test*, sort of, but not like any test *you're* familiar with; you might say you're not even being tested at all. It's just this … sort of *idea* I have, this way of thinking that I've come up with that explains why certain kinds of people … do the certain kinds of things they do. As far as you're concerned, all you have worry about is being yourself—that's pretty much it."

"But why me? Why not someone else from the ward?" I ask, less insecurely than I'd expect of myself.

He takes a breath and thinks for a moment before replying. "Well, for one," he starts, "the nurses and Dr. Cohen all had you at the top of their lists. They said you were simply a great patient.

Respectful, calm, understanding—all of that. They told me that if anyone here ought to go forth with what I plan to do, it's *you*. I've checked into your history, and you seem to be the perfect guy for the observational experiment I have in mind. No drugs, no screenings, *none* of that. It'll just be *me* watching *you*.

"A bit regarding my background: I study psychology and teach at a university that's not so far away from ... *here*." He speaks his last word with a strange sense of wariness, as if he has no clue where *here* actually is. "This semester's been cut short for a number of reasons, so over my extended break, I've decided to test a little speculation of mine that's been bugging me for quite a while now. I've been meaning to publish a work on the matter for years, but just didn't have the time to do so."

"Well, what is it all about?" I ask, overwhelmed by Darren's ambition. You see, here on the ward, goals of the sort are miserably looked down upon. In my world, it's believed that only fools try to make anything of themselves.

"I haven't actually come up with a good title yet ... hmm, maybe ... *no*, that's not very good ... or ... *no*, that doesn't work either." A pause. "Ah, I've *got* it: how about ... '*The Untold Sanity of Insane Minds*' ..." He waves a hand fantastically through the air. "You like it?"

My heart flutters with childish excitement. "It ... it sounds great! You mean I'm going to be in a book? Like ... I'm going to be ... *famous?*" Is something so stately even *allowed* to involve the likes of a poor misfit like me?

Darren offers a sincere smile. "Just stick with me and you'll have it *made*." He speaks so matter-of-factly that it sounds as if he's kidding, but some guttural instinct tells me that this guy's legit.

I begin raving about the glorious staff that so fervently tends to me each and every day. With what seems like a growl of resentment, he admits bitterly that he and Dr. Cohen are well acquainted. I don't question this unlikely matter, though I'm thrown into a mode of super-alertness. Who in their right mind is bold enough to disrespect the great Doctor himself? That's like defying God!

Darren elaborates on his blasphemy; every word he speaks makes me cringe more and more intensely. "At first, the Doctor was not so pleased about the idea of me '*interfering*' with any of his patients. He says they're all trained in certain 'patterns' of life and that any *change* in these 'patterns' would bring about emotional disaster within them. I told him I didn't buy it." He leans toward me real closely and whispers into my ear. "Between you and me, buddy, I just think Dr. Cohen doesn't want any 'Outsiders', as you call us, involved with his facility. After many weeks' persistence, though, I got through to him and forced him to agree." Darren pulls away. "Like I said, he told me if anyone's up for the challenge, it's you."

There's a bit more trivial chitchatting before our point of interest returns to the Doctor. As his previous remarks have implied, their relationship is quite sour.

" I just think he tends to his patients in a barbaric way. From what I know of him, it's like he turns you guys into *machines* or something! It's hard to imagine that he cares at all for any of your well beings!"

What? Have I heard him correctly? What in the world is Darren thinking?—it must be someone else, a *different* Dr. Cohen! Something uncomfortable arises in my gut, and I begin to feel a little bit dizzy. To divert my instant discomfort, I blurt out a jumble of unorganized words. "Oh no, no, no! You've got it all wrong! Dr. Cohen? You mean you think of *Dr. Cohen* like that? The one and only? You can't, you just can't! He's so *sweet*, he treats us *as if we're his children*! He's a man unlike any other!"

"Unlike any other, *perhaps*, but as *sweet* as you say? I'm afraid I don't think that's the case." Darren's face is fashioned with disgust.

My feelings for Darren take a slight turn—what am I to make of him? I take his daunting comments rather personally! In the great Doctor's defense, I utter: "You see, but you *don't know him*, you truly *don't.* You'd see him for what he *really* is if you were one of *us!* You'd change your mind if you were a patient like me!"

"*I know,*" Darren says sharply. "When you so passionately adore a man, it's sometimes hard for you to see him the way *others* see him—for what he *really* is."

The sudden confidence he's called upon intimidates me, so instead of arguing with this new menacing force, I try to distract him from himself. "I don't g-get it—what are you talking about?"

Darren looks away and conceals some deep, insistent emotion; with great restraint, he says tiredly, "Nothing. Nothing at all." As if defeated, he utters a sigh. Something about his troubled brow makes me feel uneasy—it seems that something terrible is eating away at him. The wrinkles in his aging face are genuine, and despite his remarks about Dr. Cohen, I cannot help but feel sorry for him.

After many minutes of awkward silence, Darren musters up strength and rejuvenates our unperturbed stroll. He continues our little interview casually. If he is willing to forget our differences, then I suppose I am as well.

"Now from my understanding, you have problem remembering things—is that correct?" he asks.

*   *   *

And so I dive deep into an account of the faults of my fleeting memory. Having arrived at worthy subject matter, Darren's previously disjointed conversing finds a firm issue to settle upon. He probes me for as many details as I can possibly give, though most of his questions are unanswerable on my behalf. One thing that greatly intrigues him is my expansive vocabulary. Because of my eloquence, Darren finds it rather shocking that I can neither read nor write.

Once I'm done explaining my weekly schedule of chores, meetings, and other variable tasks, Darren concludes that it's impossible for me to ever appreciate life itself: the "big picture."

"But I *do* appreciate the staff's love and dedication!" I admit passionately. "What else is there left in my life to appreciate?"

He laughs as we make our way around the track for another circuit. "No, no, not *that* sort of appreciation."

Darren stops our forward movement and asks, "Do you know what separates us from everything else on this earth? What is the *singular* thing that makes the sentience of human beings so special? We may have morals, but a monkey, too, knows not to harm its brothers! Ha—we haven't overridden lions and tigers and bears for *no reason at all!*" He directs my line of sight up into the sky. Its distant, azure ripples reign powerfully like a giant dome high above our heads. The twittering merriment of some playfully mating birds becomes distinctly audible. In triumph, Darren declares: "It's *art*, my friend; it's nothing more than the power and our perception of *art!*"

Art? So it is *art*, he says. Hmm. I've never quite understood its appeal. I've always reckoned it as a destructive force, as an obscene form of expression, as an … oh, I don't know. Mrs. Rory can explain this to you more articulately than I can. Art just … gets in the way! Throughout history, artists have always been the social outcasts, freaks by choice—these are *her* words, of course. She despises art just as much as I do. It's just too risqué for my tastes … *our* tastes.

I convey my disgust to Darren, but he insists that I am under quite a terrible misconception. "Why don't we sit ourselves down for a moment?" he suggests.

We settle upon one of the many benches that line the track's circuit. Despite my lack of interest in art and its profligacy, I'm still somewhat curious to find out how Darren thinks. It's not my place to reject his initiatives, anyhow—he's my *visitor*, after all.

As we sit ourselves down, he asks if I know *why* people seek out lives of art, and, inevitably, I cannot answer him.

"It's an escape," he explains passionately. "Many times it is more than art itself that allures its disciples—it's the lifestyle it entails.

When one creates art, he surpasses the constrictions of mortality; he taps into a gift, a secret world of image and fantasies. Art is the eternal language: *God's* language. It is a path toward enlightenment, a path toward knowledge, a path just as valid as any thinker's, mathematician's, scientist's, or grammarian's! It is both a way to eternalize one's self and more accurately understand life.

"I think your problem, my friend, is that you don't grasp art as a *concept* and understand what it means to humanity. Every second and every minute of everyday life can be enriched with an acutely tuned set of artistic senses. Someone like you, who lives pretty routinely, I assume, can make better use of these principles than anyone else! You see that tree over there?" He points to a massive weeping willow. "There's more to it than *just* what you see. Examine it more closely."

With no reason to object, I follow his orders.

I stare down the details of its greatly gnarled roots and slowly move my eyes upward to its great, outstretched branches. Again, Darren urges me to study closely its shape and structure.

"*Feel* the tree within you; *listen* to the song it sings; become *one* with its existence ..."

At first, there is nothing (and I mean *absolutely* nothing), but after a short while, the towering plant before me begins to imply a definite *rhythm*. Its musical language is indeed quite clear. As if my body were the skin of a huge tympanic drum, my heart flutters in synchronicity with the massive tree's tune. For a brief second, I enter a realm of absolute beauty and sense.

Darren looks over with a satisfied smile—does he have me possessed? What is this ... hidden power deep within nature that he's tapped into?

"Do you see what I mean?" he asks. "Look around. Watch things. Listen to things. The world's best learners are those willing to be taught by anyone and anything. Reckon these natural forces that surround you every day, for they've been around since the beginning of time. When you think like an artist, the most mundane perks of life become so much more *interesting*. That's what makes every second of life worth *living*. The *discovery* never ever ends.

"There's a little bit of *masterpiece* in all of us."

Something instantly clicks deeply within me. For now, at least, I can feel all the rules I've ever been taught rapidly disintegrating. A wise revelation seizes my every bone; I see *exactly* what he means!

"It's very unfortunate that you've been sheltered from so many great things, Sid. Such naïveté … is not your fault at all." Darren successfully traces my contempt back to Hanson, Rory, and of course, Dr. Cohen.

You know what? I think Darren's managed to convince me that "art" (and everything it represents) may not be so bad *after all*. Here on the ward, it's always been downplayed as worthless rubbish—but why? For *what reasons*? Art is a celebration of the greatest things life has got to offer!

I suddenly become aware of my hands' inhuman translucency. How disgustingly colorless! So putrid—so horrifying! I stammer aloud: "It's like I'm invisible! It's like I'm … a ghost!"

"I see you haven't been out in the sun for a long while," Darren observes.

A voice that I haven't been in contact with for ages desperately speaks: "No, *Darren*, it's not that—I'm actually *dead*." A severe case of atrophy consumes my body.

"Am I *looking* for something? Have you come here to show me a part of myself that's … *missing*?" The words I speak are uncontrollable, the emotions I feel cannot be held back; at this moment, I am commanded by a higher power. "Where is the corpse that this ghost must return to?"

With obvious restraint, he says, "I unfortunately cannot solve your riddles. The answers lie deep within *you*."

Abruptly, he ends our meeting.

As we head back and reenter the facility, I tell Darren that he's made me feel unlike I've ever felt before. He's shone unto me light that's never been shone unto me before!

"Then maybe it's like I've said—you're beginning to discover who you *really* are. That's part of my theory as well, that patients just like yourself are not challenged to get in tune with who they *really* are destined to be." He looks away to the sky with confidence. "You are going to be pleased with the results of my little ... *test*; I have faith in our experiment."

Out of the corner of my eye, I catch Darren shed a tear. He wipes it away quickly, but his attempt at nonchalance utterly fails. Stormed by emotional spontaneity, he pulls me in closely and presses our hearts together. He grasps me tightly in his arms and refuses to let go. A minute, two minutes, three minutes pass by. I look into the sincere eyes of this man and suddenly feel obligated to follow his every word.

Before we depart, Darren informs me of a particular book that greatly interests him. To have it read to me is his foremost goal. Apparently, it's vital to my self-discovery. He doesn't go into much detail about it, but that's okay; we may get started with it tomorrow. Oh, I'm very excited—*maybe I can pick up a few words here and there*. What if I can manage to read by the time his testing is done and over with? That'd be just *great*!

I bid Darren farewell and thank him for all that he's already done—he laughs and says that this is only the *beginning*! My gratitude is surpassed by his own appreciation of my very presence. While a nurse escorts him away, he reminds me to look into myself in order to discover the *real* me.

For a few moments, I am trapped in a silent, meditative daze. *Art*: I'm beginning to understand what it means to the world ... what it means to *me*!

*   *   *

"A *visitor*, huh?" Gary growls, snickering under his breath.

So I've informed my lunchtime buddies all about my meeting with Darren. His mindless cronies, Butch and Paulie, chortle like a pack of hyenas along with him. I told you about them earlier, *way* earlier—they're my "friends" from the lunch table. To be honest, I don't really like them very much, but we've been eating together here for what seems like forever now, so I've learned to deal with their antics. Did I ever mention how *troublesome* they can be? They're constantly making fun of me for being a naïve little "child". Though I've never taken their insults to heart, Darren's got this latent mind of mine thinking that they may be right after all ...

Our forty-five minute lunches usually proceed a little something like this: first, quite obviously, we retrieve our chow from a stretch of already laid-out meals and make our way over to the tables to eat. There are really no assigned seats per se, but everyone always sits in the same spot. Almost regularly are there various sorts of uproar. Whether it's a raging war of flying foods or just some dirty talk being hurled back and forth between two brain-dead automatons, something always seems to be going wrong.

It's a shame that I can never have a good conversation with the folks at my table. Hell, I can't even tell you *what* we ever talk about; seldom do we stumble upon a subject of shared interest! Paulie has an especial knack for always changing the focus of everything—he's constantly jumping from one thing to the next! Really, you've got to meet these guys; they make me seem like I don't belong here at our ward in the first place!

I'm trying now to impart Darren's effectiveness upon these three loony fools, but of course, it's useless. I desperately struggle to get them to understand any of it, but they're not willing to listen; they *can't* listen. Stubborn laughter is really all they're capable of.

I've been straining over my simple endeavor for a while now and decide to give up. It's hopeless.

By some strange path paved by Gary's random slurs, our attention has been drawn over to an empty seat across the room—the one normally occupied by Hank Hank. They wonder aloud where he is; no one *ever* misses lunch. Of course, Hank Hank had been taken away yesterday after my therapy session—he'd gone psycho, pulled out a knife, and nearly brought me to *death*! After narrowly avoiding being torn to shreds, I just blacked out. I don't remember everything clearly, but Mrs. Hanson filled me in on everything. I tell these three dense-headed goons about the episode, though something about Hank Hank undergoing "*harmless psycho therapy*" is incredibly hilarious to them; in unison, they predictably topple over in a fit of laughter.

"You don't *believe* that now, do ya?" snorts Paulie.

I ask him what would lead me to believe otherwise; this only riles them up even more. They go on for several minutes bashing my naïveté. I have to keep reminding myself that *they're* far crazier than *I'll* ever be. *Just keep you cool, Sid, just keep your cool.* It's perplexing, as a matter of fact—where, just where in the world do these guys pull their absurd ideas from? Okay, maybe it's *true*—there *are* favorites and I may be one of them, but by no means is anyone *mistreated.* I contradict the new dogma that Darren's unveiled to me by being so defensive, but *really*, some of the stories these guys cook up are just cuckoo!

"They prolly takin' him off for like some testin' or sometin', an' I mean like some *crazy* testin'." Butch talks in this real goofy voice that always sounds like there's a lump of clay lodged in his throat. "You watch, you watch an' den you seein' that he not comin' back for real long time, real, *real* long time, an' maybe that bein' *forever*!"

Paulie and Gary nod along robotically. Their proposition is ludicrous—what would the staff be running a "medical facility" for in the first place if the only thing they were interested in was torturing its patients? It sounds to me like these fools have confused our home and its caretakers with a slaughterhouse and its butchers!

There *may* be some hidden agenda, I suppose, but certainly nothing … *evil.*

One of them challenges me to investigate on my own; I've been dared to venture into the surgery wing during the night and sneak a peek.

"You'll be *surprised* with what you'll find," Paulie warns.

They claim to have witnessed the *evil* of this hospital with their very own eyes. They're nuts! I wouldn't doubt if such delusions landed them here in the first place.

"He's a chi-i-i-i-cken!"

"A chicka-chicka-chicken head!"

"He won't do it! He's too *scared!*"

"I'm not *scared*, Gary. I just like following the rules and making the right choices, *that's* all."

Yet I wonder for a moment … do I *really*?

My thoughts drift back to Darren. I'm reminded of the pleading agony that had confronted me, for the same sensation has resurfaced once again. I realize that deep within me, there's a *struggle*. There's a part of me that craves to defy. There's a part of me just *dying* to explode and run about rampantly like all of the others. Now it's so obvious, so un*believably* obvious! I guess in the past I … I … I *don't know*. I suppose I *ignored* it!

Eventually, I wholly accept their dare. Darren's unveiled to me the wonders of curiosity. If this is only the beginning, as he puts it, I can't imagine what the *end* will be like! I'm already a completely altered being, rechristened and reborn!

"I'm going to do it!" I proudly declare. "I'm going to stampede right into the surgery wing and explore it myself tonight!"

Expectedly, I'm torn apart with senseless laughter. They don't believe me, inevitably, nor did I suppose they would. Butch loads his spoon with a clump of mashed potatoes and flicks it at my face. His aim is pretty good, scoring a mushy bull's-eye on my forehead.

I merely wipe off this lump of processed carbs from my face, get up, and leave to blow off some steam.

Before I have time to return, lunch is dismissed.

There's an aide waiting outside the cafeteria who informs me of my afternoon chores—ugh, I'm stuck cleaning the latrines today. That's the worst of them all!

As I'm led away, I notice something riveting out of the corner of my eye.

A menacing *serpent* with exotically designed scales is coiled up in the middle of the hall. It stares fiercely into my eyes and tries to hypnotize me with a provoking, rhythmic sway. I nearly scream in terror, but it's as if this *serpent's* got its muscular body wrapped 'round my vocal chords. I try to speak, but cannot. I am limited only to fascination of this mysterious creature. Its mordant hissing starts filling up my head like a poisonous gas. What's this thing trying to say to me—how the hell did a *serpent* get onto the ward in the first place? *What the hell is even going on?*

My aide notices that I've lost myself in a daze and asks what's wrong. I try to tell her that there's a *serpent*, yes, an actual *serpent* slithering around and that something needs to be done, though what actually makes its way out of mouth is quite different than what I intended: "Oh, nothing. Nothing at all."

She chalks this off to my craziness at work, I suppose, and makes nothing of it. I glance back to where the menacing reptile had previously writhed, though now it's vanished into thin air.

*   *   *

I don't have very much to do until way later—my therapy session's not until six tonight, so I've got plenty of time to kill. I suppose I'll take my time scrubbing down the latrines. Again, my thoughts revert back to Darren. With a bit of reflection, the things he's said are beginning to make much more sense.

Am I really happy? I ask myself.

Now that I really think about it, I'm not so sure.

Am I really happy …?

Trying to truthfully answer this results in nothing more than a troubling headache, so for now, I put my contemplation to rest.

*   *   *

My group therapy session—which is now barely a group at all, being just me and Lil' Jimmy—trudges by. Jimmy pays no mind whatsoever to the leader, leaving me alone to converse with her pointlessly. She mostly interrogates me about my meeting with Darren, but my responses are purposely unclear and evasive. When plundered by Rory and Hanson, I'm able to hold my own ground just as well. I'm not exactly sure how they've interpreted this new attitude of mine; they're certainly not used to it, and to tell you the truth, I think they're in *shock*. I hope they don't get angry with Darren and scrap his project altogether. Hmm. This is something of a dilemma: if I show off Darren's effects too carelessly, I'm sure the staff will be very displeased—in turn, they might kick him out and we may never meet again. If I don't follow my instincts as Darren's advised, though, then his whole purpose of being here becomes pointless. How's a guy like me—who's always had everything handed to him so easily—supposed to make up his mind on his own?

I take a deep breath and zone out for a moment; the realization that I'm nothing short of *exhausted* has finally hit me. During the last few hours, my incessant ponderings have literally drained me of all my energy. I think I might be overdoing it. The clock beside my bed reads 9:30, a fair enough time to bring a close to the day—and indeed, what a day it's been!

Darren was right—there *is* a little bit of "masterpiece" in all of us. I've found it within myself just as he said I would! It's *always* been there, that much is for sure. Everything's unburying itself, everything's rising up again from a big ol' pile of rubbish and ash. This "masterpiece" has existed forever, but I've just never reckoned its presence! It's like he said—we here are not challenged to find ourselves. We're all capable of great things, or at least I *think*. It's the idleness and fear that eat us up alive, it's the lack of motivation that stops us patients from becoming anything more than the mindless machines we are. We're not given anything to work for! Yes, we're victims, I suppose, but why not make the best of things? Why should we suffer any more than we have to? I'm *waking* up—I've been shown some incredible sense!

The time has come at last for me to put everything to rest. I'm tired, and though I'm itching to investigate the "evils" of the surgery wing, I just can't. Not tonight; I'm simply drained. It's funny that Darren had alluded to this secret "evil" as well—something's up, that's for sure, something that I've been unaware of for many, many years. Was I too dumb? Did I just shut these things out? Did I ignore them? Had I just not been told? All of these things are beside the point. The bottom line is that I've got to find out exactly what's going on. My insecurities are of a different world, a *past* life. I'm human, a *human being*, and I therefore have the right to shape my life as I choose.

As I lay my head down to indulge in some sleep, I notice something—*someone*—out of the corner of my eye.

"Mr. Fan*dango*!"

What the heck—it's like he's materialized out of thin air! Has he taken the occupancy of the empty bunk beside mine? The one that's been unused for years?

He squirms free out of the mess of linen he's tangled in. All five feet that he has to call his own jerks up in shock.

"It's *YOU!*" he wails. I shush him immediately and (in nervy stutters) order silence—we've got to keep it down during the night! He hops out of his bunk and parks himself near my feet. Preoccupied with my other more pressing concerns, I'd nearly forgotten about this man-gnome. *How could I have?* It was his very sparkling enthusiasm that helped jumpstart this revolutionary day.

So it seems that my wish has been granted *without* the assistance of the nurses—I wanted to meet him, and here he is beside me at the foot of my bed, bustling with even more energy than before!

The two of us make small talk. Immediately, he seems anxious to "move on." I can't make heads or tails of him—he's got me totally bamboozled! I'm not quite sure what he wants out of me. Judging from that wildly anxious look on his face, it seems as if he's ready for some extraordinary feat. For at least five minutes now, he's been throwing around all sorts of gibberish that I can barely understand.

Eventually, I muster up enough courage to ask him why he's been transferred onto the ward.

With a slightly demented grin, he says, "Ain't no reason!" Mr. Fandango looks away for a moment and snickers like a madman. "*Ain't no reason at all!*"

I find his disposition rather fascinating. Intrigued by his loony character, I stammer, "There's just got to be something … *wrong* with you to be here!"

He stops to think for a moment and runs his stubby fingers through his beard. "Uh, *nope*. Not one thing wrong with *me!*"

Geez—I can't imagine what the normally dull nights around here are likely to turn into with *this* weirdo around!

"You should see me when I'm really excited, when I'm *really* over the top!" he warns playfully.

And if *this* isn't over the top, then I don't know what is. Here he goes again, spitting out bits and pieces of undecipherable mumbo jumbo. It's not before long that he intoxicates himself with a storm of self-induced laughter. As civilly as I possibly can, I try to calm him down. I conclude that this guy's out of his mind, but in a *good* way. He's not "crazy" like the kind of crazy we've got here on the ward. Mr. Fandango is … *different*. He exhibits a surging sense of passion that's really inspiring. He's untamed and raucous, but something is so stunningly genuine about him. If he goes on as wildly as this all the time, though, he's sure to eventually land himself in some serious trouble.

"You better take things down a notch," I advise. "One of these days, the staff—"

"Aww, you *worry too much!*" he declares as loudly as he can.

I find myself suddenly engrossed in a little lecture of his. Somehow, he's managed to stumble upon the topic of his own morals and philosophies. He spends the next five minutes imparting upon me his carefree doctrine of life. I can only sit and watch him, mesmerized—what *else* is there to do? The little bantam shows no sign of letting up anytime soon.

Mr. Fandango draws two quarters from out of nowhere and performs a dazzling array of tricks. I watch his stealthy hands jumble the order and positioning of the coins, but cannot catch the gist of his little show. I curiously ask him how he's doing it, but my words don't penetrate him. I try again and again for a straight answer, but I'm starting to realize that there's no way of getting through his dense skull. Instead, I sit back in awe of his hands' nonstop flurries. He entices me like a child, in a way that connects with the most primeval of human instincts. He has me on the edge of my seat playing trivial guessing games. Despite the useless nature of his sport (as Mrs. Rory would surely put it), this guy sure knows how to have *fun!*

In a speedy flash, he puts away his game pieces and enters a series of athletic stunts; he's got his stout, dwarfish body catapulting all over the place! The transitions between his outbursts are smooth, improvised, and inane, yet the youthful energy that propels him about the room is so ... so *admirable!* He's got a wide arsenal of flips at his disposal—ones to the front, ones to the back, ones to either side; I'm buzzing in anticipation just watching his dangerous demonstration!

Once he's tired, drenched in sweat, and short of breath, Mr. Fandango once again goes on talking about nothing, though this

RAYMOND

time it no longer fazes me—I'd rather absorb his appeal than wreck him for answers to my own silly questions.

By the time ten o'clock draws near, Mr. Fandango grows bored—he suggests an adventure of sorts. He demands something exhilarating.

"There's not very much to do around here," I disappointedly inform him. Let's see—we could … no, that wouldn't be much fun. Maybe if we … no, not that either. What if …? Ah, yes! That's the *perfect* idea! "The *surgery wing*!" I excitedly propose.

I reveal to Mr. Fandango the "evils" that Gary, Butch, and Paulie spoke of earlier.

"Sounds like *fuuun!*" he purrs. "Well? What the hell're we waitin' for? Lessgo, lessgo, lessgo, lessgo, less—"

"Not yet," I interrupt. Though I try to convey a calm façade, I'm teeming with the same childish excitement as my counterpart. "It's way too early; the staff's still floating around at this hour, so we've got to wait until later, much later." It takes me a while to drill this into Mr. Fandango's brain—he wants to go now, *right* now, but after endless bargaining, he agrees to hold his horses for just a bit longer.

It's a little past midnight, I think, that everyone finally leaves. There are nighttime guards, of course, but from what I hear, they're lazy and just doze off anyway; I guess they don't expect much trouble from us. Ha! And the others call *me* naive …

The cameras, though, will certainly make things more difficult. I explain this problem to Mr. Fandango, but it doesn't seem to intimidate him.

"All the more fun!" he insists. "We'll pretend we're fugitives or renegades or prison escapees or something!"

It's … it's … it's so hard to believe that any of this is actually happening! Yesterday, I prayed for the courage just to *ask* Mrs. Hanson about the loud noises that for so long have bothered me, and now I'm investigating them on my *own*! I look back on yesterday, the day before yesterday, and the day before that, and a year ago, and two years ago, and for the length of my forever and conclude that everything's false, everything's totally *wrong*. That passive creature from what seems like so long ago is not me at all! What a blind, disgraceful, imbecile I'd been!

"Get yourself a little bit of rest then, why dontcha?" Mr. Fandango suggests, usurping my thoughts. "You don't wanna fall asleep while we're out on our mission!"

"What if I don't wake up? I don't want to *oversleep!*"

"Oh, don't worry! I'll rouse you up, I'll get your blood stirring— *I'll* be awake, no doubt about it!" In a sarcastically discreet voice, he says, "I don't sleep very much, ya hear? I ain't been to sleep *in ages!* Never wanna miss a thing, ya know what I'm sayin'?"

He's obviously exaggerating, but I'm not about to question it—I'd believe just about *anything* coming from this lunatic!

A wave of tiredness storms my bones. I lie down and almost instantly drift away into a mild state of slumber.

*   *   *

MRS. BURR: You've really been thinking *big* lately, Doctor.

DR. COHEN: Well the time is right … that's all I've got to say.

B: What's this madness you're talking about now? A *digital* society? Doc, let's be realistic here. I'm not even sure exactly what you mean!

C: *(paying no mind to Mrs. Burr's doubtful remarks)* Well it's all *theoretical*, of course. The world is not yet quite at the technical standpoint it needs to be for what I've got in mind. Patience, Mrs. Burr, *patience*. It all boils down to patience. The time will come, and that time is on its way. In a hundred years or so, the kinds of ideas I have will be a part of the common American paradigm.

B: What makes you so certain? We've got activists out in the streets with their goddamned rallies and their goddamned morals … there's *no way* that our ways of thinking can ever transcend into the mainstream! Do you think those indolent *humans* on the Outside are ready to adapt to such drastic changes? Our ethics have not been taught in their culture! We won't be accepted without a fight, we just *won't*, and *that's* why—

C: *That's* why we need to make the outside world aware of what we're capable of as quickly as we can. If they only knew of the power we possessed!

B: That's insanity, Doctor! Just look at your endeavors—you'd be persecuted and put on trial! It'd be the end of all we live for!

C: It will be a rough journey to get to where we want to go, but I think it's possible; we've just got to start small, that's all. We'll ease the Outsiders into our customs *little* by *little*.

B: *(both thoughtfully and doubtfully)* Well there's no way we could introduce the kind of plans you seem to be cooking up right now to anyone, it'd just be *suicide* … in fact, what exactly *were* you talking about just before? First artificial *fish-people* and now digital *zombies* … what's next?

C: You see, Mrs. Burr, the creation of these "fish-people"—as you so call them—is just a *joke* to me, a little way of having some scientific fun. In reality, they're utterly useless. On the other hand, this so-called "digital world" that I've got in the works has the potential of becoming the way of the future!

B: And how so? Have you *lost your mind?*

C: *(proudly; arrogantly)* It's all quite simple, really

[*The doctor rubs his hands together and takes a seat*]

C: Let me explain to you, dearest: Imagine a world ... say, even the one that we live in today ... where the whole idea of "death" becomes virtually *eliminated*. A world where you've got the constant recycling of individual minds. We—

B: Oh, let's be *real* here, Doc—it's immoral and inhumane, you're just ... *I don't know!*

C: *(impatiently) Would you settle down and let me speak?* I'm not trying to brainwash you, for the love of God! The reason I *created* you in the first place is so I could have someone to talk to. You've not forgotten your purpose now, have you?

B: *(somewhat ashamed)* No I haven't, Doc.

C: *(forgivingly)* Come sit on my lap, sugarplum.

[*Mrs. Burr hops gently between Doctor Cohen's burly thighs.*]

C: The matter at hand, my love, is identity, *human* identity—what is it? Is it in our bodies? Our faces? Our expressions? The way we walk and talk? Or is it something unknown and divine? Are our identities in fact something completely integrated and intangible? *Dare I say it* ... can the answers to my questions possibly lie in such a silly notion as the soul?

[*Dr. Cohen strokes Mrs. Burr's hair gently and bites the back of her neck.*]

C: What I am alluding to is mankind's inseparable attachment to its own stupid cultures and biases! We cannot move forward without trashing our predispositions! How many scientific miracles are there to speak of that the Outside is oblivious to? These are the sorts of things the world *needs* to know about, the things it needs to *care* about! The very notion of modern society conspires against intelligence, *real* intelligence … against people like me!

C: So what I've been thinking about lately is how mystifying the notion of life after death really is … *mortal* life after death. A while back, as you already know, we developed the means to "photocopy" any given mind. We have the ability to run scans that read and compute every genetic nook and cranny of any and every brain. This equipment, however, is terribly expensive and difficult to use. As of late, I've been trying to modify this already brilliant system into something even greater, something more accessible.

C: At any given point, if permitted to do so, we could assemble a completely digital database of the entire country! Every single mind would be invariably stored as a computerized code. May anyone die at any point in time, their "information" will never be lost—all they've ever known, seen, and felt will be preserved in this massive databank. It will not be long before the physical and technological worlds will join together to form a single ultramodern race. This marriage can allow virtually anyone to live forever!

C: My dear Mrs. Burr, have you any idea what that means?

B: *(after thinking a few moments)* That we've discovered the key to immortality?

C: *(beaming with ecstatic optimism)* Bingo! Yes, my lovely honeybunch, that is correct! Isn't my mind just grand, Mrs. Burr? Aren't I a fucking *genius*?

B: I've never been more proud of you, my love!

C: Are you up for a round of the Game?

[SEDUCTIVE, PERVERSE LOOK FROM MRS. BURR.]

B: How 'bout a dose of morphine first?

C: (Sighing; not in the mood; he surrenders to the thirst of his sexual desires) I suppose just one shot can't hurt …

*   *   *

Just as the clock strikes midnight, Mr. Fandango eagerly rouses me out of my nap.

We silently make our way around a few halls. I lead the way. Cautiously, the two of us slyly dodge the dozens of mechanical eyes that probe the grounds for intruders. My body is learning the art of mischief—and it's about time. Why, I've got a whole lifetime worth of troublemaking to catch up on! Who would have guessed that this sort of thing could be so much fun?

After a few minutes, we run into a security guard; as expected, he's completely asleep. Mr. Fandango and I exchange an optimistic little giggle, pressing onward wordlessly. I seem to be driven by my newly unleashed desire for the unknown. We are predators in search of a fresh, bloody meal. I've not eaten for days, years—my entire life—so I'm just about ready to sink my teeth down into my anything.

It doesn't take long for us to reach our destination. Presently, the only thing standing between ourselves and the mysteries of the "surgery wing" is a giant, metallic door. Mr. Fandango begs to go in first, so I allow him to pass me by. To my surprise, there are no perceptible defenses here of any sort—no lasers to trip, no cameras to be caught on, and no sensors to activate. I somehow feel as if we're entering a trap, but I shoo my pessimism away.

The door opens with a startling screech. Mr. Fandango can't help but gasp and topple backward into me. We land together with a deafening crash. There's a ferocious rumble, something like an atomic bomb exploding in the small proximity of the corridor—instantly the animal-like drive roaring all throughout me has died in a rush of fear. Our stares meet in apprehension. I can see that his mind is racing as well, calculating the worst possible of outcomes and their consequences. I close my eyes tightly and pretend to disappear, pretend to melt away.

It's quite some time later when my troll of a counterpart comes rapping upon my chest. I reopen my eyes, and, to my relief, it seems that the coast has remained clear.

What a rush!

I've never before quite experienced fear, *real* fear. It's a funny thing, I now see; it gets your body and mind all twisted and bent out of function, yet something about it is so *thrilling*. Despite the tension, there's this tremendous, explicit exhilaration. I'd felt vigorous and alive! If only Gary, Butch, and Paulie could see me now … they wouldn't believe it, not in a million years!

In synchronicity, Mr. Fandango and I venture into the dark realm concealed behind this menacing door.

In the dark, we grope around to find a source of light. Mr. Fandango stumbles upon a light switch and everything illuminates. Surprisingly, the room we've found ourselves in is small and uninteresting. There's another door beside the one from which we've entered, but that's about all this small space has to offer. It's a bit disappointing, but a voice deep within me promises something more beyond this second door. Wrought with both apprehension and suspense, I decide to proceed.

The lights are already on. Fandango and I scan our surroundings confusedly. *What the heck is this?* We exchanged astonished glances. It's been a wasted journey—a decoy! This isn't the *real* surgery wing. It's just a detour, just a storage room or something! There's nothing here but … sky-high piles of dismembered *cardboard boxes*!

"This can't be it!" Mr. Fandango cries. He leaps over a massive heap of garbage and desperately explores the rest of the room. "It just *can't* be!"

He's very agile, so I have some trouble keeping up with him. In spite of his determinedness, it's difficult to find the motivation to move on. There's really no point; it's obvious there's nothing more to see. I mean … just *look* at this place! What a letdown!

Mr. Fandango turns 'round on the highest peak of this cardboard mountain range, so for a while, he disappears out of sight. After a few moments' silence, he begins shrieking in a restless tone.

"Sid! Sid!" he calls anxiously from a distance. I follow the sound of his voice hurriedly, for my dying wick of hope has been relit.

"Quick, quick, come here! Come here now!"

I find myself relocated in a distant corner of the room. Mr. Fandango's attention has been won over by a giant, shield-like curtain. Instantly, our efforts are aimed at throwing it aside. Once we get it out of the way, we step back and behold the horror it had concealed moments ago.

My God!

My gut performs a fanfare of circus tricks that leave me sickened. Where can I even *begin* to explain the sadism kept behind this cursed drape?

Undoubtedly, this is the most horrific sight I've ever set my eyes upon. Floating around in fluid-filled vats are body parts—*human body parts*. Suspended inertly in their watery atmospheres, I am stared down by lifeless arms, legs, torsos, and even severed heads! Disconnected brains—intricately wired and kept alive by currents fed into them by giant machines—are seated in neat rows contained inside some oversized incubator. The gnarled head of a bodiless baby struggles to break free of the strange, jelly-like substance it sprouts from. Dismembered torsos hang from the ceiling, and they lifelessly dance to the rhythm of the room's current. I turn to find Mr. Fandango, but I see that he's disappeared—I can only imagine he's already bolted away from this horrible freak show! I try to shift my legs into motion, but they are frozen and numbed.

Behold!—Great, clanking, metal machinery ... Chimera-turned children preserved in icy holding cells ... De-skulled robotic men, naked on the floor, brainless, their hollow heads filled with metal and pulsing electricity ... A genderless creature, not quite man, not quite woman, laced with intricate tubes and knobs, hooked up to some piece of monitoring equipment ... Mindless clones bred in placental tissue culture ... A half-man, half-aquatic life form resting peacefully in the confines of an aquarium ... A large, plastic container overfilled with disheveled, torn-apart *hogs* ...

My attention turns to a bedridden man—he is secured down savagely by a number of clamps, straps, and holding devices. His face is distorted with permanent agony. I know who this is—*was*; there is no life to be attributed to this pile of forsaken flesh and bones. Here lies the man once known as *Hank Hank*. His chest is a yawning cavern, and it is filled with something inhuman: an overblown, inflated heart. It beats rapidly and is on the brink of exploding.

I screech, consumed in fear, for I've just realized that I'm not alone.

I've awakened someone—some*thing*. It's a bodiless head connected to a long, transparent, gas-filled tube. The torn flesh around its neck is secured by bolts to the brim of this pump—the two have seemingly merged as one. Its eyes are devoid of life. It *breathes*, it *thinks*, but its actions are purely mechanical. Its realized state of being brings forth a howl like that of a dying beast. This head shakes feverishly and begins foaming from the mouth. The machinery which with it has fused teeters from one side to the other. It reaches out to me desperately during the last moments of its life: "*Save me! Save me! In the name of God, somebody fucking save me!!*" The earth rumbles beneath my feet, and I soon find myself charging back through the cardboard maze from which I've come.

What in the world? What have I just seen?

What propels me forward is nothing more than the instinct to survive. After a few moments, something (or some*one*) wallops me in the back of the head.

I vanish off the face of the earth.

*　　*　　*

And then there?s this dream_the one that?s always there_with the probing_ and the poking_and the numbness all up in you__try to move_but there?s no place to go_something like being trapped in quicksand_too tired to think about anything_so it all becomes okay_ too tired_too! too tired! tiredpoke_ tiredpokepoke in the head_and it feels like a drain, sort of_ but_can?t fall asleep just yet ?cause i?m listening_ and she says (look what you?ve done to him)(it?s been only a day!)_and then he defends himself_and they?re all getting angry_so very very angry!!!!_(one more slip up like this and you'll be packing up your bags and getting your ass out of here)_but i?m trying and trying to move_but_just can?t_so they start fighting_but there?s nothing I could do ?cause i?m fucking trapped!!

… can?t even … move … a muscle …

*　　*　　*

DR. COHEN: And how is our friend Poseidon doing, Mrs. Burr? Have you checked up on him thus far tonight?

MRS. BURR: Oh, he's just *fine*, Dr. Cohen. He seems to be getting more and more mobile by the *second*! There's no impending problem with the genetics, either. It appears that the use of gills is quite natural for him.

C: Part crustacean, part sea mammal, part human—it amazes me sometimes what we're able to achieve!

B: If everything turns out okay, I have the data for his duplicates just waiting to be grown. There are also…

[COHEN STOPS, GLANCES DOWN THE HALL; ATTENTION IS DRAWN TO THE SOUND OF APPROACHING FOOTSTEPS.]

B: Is that who I think it is?

C: *(irately)* So the bastard's come again. *Sigh.* Can you do me a favor, Mrs. Burr? Just leave the two of us to ourselves for now; we've got some serious business to take care of.

B: You got it, Doc … be back in an hour?

C: That's fine.

[MRS. BURR EXITS.]

[ENTER DARREN.]

[THE MOOD IS AWKWARD AND STIFF; THERE IS AN EXTENDED MOMENT OF SILENCE BETWEEN THE TWO OF THEM.]

C: **(blatantly; the Doctor is overly direct.)** We're going to have to start Him over again.

DARREN: I thought we had a *deal* going on, a solid man-to-man deal!

C: We do. But that doesn't permit our friend here to go snooping around wherever He wants. We have *rules* here, and if you're teaching Him not to follow these *rules*, then I'm afraid I'm going to have to ask you to leave!

D: I never told Him to do anything! He's finally thinking for *Himself*!

C: In a matter of one day's time? That a lifetime of efforts here at this place can be overthrown by *you* in less than twenty-four hours is just ridiculous! An absurdity!

D: I've only introduced myself! We haven't even begun the relearning process!

C: I know, *Darren*, and that's exactly what's most frightening of all. How 'bout we just scrap this whole idea and forget about it? By sunrise, we'll have you relinquished from His memory altogether.

D: *(anxiously; desperately)* You c-c-can't! You *can't* do that! I'll … have you *busted*, I'll have the whole world know of your sick and twisted ideas!

C: Are you saying that I don't have the power to wipe you off the face of this earth right now in but a mere instant? If you'd like, I can *easily prove you wrong.*

D: That's *not* what I'm saying!

C: I told you long ago, *years* and *years* ago, that there's no way you can win this fight. Ever.

D: If only He could hear you now. Do you know what He'd do, do you *have any idea what He'd do?*

C: Of course, and that's *precisely* why He is where He is today. Never knew how to keep His goddamned mouth shut. You know just as well as I do that our troublesome little lout here was one of the most dangerous thinkers of His time—He was our first priority to snatch, He needed to be cleansed immediately. Had we not stopped Him while He was young, *who knows* what the world would be like today! He was on his way to becoming something of national affair, wouldn't you say?

D: He was bringing the world back to how it should be.

C: How it will *never* be, is what you mean to say.

D: With you around, I'm starting to believe that might be true.

C: Good. Then at least you've acquired some kind of sense.

D: Will we resume again tomorrow?

[LONG, SUSPENSEFUL SILENCE]

C: Being a righteous man true to my word, I suppose so. We're all very upset here, the nurses especially. It's a shame for them to see all their dedication and hard work go to waste. Heartbreaking, actually. Like they'd never made a difference in His life at all.

He'll be reconfigured and transformed into a totally different man, more *stubborn*, more *naive*, and more *robotic* than ever before—the process might take some time, a few weeks or so. My vow to you is that we'll give Him full reading capabilities and a solid, infallible memory, one better than He's ever had in the past. We'll keep it intact and swear not to alter it. Since He'll be entirely literate, you may give Him your little book and He may read it on His own. To prevent Him from causing any more mischief, the nurses and I have agreed on *paralyzing* Him; that should be enough to keep our dear friend in line.

Until His reconstruction is complete, you'll just have to sit tight.

D: What makes you think you've any right? Who ever gave you permission to play God?

C: God? Ah, yes. He will come and go as well. There *is* no God—His era will soon be a part of the past. We live in a new, biosocial age, my friend; humans have *surpassed* the unknown; we ourselves have become the *gods.*

D: So what is to become of me in the long run? Whether or not I succeed in having Him relearn His past, what do you have in store for me?

C: You've avoided us long enough—you're the *last* of them. We've cast our bait and have got you right where we want you. Nice façade: someone like you—a professor? At a university? Ha! For the past twenty years, you've been running in circles like the blind rat you are, and at last you've run right into our hands. It's a game, to be honest, that's all it really is—a round of Russian roulette, and sadly, my dear Darren, you've already lost.

*   *   *

I didn't sleep well last night—it feels like I haven't slept at all! I'd fallen into slumber no later than usual, but I presently feel absolutely lifeless. Even to jerk open my eyelids costs me more energy than my body's willing to spare. Not only am I tired, but I ache terribly as well—there are these blaring sore spots all over me. Hell, I can barely move! Slowly, I attempt to rise up from this mess of sheets, but it's useless. The rest of my body's been cut off from my brain.

What in the world …?

With all the might I can muster, I try to lift a single finger but achieve little success. I've become something of a statue, a concrete ornament pasted upon this bed. The weight of the world ties me down to my captor. I try to scream, but the message is intercepted by some tainted chemicals brewing within me. I can *feel* the biological compounds swirling mockingly through my blood stream. That bastard Cohen, that selfish little *bastard*! My whole life wasted here on the ward and *this* is what I get?

Darren!

Though I can't budge, my mind is kept in functioning order. I jump back in time for a moment and recollect everything I can. Yes, yes, it's all there: Mr. Fandango, my congregating outside, the meaning of art, the meaning of *life*, the treacherous truths behind this hell-house … in my secluded brain I cry out for help, but no one can hear me. I feel a bit frantic now, *paranoid* even; I'm stuck here lifelessly, my body its own prison. My breaths slowly disintegrate and I am cut off from the air around me. I hear footsteps approaching—hovering over me now is the unholy trinity, Rory, Hanson, and old man Cohen. They're laughing, overflowing with bubbling ecstasy as I am left here to rot. If only I could shed my skin and free myself! I wouldn't mind if all three of them were beheaded and sent to waste away in hell. I'd rather *die* than ever set my eyes upon these devils again! The fury within me manages to awaken the mobility of my fingers, though just my fingers alone. This animal instinct causes me senselessly to dig my unshaven nails into my palms—deeper, deeper—until the flesh is ripped, torn, and destroyed in desperation.

Alas, after a moment's rage, this spontaneous power fades away.

I am buried alive in my motionless stupor. Helplessly, my frozen, paralyzed body shuts down.

part 2

The black of sleep slowly wanes away.

It takes me a while to fully come to—it feels like I've been out of it for days; *weeks!* Before things get too busy, allow me to introduce myself. My name is Sid Tate, and I'm a patient at a highly advanced mental institution. I'm rather shy and never ask for very much … all I really need is the dedication of the extraordinary folks that run this place. I'm paralyzed from the waist down, but that never really manages to bother me. Sure, getting around is a bit of a chore, but honestly, where is there to go that the lovely Mrs. Hanson wouldn't be willing to take me herself?

If you're unfamiliar with the staff, I'll give you a quick rundown: Mrs. Hanson is my personal assistant. She loves me more than anyone else in the world. Whenever I need anything, she's always there to help. Rarely does she concern herself with other patients, for I've always been her number one priority. Then there's Mrs. Rory; she's the main secretary. You can find her office directly in the center of the ward. Oh, she's a gem, as well … without her, I don't know what we'd do! She keeps track of patient histories, medical information, scheduling, the distribution of our medication, and so much more. Honestly, I don't know how she does it. Lastly, of course, there's Dr. Cohen. He's handpicked the staff himself. As you might have guessed, he settles for nothing less than the best of the best. This is *his* ward, we are *his* patients—I owe my *life* to him. Since I'm his favorite, he makes sure that I always have the best of everything. I'm docile, tolerant, respectful … what more could one ask of a mental patient like me? Oh, and just so you know, I *never* break the rules. Unlike many of the others here, I'm not very much of a troublemaker; in fact, troublemaking makes me physically *sick!* The slightest bit of conflict transports me to a nightmarish, delusional world of horror. Because I'm so sensitive, Mrs. Rory has it arranged that I interact as little as possible with the other patients. I don't really mind this, though, for it allows me to spend more time with my dear, dear Mrs. Hanson.

What makes this morning so different is that I am anticipating the arrival of some "visitor." I was informed last night that I'd be meeting with a stranger from the *Outside*. The notion summons a swarming cluster of nervous butterflies in my gut. An Outsider … what could an Outsider possibly want with me? I'm actually quite apprehensive of this strange, strange event.

Ugh. Unless I'm dealing with Mr. Fandango, socializing is just *not* my thing; he's another story altogether, though. Boy, what a maniac! I'm sure you'll get to meet him later on tonight. I won't even try to explain that loon in words. You have to see him for yourself! He's crazy; he's a living elf-man!

Wow … *an Outsider here on our ward.*

Geez, I feel weird just *thinking* about it! We never get to communicate with the Outside, but I suppose everything will be all right. If this were going to be a dangerous affair, I'm certain that Dr. Cohen would not allow me to be a part of it. He would *never* let anyone hurt me!

At 10:30, Mrs. Hanson arrives and helps me into my wheelchair. Somewhat unexcitedly, she reminds me that my visitor will be arriving shortly. Her lack of enthusiasm is a bit odd, but I don't bother to question it. Her eyes seem slightly bloodshot, too, and a significant tremor has seized her hands. She probably didn't sleep well last night, that's all … I'll try to trouble her as little as possible today so she can catch up on some rest!

Before I head down for breakfast, I'm given my morning medications. It's quite crucial that I keep up with the drugs I'm prescribed; without them, my body wouldn't run properly! If I'm not constantly medicated, my fragile framework is likely to ruin and crack! In case you're wondering how bad my condition actually is, I'll explain: my legs are completely useless, and though my arms and hands are fairly futile as well, with some great strength, I can operate them clumsily. These handicaps may sound burdensome, but believe me, things could be *way* worse—in my little world, there's nowhere to go, no one to see, and absolutely nothing to do.

I enter the cafeteria and immediately fill up my plate with my favorite yolkless omelets. Mrs. Hanson sits by my side, as always, and watches me greedily pig out. (It's just the two of us—it's been arranged so I have the cafeteria entirely to *myself* for breakfast ... isn't that just great?) I'm especially hungry this morning—it's like I haven't eaten in *weeks*!

I'm given a short lecture on how to deal with my soon-to-arrive visitor. "Just be yourself," she passionately explains. "Don't allow him to take advantage of you."

When we're done, she directs me back upstairs. Did I tell you that I've even got a room of my own? The other patients are restricted to cold, uncomfortable bunks, but I've got a little, tidy haven completely to myself! My room is rather plain, but that's perfectly fine; it's right next door to Mrs. Hanson's personal office, so that's all that matters.

"Just remember," she says firmly, "don't believe anything your heart doesn't want you to. Follow your instincts. You *know* we love you. We always have—and always *will*."

*　　　*　　　*

I'm allowed some time to meditate before the arrival of my visitor. Trying to remain calm, I close my eyes and intentionally zone out for a bit. Now that I'm alone without Mrs. Hanson's maternal reassurances, the notion of congregating with an Outsider seems mightily intimidating. *Don't be afraid—there's nothing to be afraid of.* Her words resonate clearly in my head. *We're here to make sure that everything is okay.* I know that she'd *never* want to see me like *this*. I sober up and put aside my fears, knowing this would make her proud.

Why, just why am I such a living wreck? Dr. Cohen—the great

man in charge of this incredible facility—has sought after many prime psychiatrists throughout the country, but no one seems able to penetrate my terribly diseased psyche. No man ought to be as apprehensive and insecure *as this*. Take a good look at me! Behold this shameful excuse of a man! Here I am trembling like a child in the confines of my wheelchair, here I am on the verge of breaking out into a deluge of salty tears! Nothing can help me—indeed, what a terrible fate. I'm pumped with the most advanced drugs and given an abundance of care and attention, yet still, I remain hopeless. The only cure is to come from "within"—I am my *own* cure, though I'm not quite sure how to unlock this potential. It's inside of me somewhere, buried deeply beneath the pile of unconfident rubbish that pollutes my soul … *it's just got to be!*

In spite of all these terrible truths, I *am* happy. *Really.* Thanks to the ward's overwhelming attention, I'm allowed to rot away in my screwed-up little head while feeling great about myself at the same time. They let me forget, and isn't that most important of all? Does it really matter if I ever face the truth? As long as I'm able to remain happy in my warped little world, does *anything* else matter at all? Only ignorance questions bliss.

The false colors are unchained and instantly I am lured into a secret world.

Something strangely external compels me to lift up my head, open my eyes, and take a peek out of my open door. The corridor is blank as usual, but some unidentifiable voice calls out to me—it is not a voice I can *hear*, in fact it is not a voice that connects with any one sense in particular; it is an elusive yet inclusive channel of communication.

I chalk it off as nonsense (you learn to deal with delusions like these when you're as crazy as me), but its presence lingers and refuses to depart. My childish fears of the visitor from the Outside wash away, exchanged now with fear of whatever this phenomenon may be. With all the strength I can summon into my weak, paralyzed hands, I set the wheels of my mobile chair into slow (but eventual) motion.

At first, I advance sluggishly. The things around me begin to acquire a somewhat reflective, *cartoon-like* appeal. Dazed amidst this slick and slippery world (still drawn by an obscure and distant calling), I find myself pushing unintentionally through the doors of our resident spa/work-out room where physically suited patients can spend their leisure time keeping in shape.

Upon entry, every head turns and focuses in on me; the energetic flow of their exercising halts immediately. The nuances of their faces distort, though I can still clearly make out their perturbed expressions staring me down. My eyes widen confusedly; *fearfully.*

What are they *doing?* What in the world are these masked faces looking at so *strangely?* It's like they've never seen me before, like I am foreign, like I am alien! A troubled wave of discoursing sweeps them—I don't understand! What's gone wrong? It's just me, Sid! *Sid Tate!* What more or less do they expect?

I hear the exchange of doubtful questions like *"What's happened to him?"* and *"Is that who I think it is?"*, though I can't find any reason for them to be exhibiting such shock!

Heated by a blazing, anxious flame, this waxy world instantly melts into nothingness.

*   *   *

DR. COHEN: *What?* You cannot be serious, my dear ... He's blacked out *already?*

MRS. BURR: Yes, Doctor. It's quite unfortunate.

C: Have we perhaps reconstructed Him *too* insecurely? *Too* responsive to fearful stimuli?

B: As of now, we cannot be quite sure. We must allow Him time to grow accustomed to His new "adjustments."

C: Oh, *Christ* ... just think of all the others that have seen Him! I suppose we'll have to rework their memories tonight. What a *hassle* ... *[The doctor angrily pounds his work desk.] He needs to stay locked in His cage where He belongs!* I can't imagine what would ever get Him to wander off like that! Is it necessary to inhibit His thoughts even more? Something's not right, Mrs. Burr, something is definitely *not right* with Him.

B: *(as she re-buttons her outfit and slips her shoes back on; she speaks with a surprising sense of wisdom)* I think you hit the nail on the head, Doc. Just the other day while I was cleaning out His memory bank, I ran a scan of His brain and noticed that, quite interestingly, our dear friend is beginning to ... *lose* it.

C: *(curiously) Lose it?* You mean His sanity?

B: Yes. Our experimentations have finally caused Him to lose all communication with His own already distorted "realities"—He's at last gone "insane" on His own, by virtue of *Himself.*

C: Why, that's ... that's just *terrible!*

B: His world has been transformed into one of mirages, illusions, fantasies—things *beyond* our comprehension.

[DEEPLY CONCERNED EXPRESSION FROM COHEN; FOR THE FIRST TIME, HE EXPLOITS A SENSE OF WORRY—HE IS TRULY APPALLED.]

C: Is this a sign?

B: A sign of what?

C: *[delayed response]* ... I'm not *sure.*

B: Well, what are we to do?

C: Nothing, as of yet. We will keep Him under intense surveillance at all times. Once Darren is finished wasting our time and we rid ourselves of him, we must return our focuses to more pressing matters.

B: Maybe I've given you the wrong idea, Doc—perhaps the situation's not as bad as you're imagining it to be.

(EXAGGERATED, PENSIVE SILENCE.)

C: No, maybe *not.* However, the end of our most prized possession draws near. *[Thinks to himself for a moment.]* After more than thirty long years, at last the battle has been won.

*   *   *

His name is *Darren.*

He sits in a chair beside my bed, contemplating the cover of a recent news periodical. I think I've previewed that one already; Mussolini's the main feature. As he skims through the pages, his face distorts, aghast at the context before him. I find no reason for him to be in such awe—the stories covered in those magazines deal with *his* world, the *real* world: doesn't he know of the war? Is he not aware of the international conflicts between the global superpowers? Can it be that we here at the ward are kept in better touch with the news than those on the Outside? Ha, I wouldn't doubt it—that just proves how on top of things Rory and Hanson are! But whatever. I suppose the matter is irrelevant.

Upon my arrival, he sets the magazine down, exchanges greetings, and rids himself of any trace of puzzlement or shock. To my surprise, we don't exchange very many words; he speaks quite sparingly.

Darren explains his purpose for being here: it has something to do with a theory of his that he's interested in testing. The basic idea is that patients such as myself are not *challenged* to reach their full potential as "human beings"; he claims that I, just as he's suspected, have not fully come to understand the "meaning of my own existence." Who does this guy think he is? You can't just barge into somebody's home and tell him or her how to live! Suspicion provokes my senses …

"We'll be meeting again tomorrow and we'll be able to elaborate on more personal matters then. It'll just be *me* observing *you*," Darren explains.

His outright (and seemingly *anxious*) presentation takes me largely by surprise.

I'm not sure how to judge this fellow. At the very least, he is approachable. The rate of my heartbeat has not veered into a fearful, fluttering crescendo just yet, mind you, which in itself is quite a feat. Most importantly, the man is *genuine*, or at least he appears to be. Despite my initial wariness, it seems that he's unintentionally managed to charm me. Darren articulates his words in such an unwavering manner that directly gets his point across. His expression, the curve in his brow, his interesting hand gestures—all are unreadable. It's clear that this man is *dense*, that a lush, impenetrable barrier surrounds him like a forest. I've encountered in him something special and unique, though I'm not sure *what* this quality is.

Our meeting ends abruptly. He leaves just as quickly as he's come. Darren sets a small book down beside my bed nonchalantly—my first "assignment" is to read the first two chapters. I'm not so enthralled, but really, it's not like I have anything *better* to do. (Usually patients are assigned daily chores, but considering my damaged physique, I'm fortunately exempt from these.)

For about two solid minutes, he talks wildly of the story's

purpose and its "hidden meaning"—really, how mysterious can a *book* possibly be?

After a cordial handshake, he departs with a farewell.

Deeply beneath Darren's candy-coated expression, I can see there's disaster written all over his face—he's a troubled man, quite obviously. He drifts out into the hall like a specter, a lost and weary apparition.

Something's *fishy* here, something doesn't feel *right*. I'm certainly not brave enough to ask the nurses about it, but I've instantly developed feelings for Darren. I'm not one to look deeply into things, but there's *definitely* more than what meets the eye. Just the way he so effortlessly vanished into thin air—he's not ... *normal*, to say the least. There's something ... *special*, something *different* about him ...

Once he's gone, I roll myself over to the head of my bed and pick up the book that he's left. It's an unpublished manuscript, old and faded. There's no title, but near the bottom, it says "*by the savior.*"

It's a curious work, but I set it aside for now. I'll get a go at it tonight before I go to bed, I suppose.

I grab the television remote and tune in to my favorite station—I'm a newshound. There's some reporter over in Britain interviewing Churchill about the war. Ah, he's quite a character. Politics are real confusing, so I don't get too involved with them. To be honest, I don't know why this warfare is even raging in the first place; I just get a kick out of watching the famous people from all over the world enter my life on behalf of the television screen and magazines. I don't need to make sense of what I'm watching or reading to enjoy it. The sounds and colors, it seems, manage to pull me in on their own.

*   *   *

All throughout the day, the nurses have kept their distance. They're very on guard and cagey, which is not like themselves at all.

I've been escorted to lunch and back, attended a physical therapy session, watched some more television, and took part in a grand, orchestrated orgy. As you can see—sans Hanson and Rory's overwhelming affection—it's been a pretty average day. Perhaps it's because they know I have some homework to do and they want me to get it done—ah, why of course! *That's* what it is! The staff doesn't want to distract me from my *reading*! I'd nearly forgotten all about my elusive visitor! Since I've already gone forth with everything I'm likely to do in a single day, I take it and open up to the first page. Normally at this time, I take a nap, wake up in an hour or two for dinner (which Mrs. Hanson delivers to me personally), and then fall back asleep for the night.

There's something prophetic about it, though I can't pinpoint exactly what's making me feel the way I do as I hold it tremblingly in my hands. I move my body into a relaxed slouch, take a deep breath, and dive headfirst into this ocean of tiny words. I don't know why, but some instinct anticipates a wild ride.

CHAPTER 1

A familiar smell embedded into my worn-down shirt jumpstarts a slew of red-hot memories.

There's something so irresistible about that buzzing, narcotic-esque heat once it spreads out and fills up every inch of your body. Kind of like a warm, soothing bath that makes you forget the rest of the world exists. It's cultural, you know, it's more than just getting your "high"—it's all about unity, if you catch my gist. You merge with countless others around the world of different colors, ages, and lives. Marijuana is a *common front*, really, a common front against a singular enemy, that enemy being none other than the unbeatable real world itself. There's no way to really get it through those narrow-minded ass-kissers' heads anyway; they're just not in the "know." Big difference between a pothead and an educated ganja smoker, too; I've been argued against this plenty of times, and I could see why, 'cause I really can't explain *what* the difference is in words alone; you can just *feel* it and *see* it; it's in the way those grimy druggies pull that smoke into their lungs, it's written all over their mindless, droopy faces … honestly, they turn it into a disreputable affair, and it's a *shame*. All the twisting and twirling of that grey, smoky cloud becomes *more* than just a looming cancerous smog—it gains *life*, it becomes *sentient*, and eventually, a companionship arises. That aromatic burning leaf is always willing to offer you some good advice. As with most things in life, it's all in the way you approach it.

This is no bullshit, that's for sure—ask anyone, anyone *respectable* at least, and I guarantee that they'll tell you likewise.

Well, I suppose it's time for me to kick off my tale. More than anything, it is a dramatic story of loss. It tells of the dissolution of a set of friendships that should've lasted a lifetime, it tells of the destruction of a band of brothers. I'd expect myself to be angrier and more frustrated with the matter than I presently am, but at this point, things are too far gone. It's a lost cause. We are beaten and without redemption. These past few weeks have been unbearable, and I'm lucky not to have lost my mind yet. Though I've finally come to accept our disgraceful loss, there's one thing that I've still got left, a thin sliver of faith that manages to weakly illuminate the little hope I still cling to.

I don't believe in God (or at least in any conventional sense), but I sure as hell have *faith*. Not faith in any one thing in particular, but a universal faith that I believe is in my best interest. The conviction that everything will eventually be okay is an ideal that has helped me through the hardest and most daunting times of my life. You might say I'm crazy, a stupid, adolescent dreamer, but I'll have you know that you're wrong. Things *always* work out when you believe they will—people are just too blind to see this, that's all. Many of life's most well-kept secrets are easily accessed with a little trust, with just the slightest bit of submission. All the right and wrong things

RAYMOND

happen at the most opportune of times. Sometimes things are *supposed* to go wrong; c'mon, we all know this. Attribute it to whomever you want, Jesus or Moses or Muhammad, any of them guys are all the *same person* anyway. Life is honestly not as mysterious as we think it is, my friends—it's just one big solution, s'what it *really* is, one huge *answer* to everything. Some crazy scholars spend their whole lives asking themselves these far-out, philosophical questions … can't they see the answers to their questions are here? *Right here*? They're in this paper you're holding, they're in the very ink that make up these letters! *Everything* is the answer; you'll never understand it 'til you totally believe it, but it's the truth. In the universe, there exists only one thing, and that thing is the synchronic energy that binds us all together.

My friends and I used to have a blast *all the time*. Okay, maybe we *were* a bit troublesome, but we seldom got in anyone's way but our own. Criticize as you will, but there's no denying that our friendship was something genuine, beautiful, and divine. We had a culture in a time of *no* culture, we rebelled in a time of *no* rebellion, but everything we ever had just fell apart. More than anything, as I've already stated, that's what I'm here to tell, *that's* my story's purpose: to impart our shameful ruin. It may sound too melodramatic or cliché right from the start, but it's a story you just *need* to here. We grew up in a time where we *could have* made a difference. We got so close—*so fucking close*—but in the end, it all crumbled.

And that's why I'm writing this now, as quickly as I possibly can.

There's not much time left. I may be the last one. If I don't get this down on paper and into safe hands, my life might as well never have been lived.

.   .   .

Scripting this is not a pleasurable thing; if I'd written my story out of leisure, right now you'd have a far more detailed and exaggerated account of my life—that's not at all the case. This is for posterity's sake and the sake of posterity alone. I'm not about to dive into specifics, so use your imagination to fill up the gaps that I unfortunately can't help but leave you with. I might forget to say something and not realize it until way later, so expect my storytelling to be annoyingly loose and sketchy. If I decide to get lost in some side story of mine, then so be it—it'll only enhance your understanding of everything else. It's just a big puzzle, trust me on this, and by the end, it'll all eventually click.

Okay, okay ... enough. Time's running out.

First let me brief you a bit on the time period we're all living in, the byproduct of a national mess. Generation *Shit*. Really. It all began about eighteen years ago; I was born during the planting of this evil moral seed. We're in the year of 2037 now, and I'm on the verge of seventeen—allow me to spare you some history:

America finds itself in a bit of a disaster, where I'm from especially, that being the suburban Jersey world right outside of New York. I'm not exactly sure why or how things got as bad as they did, but what's come to be has come to be. From what I understand, the nation was overtaken by a plague of despair—an epidemic of melancholy literally infested the everyday lives of most American citizens. I suppose it was the result of a multitude of things: the predecessor to our current culture had allowed trashy media, politics, and rotten consumerism to get the best of its people. Keep in mind this no work of fiction and that I am writing out of *fear*—fear that all I've ever stood for will be lost. The rate of crime across the country skyrocketed, substance abuse was no longer taboo or obscure, sex lost its lust, art became drab and uninspired ... pretty much even the most exuberant of lives had become monotonously painful to live. It sounds like something out of a ninety-nine cent futuristic tragedy, in fact it's an overall unrealistic notion, but you've gotta believe that this is all true. No one can say for sure why it all gave way, but like a weak bridge's imminent collapse, the hopes of millions of people nationwide were shattered. Basically, everyone was desperate for some help, any help at all. At the time, I was too young to understand any of this completely, but I always knew something wasn't right.

Politics couldn't help, either; we Americans had become the laughingstock of the world. I wouldn't doubt that at this very moment there's a pair of European coffee shop intellectuals somewhere overseas giggling over how moronic we "lethargic American fools" are.

So it's Dr. Dawson to the rescue.

That motherfucker. There's not a single person on this earth that I've ever hated more in my life—he's dead now, thank God, that good-for-nothing cocksucker's finally dead. Died of cancer seemingly overnight; I'd much rather have seen him skinned alive and roasted over a crackling, orange fire. Dawson: if anything, I'm sure you've heard of *him*, the bastard, the "All-American hero." Oh, he'll be in every history textbook in a few years from now, that's for sure, alongside all the other greats: Washington, Lincoln, Kennedy, King. Although just mentioning Dawson's name makes me furious, in case you *don't* know who he is (which most likely *isn't* the case), I'll give you a synopsis of his rise to glory.

So like you already know, America was crying out for help. Out of nowhere comes Dr. Fredrick Dawson, the Christ of our era. His primetime television show cast a hypnotic spell on millions of lives across the country. (I refuse to believe he had any knowledge in the field of psychology whatsoever; I can almost guarantee that he was nothing more than a quack trying to cash in.) His success was something of an overnight spark. He'd first published a short and simple book on the current state of the world and how we Americans should be fixing our lives. It turned out to be a smash hit—written with prose for a retarded fourth grader, it offered a sparkling sense of hope. Instantly, television corporations clamored over the legal rights for a network show, and months after his book hit shelves, that son of a bitch was gracing the screens of televisions across the country. With great pain, let me inform you of some of his ideals.

The world of adulthood is now one of stubborn paranoia, and adolescence is all about *fear*, fear of straying from "The Square." The Square is a mess of absurd principles cast forth by Dawson himself; had they been introduced to the world at any time other than this state of disaster, Dawson's ass-pink face would've been laughed at and shunned. Each move of his twisted schemes was plotted so strategically, every shot he called was at just the right time. His philosophies were sickeningly plain and simple. He preached that all people were (get ready for it) ... *eviiiiil*. Yes, that's right, innately *evil*. Like that's not been said a million times before. Every human being, he believed, was so tainted with malevolence that we as a race have ceased to understand or acknowledge it—we've come to personify the wickedness of sin itself. Great. Just great. And *original* too.

And there you have it: the beginning of the transformation of America. Struggling parents and counselors of all shapes and sizes turned to this wonderful figure like he was a god; in all truth, Dawson was—*is*—a god. He'd taken his very own flesh and blood and made out of himself something divine.

Everything was based on fear. I saw this principle materialize when I was just about six or seven years of age. Back then I didn't fully understand what he stood for or why he'd become so popular, but man, Dawson was *everywhere*! (My very own mother, of course, had sunken into this national stupor, and just as everyone else had become overly delighted with Dawson's triumphant rise, she too could not resist his allure.) So yes, I was raised in the midst of his zenith. To have denied his way of thinking was to be an outcast, to be a heretic. The scariest part of it all is that his methods actually *worked*! Just months after his prophetic television airing, it became evident that the American people were getting back on track. Over the next few years, everyone's problems had suddenly been solved!

Okay, more on his 'fear theories'. Once he'd taken off, Dawson released plenty of other books crammed with all sorts of pseudo-moralistic bullshit. I was taught in both my home and in school to *fear* mistakes, and for a while, I actually did. We were raised to be uncurious machines, slaves for the sake of a perfect society. I saw how my classmates unquestioningly adhered to this, but it always felt wrong and disgusting to me, even at that nascent age. How else is one to learn without faltering? There was *no* learning, you see; advances of any sort had ceased. He paralyzed America in a singular mode … even today, everyone's still stuck in it! Both the young and the old are tangled in this deceitful, blind web.

At the expense of everyone's individuality and thoughts, yes, I suppose you can give Dawson credit for getting America up and running again. On the outside, everything seems okay, but deep down, and I mean deep, deep, deep down, I know that everyone is still an emotional mess. He created a much-foreshadowed mechanical culture for the new wave of American families: they walk with fear, talk with fear, they live every second of their meaningless lives with fear. Fear of what? No one knows. I don't even think the Dawsonites themselves know what they're afraid of. They're just fearful because it's what their master has demanded of them. You'd imagine that his death would've changed things, that people would've started to wake up and stuff, but no. Hell, his dead and rotting carcass has made things worse! Now more than ever is the world clamoring to suck the doctor's dead, decrepit dick!

That is where we stand today. This is the world I've grown up in. I've spent my whole entire life watching my peers get slapped across the face (gladly, too!) by the iron fists of authority. Whatever happened to the glorious teenage lives that kids *used* to live, the kinds that you read about in old books and movies? Oh, and that reminds me! Get a load of this— slowly but surely, past cultures are being erased. Controversial books, films, movies, and art are all beginning to disappear. It's all done real sneakily, so nobody really knows about it: no one bothers to care, either. We've been saved by the censorship and overprotection that has in fact destroyed us—the end result is a condition far worse than that which we'd begun with.

I fear nothing but the *future*: not even death itself could overshadow the monstrosity this new age of America foreshadows. It's a scary, scary world out there.

So there's a bit of back-story for you. Now on to my *own*

private life amidst these wretched times.

Wow! Is all of this really true? What a strange tale! I can't imagine myself in this world, that's for sure. You've got to be free to *think for yourself*, you know? You can't let other people control you! This is a real interesting read. I'm not sure why the heck Darren has given this to me, but I'm compelled to press onward. The narrator's story is likely to get even *more* interesting. With a life as grand as my own here on the ward, it's somewhat tough to relate to his troubles. Is this what it's *really* like on the Outside? I'd never have imagined!

A whole load of ponderings have overtaken my mind, but I try to divert my curiosity. Mrs. Rory doesn't like when I look too deeply into things—it's not good for my state of being.

Well, all right, I'm going to read some more.

CHAPTER 2

My name is Raymond James. Five foot eight, medium-length brownish hair, average build, stereotypically Italian in heritage. I'm a writer, as you can see, a drummer, a music fanatic, blah, blah, blah, not like any of that really matters. Fairly intelligent, to say the least, and despite my hatred of the school system, I've always been a top-ranked student. Okay, so those are the basics.

My parents never married, so I was raised by a single mother who'd unfortunately fallen into the Dawson state of mind—oh, she's very malleable to the media. I used to see my father about once a week; he's a surprisingly cool guy. He wasn't as strict a devotee as everyone else, but he still, in the end, was victimized. By virtue of his age, he'd managed to hang on to some of the *old* liberties, though never encouraged me to exploit them. I, being something of a "thinking man," have always fought with my narrow-minded mother. Prior to my (for lack of a better word) *abduction*, we had something of a good relationship, despite the impossible era we live in—the Doctor managed to rupture the standardized functionality of the family unit as it once was known. Trying to satisfy my mother's overprotective desires was, nonetheless, always quite a chore for me. For a very long while, I believed that my true identity was unfeasible in the world that I lived.

For most of my grade school years, I was just as mechanical as everyone else around me. It wasn't until about fifth grade or so that I gradually began thinking on my own. When I was unsure of something, I checked it out. I was always curious about everything. That's when people started noticing I was different, "dangerous," if you will.

For a while, I was miserable. Really. The few childish friends I made slowly began to fade away, and no one else bothered to talk to me. The truth is that I was feared! The other kids were scared to be my friend! I'd go home every day crying my little ass off in secrecy. I never told my mom about the way I was really feeling on the inside, but now that I'm older, I can reassure myself that it was for the better. I'd probably not be half the person I am today had I crumbled in her maternal arms. I can imagine her bringing me for "help," going to counselors, and flooding every corner of our house with Dawson's useless books. What doesn't kill you makes stronger, or so the old saying goes. It's a good bit of truthful advice. I needed those lonely, introspective nights in order to awaken the beast inside of me.

Along the way, I'd taken an interest in music. For my ninth or tenth or eleventh or something-or-another-eth birthday, I saved up enough money and bought myself a drum set. My mother was very displeased with this: already somewhat aware of my social problems, she *knew* this would only make things worse. And it did. It scarred me with mark of Cain, but I was beginning not to care. Music was something from the *past*. I was getting used to being shunned. I was getting used to being the *outcast*, so as a whole, things got easier. I'd stay home and practice all day—it genuinely entertained me, plus I actually *got* something out of it.

My leap into musicianship was symbolic in many ways; it represented me doing what *I* wanted to do, it showed me being *myself*. I had finally come to an age where I was beginning to make sense of things, *everything*. At last I'd found my niche in this fucked up world.

All life is really about is the pursuit of happiness.

Some bonehead could lecture you for hours about the meaning of life, but I'll tell you right now what it is: nothing else matters unless you're happy. That simple. People are all wrapped up in trying to save each other and helping each other and trying to root for this cause or stop this or stop that—bullshit, man it's all just *bullshit*. *Be* a little selfish. Find satisfaction in *yourself*. In most cases, you are alone in your time of dying. That's how we got into this whole Dawson mess in the first place, I think; we all became too dependent upon one another. If you never *stand* united, you'll never *fall* together.

Had I grown up in a different time, maybe my views would differ, but that's just the cold hard truth. I live in a world where everyone tries to do everything for each other, where everyone's dick is up everyone else's ass … it's just a sorry mess. Really. It's a fucking shame. It all sounds much better on paper.

So let's fast forward to seventh grade—that's when the gears that operate my current state of being were thrown into motion. There comes that period of revelation in the life of every youth. You either go one way or the other. It's that simple. I, as you can imagine, was a very confused adolescent coming of age.

As I looked around at my peers, it was evident that none of them faced the same struggles that plagued me. This pissed me off. At first it didn't bother me, but as I looked into their mindless stares and saw not a single hint of pain or suffering, it *really* managed to get under my skin. I felt that I actually had some sense, but my sense had given me nothing more than a

RAYMOND

big fucking headache.

My mom slowly started losing her mind: she's not, like, *crazy*, but she's not altogether, either, that's for sure. She's like all the other Dawsonites. They're all so *insanely sane*, if you know what I mean. It's weird. I can't express it any other way. The matter is simply ineffable. This was when my mess of a life was at its worst. Everything was so abstract and made no sense to me at all.

And then I met Allie. Oh, Allie, my dear, Allie my *love*—I've never felt for anyone like the way I felt (and still feel) for her. For most of my life, she'd been my best friend. We're not "together" right now, per se, but we dated for a real long time. My Allie: she was the first step toward reaching the Ray that's writing to you today.

Our friendship came out of the blue, really. We helped develop each other into better people. Like me, she was something of an outcast. The things we valued were similar, so that's what I can assume helped sparked everything in the first place. We fell in love, like really *really* in love—we'd both been searching so desperately for an emotional outlet, and we'd found each other. Man, everything just clicked from the start.

We became magnetized; going to school now meant something to me, suddenly I found a meaning to life! Wherever you turned, you'd be sure to catch us sticking our tongues ten feet down each other's throat. In short, we were inseparable. We *wanted* to be different; we were disconnected from the majority, anyway. The principal hated us, the teachers hated us, fellow students hated us—we were put through such ridicule. Fuck 'em all … the main point I'm trying to make here is that we made each other's lives complete. I'd go home every day delighted and proud 'cause she was mine, all mine. We defied everything; while everyone else around us was wrapped up in Dawson's wretched dogma, we were either skipping classes or hiding in janitors' closets jerking each other off. It was more than *that* sort of stuff though: we absolutely adored each other.

So you get the idea.

Fast forward to eighth grade now. A full-blown pubic bush begins sprouting from my ball sack—I'd become a man. As our relationship grew, Allie and I starting fighting more frequently, but we stuck it out and remained together. As far as either of us knew, we were the only two people on the face of the earth of our sort, so to foil our love was inevitably unwise. We soon learned, however, that we *weren't* alone.

Seth, Greg, and Juan entered our lives completely arbitrarily. Greg and Juan were both our age, though Seth was a year and a half older than his brother, Greg. I'd known these three guys my whole life, but always just assumed they were Dawsonites like the rest of 'em. They didn't talk much and were real reclusive. I'd never have guessed they were anything like myself.

I remember clearly how our lives intersected: it was the middle of winter, real snowy, and Allie and I were walking home from school. Being the little rebellious louts we were, anything that defied the Dawson doctrine even in the *simplest* of ways appealed to us.

Over the past few years, the tobacco industry has been suffering. Along with all the other chastity he demanded, Dawson taught that smoking was of course a sign of individual weakness. You can't even begin to imagine how quickly (and easily!) American smokers began kicking their habit. Only the serious addicts clung to their dependence, of course with much dissatisfaction. So you can imagine how badly Allie and I wanted to get our hands on a few smokes.

On this bitter, freezing day, we catch sight of Seth, Greg, and Juan huddled on a street corner casually puffing away at a searing cigarette. Allie and I knew that a chance to smoke like this might not come again for a very long while, so with all the balls either of us could muster, we nonchalantly approached them and introduced ourselves. Pretty blatantly, we asked to join in and implored them for a smoke.

They were all too happy to have our company. With introductions long overdue, we exchanged stories and listened

RAYMOND

absorbedly to one another. We learned that Seth and Greg's dad was an extreme smoker and had purchased an overabundance of cigarettes in fear that they'd soon become taboo. The brothers would snatch a few here and there and commonly indulged. After smoking an infinite amount of cigarettes since then, I no longer find them so childishly enthralling, but back in the day, they provided me with a thrill unlike anything else. When something's completely out of reach and is so goddamn prohibited, I guess it makes you want to try whatever that might be so much more. When that paper roll of shredded tobacco and tar made its way into my fingertips, it was as if all the power of the world had been placed into my hands.

The five of us agreed to keep in touch. After lighting up and passing around two more cigarettes, the harsh weather had driven us home. Ha. I strolled in through my front door that evening like I was ten feet tall.

I remember not wanting to go to bed that night. I knew for sure that my life was headed for a change, a shift in a better direction, and oh, how *right I was*. So many great things suddenly seemed to await me.

And so our little *cult* was born; ah, now this is where the REAL adventure begins.

(Though I've only been told to read the first two chapters, I'm finding this hard to put down! I haven't read a good story in ages, so I'm getting a kick out of the narrator's fast-paced, first-person account. One more chapter, just *one* more, and then I'll give it some rest.)

CHAPTER 3

That day initiated a monstrous shift in all our lives. Amidst the other schoolyard dupes, we lived proud, organic lives. It was great to see my ideas of what a childhood was *supposed* to be blossom in the real world. Things took control of themselves, and this is what made our friendships so special; no one *tried* to be anything more than what he or she really was. Our bond gained a mind of its own, and unknowingly, we were taken over by it—after a few weeks, my gut instincts told me that *this* is where I was supposed to be and that things would *never* change. For a very long while, I must admit to actually believing that.

Let me tell you about those first few months. Boy, I wouldn't give up those memories for *anything*; they've literally become an integral part of me! I still get a warm feeling when I reflect upon them—they represent the carefree and purely joyful part of my life that unfortunately can never be relived.

After congregating on that fateful, bitter afternoon, many days of the sort soon followed. I can't admit to having engaged in anything particularly productive in the beginning of our rebellious odyssey, but those simple, absentminded times we lazily wasted away together mean *more* to me than *anything else*. The very knowledge that we were the *first* of our caliber is the most satisfying of all. We were fearless and just didn't give a fuck. More and more frequently, we'd earn ourselves weeklong strings of detention and boring lectures from the principal, but these things just reassured us that we were doing something *right*. We got out of the Dawsonites exactly what we *wanted* to get out of them.

Now that I look back on matters, in comparison to what our radical natures would evolve into, those preliminary, semi-subversive months of ours seem like child's play! Keep in mind, however, that we never deliberately caused trouble with those around us—like I said earlier, we seldom got in anyone's way but our own, and even that is somewhat of an overstatement. That very fact, though, was of course not enough to prevent the school from unfairly penalizing us for every little thing we did. If our teachers could've issued us the death sentence, they sure as hell would have. We were punished for the most ridiculous of things and they hated us for no good reason at all! Things like these are what primarily drove us to take our mutiny to the next level, but before I proceed, allow me to elaborate on some specifics. Here's how we'd spend a typical day:

Until school was dismissed, we'd miserably sit through our various classes. Every course was virtually the same—all we ever learned about was Dawson's half-assed principles. So little curricular work was enforced that eventually our school days transformed into a single, ongoing quasi-philosophical sermon. Once dismissed, we'd usually just walk around town aimlessly 'til the day waned away.

You might be wondering how the hell we were anything *special*, but you've *gotta* believe that we were. The essence of what a teenage social life was supposed to be had been destroyed. We'd watch everyone else pack up their bags and march their ways on home, only to decay alone like rotting vegetables. It's something how I'm accusing everyone else of doing nothing at all when our little group was guilty of zilch as well, but at least we did nothing with *some fucking balls*. Goddamn it, we were *kids*, kids on the verge of adulthood, and it was as if everything had already run full circle! Zombies, I tell you, *zombies* ... s'all they really were! They had no souls, they had no minds, they had nothing but the rules beat into their brains. Ray, Allie, Seth, Greg, and Juan—we were both nothing at all and everything the world had to offer.

After a while, I'd come to totally forget about Dawson and all his wretchedness. The real world had melted away. We had reached a brief state of living where nothing mattered but ourselves and each other. It was a beautiful realization—we'd led ourselves to genuine happiness. We hadn't searched for it—it cast *itself* upon *us*. We'd gotten in touch with some greater essence that breathed into us meaning, purpose, and most importantly, love. How pure it was, too. When everything's that damn good, you refuse to believe it can get any better. No drug could ever overshadow that feeling when external life so effortlessly fades away on its own.

You'd say we had absolutely nothing, but I'll tell you again and again—*we had it all.*

Oh, there's something I forgot; I hadn't planned to include him in my little story, but all this writing about the good ol' days has got me thinking 'bout how much I really love D.J. Okay, so D.J., at one point, was one of us. He was there when Allie and I first smoked with the other guys, he hung out with us every day after school; he was in fact Seth's best friend for as long as either of them could remember. D.J.—what a character! He had a full-grown beard by the age of ten, suspiciously long fingernails, and a witty knack for debating; though he could stand up weakly, he was unfortunately nearly paralyzed from the waist down.

(Hey, he's just like me—finally, a character in this story that I've got something in common with!)

He really doesn't play an important role in any later events, but I should acknowledge that he started out as one of us. Even back then, he was always warier than we ever were, was always questioning what was *right* and *wrong*—he spent so much time analyzing every damn thing! I think he burnt out his brain; I ain't ever met another guy just like him … always thinking, always always thinking, round the clock, twenty-four/seven, even about nothing at all, just thinkin' nonetheless. I bring him up because he's a great example of how deeply Dawson's filth inhibited our culture.

D.J. had a good head on his shoulders (and I'm sure he still does), but the Doctor has penetrated his conscience too deeply. None of the great things we did ever sat completely well with D.J. Slowly, he drifted away from our lives, further and further into the dark abyss of no return. We tried to save him, but he had to follow his own path. In the end, I'm sure there will be a reason for it. The thought of D.J. rotting away under Dawson's command makes me feel just *awful*, but I suppose it's in his destiny. He'd almost made his way over the fence but chickened out at the very top. Looked down, saw how far off the ground we were, and just couldn't take it. I miss him,

I really do; he's on my mind a lot, but if he's convinced he's happy under the rule of Dawson's iron fist, then so be it.

It was around the time when D.J. faded out of our lives that our simplistic thrills began growing a bit dull. Not to say that our friendship itself had diminished in any way, but nothing seemed as grand or daring as it did before ... you know, sort of a been-there-done-that kinda thing. Our lifestyle had become so natural that even the ones who despised us most had seemingly come to accept our ways. We wanted something fresh—the school year was drawing to an end, and summer was merely weeks away. Quite simply, we wanted more power; we wanted to cover more ground and expand. At the time, we conceived our hopes out of nothing more than wishful thinking, but we wound up *amazing* ourselves with what we actually were able to achieve. Ha! I'm sure you're dying to know what we eventually grew into. Don't worry, I'll get to that later.

Eventually, we exposed ourselves to and embraced a life of drugs. Ah, yes. As you may have guessed, intoxicants of any sort are a rarity nowadays, so *of course* we were dying to get ahold of some. Through some far-flung, untraceable connection, Seth managed to bargain with a bunch of urban lowlifes and scored a load of fresh cannabis seeds. With nothing to lose, he amateurishly gave planting them a shot.

Drugs were never discussed in our pitiful world; they were totally off limits. With this new addition to our lives, things became lively and daring once again.

If you recall, I opened up my confession with a little blurb on marijuana. Now that you're better acquainted with me, it might be opportune for you to jump back a sec and reread what I've written. Mid-July, Seth's first plants successfully bloomed. With very little knowledge concerning the proper harvesting of pot (and little resources to turn to for guidance), we cultivated about an ounce of homegrown weed. This, of course, was done in secrecy—Seth and Greg's parents had no idea about this clandestine operation. None of us really knew anything about smokers' etiquette or how to roll joints and such, so we basically educated ourselves. (As a side note, Greg was always the best at joint-rolling—not too tight, not too loose; just *perfect*. It took him a while to hone his craft, but after a few months of herbal experimenting, he took pride in becoming the "go-to" roller.) Our first intoxicated experience together was such a wild ride. I didn't know what to expect or when to expect it, but once I'd smoked and my high had sneakily crept on me a few minutes later, I immediately thought to myself: this is the greatest thing *ever*!

From what I understand, pot smoking was not so unheard of twenty or thirty years ago, even amongst adults. Illegal, yes, but something completely taboo? I don't think so. Imagine yourself living in the times that I do—smoking a fucking joint is socially equivalent to mainlining a derivative of *opium*!

There is no way to describe the feeling of that first full-blown high. It's a little different for everyone (some get it better, some get it worse), but it's something extremely special. As with anything else, our smoking began to lose its initial impact, but there's no denying that pot has truly helped me better understand myself and the chaotic world around me. It's something you either totally get or you don't get at all; there's really no in-between.

Like I alluded to before, about halfway through August, we started to dwell on "power." As if we were some sort of prophets, we desperately sought to recruit others into our kind of life. We just felt that the way we lived was too *good* to be spent alone—we wanted to share the joy we'd discovered.

Eventually, our imperialistic dreams began to find fruition. I entered high school that September as a freshman (along with Greg, Juan, and Allie), and Seth was beginning his junior year. We instantly spread the word about our little newly discovered lifestyle, and of course, the school system tried to retaliate. We were often scolded for trying to poison the other children's minds and were accused of absurd fallacies such as spirit worshiping and voodoo. Spirit worshipping? Voodoo? What fucking nonsense!

We, in all honesty, made ourselves out to seem like nothing short of the greatest union of friends there ever was. I suppose we may have come off a bit pretentious in the beginning of our affairs, but we had a mission in mind and were determined to deploy whatever methods would work. It was almost impossible to avoid us; I assure you that we were nothing less than *a hundred feet deep* down everyone's throat. In time, we were approached and questioned about our "lifestyle" by the other students around us—some came like sinners begging to be cleansed, some like guilty murderers pleading for justice, and others like top-secret mercenaries embarking on a forbidden mission. It was exhilarating, a reward unlike any other—it started off with two, maybe three classmates interested in shifting away from the mundane autopilot they were set on, but suddenly, all at once, we'd broken out into a town-wide phenomenon. The weight crashed down upon us with no warning at all, but it was a load we were willing to carry.

Things were a bit overwhelming at first, but after a month or two of rocky proportions, our affairs began to run smoothly. The first of our converts was a fellow named Allan Burns. He instantly proved himself worthy of our respect and became "one of us."

You now know everything you need to know—the key events, the key players, the history, and the causes and effects. I can now unveil to you the cultural significance of the short-lived but ever-so-powerful *Cage Breakers*. There's more on that awful, awful name and how it came to be in just a bit, but first, here's how things got started:

While ordinarily walking 'round town one random afternoon, Juan took notice of something peculiar: situated in the corner of a tributary avenue right off the town's main street was an old-looking, boarded-up building. Something about it just called out to us. We'd passed that same spot many times before, but not once had this oddity ever caught our attention. We later found out it was nothing more than a lot that was constantly (and futilely) being remodeled or repurchased by different businesses. I think most recently it had been an unsuccessful ice cream parlor or something. In retrospect, I've come to realize that that damn place had to be cursed; no single residence could ever stay there for an extended period of time. Without taking that into consideration, we set our eyes upon it and contemplated a slew of promising notions.

We nonchalantly snuck over to the back of the building and smashed our way through a series of splintery, wooden boards. Expectedly, the joint was utterly desolate. Amongst other positive first impressions, we unanimously observed that this forsaken property, with a few adjustments, could lend itself rather auspiciously to our future operations. "With a little cleaning up," Greg said, "this place can get *pretty* interesting."

We spent the next few days completely refurnishing the interior of this newly discovered dump into what eventually would become known as the *Cage*.

As our group of devoted followers began to grow, I started noticing a striking common denominator prevalent in all of them—they all seemed so terribly relieved after wholly submitting themselves to us. An entire generation consumed by fear was at last allowed to take a step back and breathe.

For just a moment, my narrative is about to take a grim turn. Just when things started looking brighter than ever, there arose a few internal struggles. The first of these that I'll mention is the breakup between Allie and me after two long years. I'm not really sure what primarily initiated our dissolution, but things eventually *exploded* between us. That really got to me, and for quite some time I was a sad and lonely motherfucker. Some other minor complications were Seth's sudden depression, the divorce of Juan's parents, but most devastating of all was the terrible sickness that took the life of Allan Burns' mother.

Recall that Allan was the first of our new followers. I connected with him unlike I've connected with anyone else in my life. There's something about him … I'm not sure what it is. He just *understands* things for what they are. Something very special immediately developed between us, and it's safe to say that, aside from Allie, Allan's the best friend I've ever had. We differed in many ways (there's no denying that), but what drew us together was a power too ineffable for words alone. Keep in mind that most of us developed resentment toward our parents; they all fit the stereotype, they all stopped thinking for themselves, they all got in the way of what we pictured good lives were supposed to be. Allan, however, *loved* his mother with all of his heart. He wasn't like us—we'd come to shun and ignore our makers invariably. He never was able to explain why his affection toward her was so great, though I'm pretty sure it had something to do with the passing of his father at a young age. She raised him amidst poverty and inconceivable illnesses. This, I'm sure, was why he hadn't rebelled against Dawson on his own. This emotional soft spot was ultimately his greatest weakness. He had the fury, he had the rage, but he also had the *fear*, the fear of bringing shame to his dedicated (though brainwashed) mother, the fear of failing to meet her expectations, the fear of losing her altogether.

Allan and I talked of things such as this quite often. My heart went out to him, it really did. I've never seen someone caught in a stickier dilemma. Every step he took just confused him more and more. Once his mother died (that being about a month or so after he joined our group), he nearly *lost it*.

I felt his pain, I really did. Unless you've been involved in a similar situation, there's no way of getting you to understand how sorrowful something like this is. It's one thing when you lose a loved one yourself, but when you watch it happen to someone close to you, someone who's always coming to you for help and guidance, someone whose safety you *fear for*, things are a bit different. For me, Allan's tragic loss became a very personal experience, so I felt obligated to help him cope.

All he really had was his mother—the rest of his family was living somewhere out west, and they were in no financial situation to continue raising poor, tormented Allan ... not that he'd want that, anyway. To make a long story short, he was tossed over to a set of legal foster parents. Allan never said they were unkind, but he despised their detached, cold, robot-like nature. Sooner than later, he expectedly rebelled and dedicated himself to a life of homelessness; he became a full-fledged vagabond, a *bum*.

For a while, I stayed away from the Cage Breakers'

expanding affairs to spend time alone with Allan. He was nothing short of a mess. Over a short period of time, I watched him rapidly grow worse. He skipped school frequently and became something of a thug; he learned the art of thievery and was reduced to a diet of stolen alcohol, cigarettes, candy, and cheese crackers. You could even see it in face, you could hear it in the way he talked, you could *smell* it in unclean clothes— Allan had totally lost his grip on things.

Then came his attempt at suicide. Man, did that kill me. It broke my heart! I never imagined the thought would've crossed his mind, but he unfortunately proved me wrong. He called me up one afternoon crying hysterically, wailing and wailing like he'd been shot in the belly—I couldn't make out a word he was saying. Immediately I knew something was wrong. I found him camouflaged amongst sacks of stinking garbage in a rusty dumpster. Smashed bottle of vodka in one hand, clusters of torn hair in the other, red flowing blood splattered everywhere. He was silent, motionless: I honestly thought he was dead.

I did my best to help pull him together. The day was appropriately dull and gloomy, in fact I'd not until then realized the drizzle that had cast itself down from the skies. I washed him up, got him to his feet, and hurried over to the abandoned home that we'd recently turned into our own. Though not quite immaculate just yet, our desolate, newly converted hangout was comfortable enough for the two of us to spend some time to get a grip on things. Allan often cried softly and faded in and out of consciousness. I got lots of water from an icebox we'd all chipped in for and encouraged him to drink up. *Gotta keep things together*, I kept telling myself.

It took a while before he could speak anything more than painful barks of grief. If I've not mentioned it thus far, let me inform you that I'd managed to stop the flow of blood from Allan's wrists by wrapping them in my shirt and applying tons of pressure. After he'd settled down, I stepped back silently and meditated.

And waited. For something—anything. A response of any kind.

The minutes passed like hours, the hours like years. Two very simple words were all he spoke before falling into a long-deserved sleep:

"I'm sorry."

Allan drifted away into unconsciousness. I was afraid to leave him, but the better part of my faith in things told me he'd be okay. I trudged home that night with my mind abuzz and whirring, though something deep inside me was warm and satisfied. It's safe to say that I saved his life. If not for me, *who knows* what have become of Allan's troubled (yet brilliant) mind.

It took a while for him to get back on track, but once he did, Allan found a new meaning to life: art.

Wow, is that what I call *intense*! What a nerve-wracking situation the narrator's thrown himself into. I've never read anything like this in my life! Darren's sure got good taste in literature, that's for sure. I still haven't figured out *why* he's having me read this, but it really doesn't make a difference to me. I haven't had a rollercoaster ride like this through the pages of a book in I can't remember *how* long ... *never*!

*   *   *

"Authors are *allowed* to twist the truth, Sid," Mrs. Hanson says as she carefully feeds me. "Just because you read something doesn't necessarily mean it's true."

"But that's the thing!" I exclaim. "It seems that the author's main purpose is to get the reader to believe that all the stuff he's talking about has *actually happened*."

Mrs. Hanson seems disinterested and shrugs it off. "That's what makes this wacko a good writer, I suppose. In the end, a story's *just* a story—fictional rubbish that rots the brain. Don't take the author's words too seriously. My counsel, as you know, is always in your best interest, and I advise you to read that trash merely for kicks." As she pours me a glass of cider, I'm met with a rather astonished look. Somewhat unpleasantly, she says, "My, Sid, you've *really* taken this little bit of what you've read so far rather personally. It's as if you know the author himself or something!"

I simply explain that I find every darn word so powerful and convincing! We discuss its subject matter, and immediately, she deems Dawson as the story's supreme hero—the narrator and his weak-minded friends are nothing more than troublemakers in a time of peace. "Can't you see how smoothly the world had run until those silly kids decided to take things into their own hands? Life works in a way where the *big* people always make the *big* decisions. Things are certain to go awry when others try to interfere. I'm actually a bit surprised that you're giving this narrator the time of day in the *first place*. He resembles many of the troublesome fools that we've got here on the ward ... you know the kind of idiots I'm talking about, the kind of idiots we *despise*. Some people simply can't accept the fact that they're wrong and that they're outcasts, and this author is no exception. *These* are the people that constitute the scum of the earth."

As my nourishment continues, Hanson elucidates the many trivial difficulties that burden all Outsiders' lives. I'm starting to understand how miserable it really is out there. Passionately, she explains, "In the grand scheme of things, Sid, your disastrous social and medical flaws have saved you ... if not for your wretched insanity, you'd be another victim of the mess that rages on forevermore on the Outside."

Gulp. I gratefully swallow a meaty chunk of glazed chicken.

Very clearly do I see Mrs. Hanson's point, but the situation in the story is *different*; the setting is nothing like that of my beloved ward, or at least so it seems. Wow, has Mrs. Hanson really opened my eyes—I've never understood how *lucky* I am. Honestly, can you imagine someone like *me* making it out there in the *real world*? I can't even fathom what sort of terrible life I'd lead! With Rory, Hanson, and Cohen around, what more could I possibly ask for?

"There are thousands of men and women struggling out there every single day ... they'd all give *anything* to be in your shoes," she reassures.

It soon becomes evident that I've been wrong all along. For quite some time, I was wholly deceived by a childish misconception of what the Outside was really about. Ha! Sometimes my naïveté even astonishes myself. Without the staff's aid, I don't know *where* I'd be or *what* I'd ever be doing!

"I'm not saying you shouldn't enjoy reading that book," Mrs. Hanson concludes. "I'm sure it's a fine work of literature. Just keep in mind that the author may be a lunatic, a madman, a psycho, a killer—you'd never want to be influenced by the likes of such maniacs, would you? Remember ... when people of this caliber are wrong, very seldom are they aware of the fact that they're wrong in the first place."

Satisfied, she wipes my greasy mouth as I gobble up my last bit of dinner. I thank her, as usual, and am propped up on my bed for the night. Once she departs, I seize my TV remote, tune in to some mesmerizing bit of news, and sink comfortably into position. I give that old manuscript a glance, but decide not to read any further today. My eyes are weary from having left them in focus for so long—like I said, *ages*, it's been *ages* since I've read anything so engrossing. Though I'd originally rooted for the Cage Breakers' fight against the abominable Dr. Dawson, Mrs. Hanson's got me thinking that maybe the rest of society was right *after all*. It was never the children's place to make a difference—hell knows *I'd* never be gutsy enough to engage in their affairs.

Life works in a way where the big people *always* make the big decisions—she could not have put it any better. That's the world of which I'm from; that's the world of which I know best; this is the world in which I am loved.

*　　　*　　　*

I am thoughtlessly sprawled out upon my bed.

As I engage myself in a series of finger-stretching exercises that help better my state of paralysis, my attention is drawn to a pair of bloodied wounds in the center of my palms. I've never noticed them before; it seems that their formation has been a recent affair.

How in the world did they get there?

Instantly, a tingling sensation compels both hands and a strangely inhuman conversation is initiated between them. The language exploited is not one of words, but of helplessly terrified shrieks. For a moment I am displaced from reality, but as soon as I am aware of this absurd phenomenon, my body convulses and the voices disappear.

I'm left with an odd sensation awakened in my wounded palms—what could such an absurd feat possibly mean?

I remain in an uninteresting daze for a number of hours until the night inevitably comes to be.

There's neither much left to do nor anywhere to go. I scan my quaint living quarters for a point of interest. Nothing manages to grab my attention until I stumble upon something I'd not noticed before. I realize that I've forgotten to drink and discard of my daily glass of milk. It sits patiently upon my windowsill with a mind of its own, waiting and waiting for nothing at all. Something about it is so *dull*. It's the same all throughout, a monotonous shade of pale bone. I can't help but to be drawn into its milky void. At its height, curious little bubbles swim around, bunk heads with one another, break, reform themselves, and begin their voyage anew. The glass of liquefied dairy seems tired and bored, both with itself and its surroundings, but there's obviously nothing it can do to change this. I see myself reflected in that spacey emptiness, but yet there's no image at all. The purely white milk is something of an empty slate, a blank piece of paper to be written on, crumbled, or destroyed; I feel at one with it. I've come to learn that you can see a little bit of yourself in *anything*.

When there's not much to do, you find yourself overanalyzing everything like me; you've gotta keep your mind young and healthy somehow, you know? I may be helpless and immobile, but I'm sure not going to let my brain (of all things!) decay.

Just as I'm sucked into this magnetic, milky void, my concentration is shattered by a knock upon my door. I turn slowly and find that my elfish friend, Mr. Fandango, is easing his way into my room. He comes 'round faithfully every night. Allow me to tell you a bit about his crazy antics!

Fandango is, to say the least, an ill-behaved lunatic, but never once has he landed himself in any trouble. He's just so sly, so good at what he does! I can confidently say that all the transgressions of every other patient *combined* are nothing but a small fraction of Mr. Fandango's monkey business—in just the short time he's been here with us, too! (That he and I have bonded so intimately is an intriguing matter in itself ... why would anyone so wild want *me* as a friend? Of all people! I'm a cripple, a nut, a helpless freak of nature!)

Fandango usually talks in mindless metaphors and babbles on and on. His rants are poorly structured and often leap from one thing to the next, but he, as the deliverer of this lunacy, never seems conscious of his incongruous storytelling. He's rude and crude, a tad too adventurous for my tastes, but something very genuine in me appreciates this. Some heartfelt emotion of mine just *loves* him.

At this point, it's become routine: Fandango slips past security each and every night (don't ask me how he does it!) and makes his way into my room. This is when we spend our time together, in fact I don't think I've ever once seen him during the *day*. Maybe he's off spreading his humorous mischief 'round the clock ... I don't know. I'm always asking him where and how he spends most of his afternoons (he's the only one I dare to question like this, by the way), but never once has he given me a decipherable answer.

Whatever: it's not his personal life that concerns me, really, for the very fact that he charms me is enough. I want nothing out of him more than his natural craziness, and it's a *good* kind of craziness, in case you're wondering. Mr. Fandango shows defiance that I never will and exploits folly that I never will—I vicariously live my own playful fantasies through his actions. When Hanson or Rory ask me how I manage to remain so well-behaved, it takes a lot for me not to mention Fandango's name—you see, I've made a promise to him, and that promise is to never *talk about him* to anyone else. I'm not exactly sure why he wants our friendship to be so secretive, but if I break my vow, he swears to never visit me again! I'd never want that to happen! It's a simple request—I just keep his profile low.

Upon entry, Mr. Fandango performs something of a jittery back flip. Despite his height, he's surprisingly athletic; he's always twirling and whirling around. He hops onto my bed and lights up a cigarette. He offers me a puff, but, as usual, I decline … smoking is bad for your health and against the rules! I constantly tell him that he should quit, but as you might have guessed by now, there's no penetrating his stubborn will.

Fandango's wild antics used to worry me, but I've grown used to them over time. He talks about "faith" a lot, which I've now just realized is quite ironic—the narrator of Darren's story builds his morals around a similar ideal. A coincidence, I suppose, but what a mighty large one indeed! If Mr. Fandango were to meet this narrator in real life, they'd surely get along quite well!

He's currently talking up a storm, something about aliens, I think; I can never make heads or tails of his zany narratives, but it's not his words that matter; it's all in the *delivery*. I could honestly care less about the spaceships and abductions and laser beams he presently speaks of, but the solid dedication to his storytelling is what makes me feel like a *king*. Every tall tale of his seems especially crafted for and addressed to me, and *that's* what's so special about him. Nope, not even *Dr. Cohen* can relieve me of the real world in the manner that Fandango does. This troll's just got a knack for his nature, I guess. The best part about his visits, if I may add, is that I never need to chase him out, regardless of the time! Whenever I wake up in the morning, whatever mess he's made is always cleaned up like he'd never come in the first place—isn't that strange?

Out of nowhere, I catch sight of a soaring glass of milk, seconds before it careens into my television screen and breaks into a dozen pieces.

"Dammit!" Fandango cries, pouncing on all fours. "Almost had him—almost nailed the little bastard! *How did that stinking fly manage to get away?*" He declares a war cry and playfully somersaults into a strange contortion.

Ahh ... he has me intoxicated.

Together, we laugh the night away for what seems like hours. Once I grow tired, I shut my eyes and listen to him start up a new bubbling wave of thoughts (something about insect life, if I'm not mistaken). The fine line between reality and sleep is blurred as he helps me drift through a medium of time unknown to any other man.

*   *   *

Why? Why in the world is Mrs. Rory so skeptical of Darren? She talks about him as if he's a *criminal* or something! He's just a teacher at some university, I think, not the mind-controlling freak she says he is! I mean, don't get me wrong, she's *always* right about *everything*, but I just don't see the *sense* in her right now.

"He's trying to *trick* you," she ardently stresses "Don't be swindled into his nonsense ... just be *mindful* at all times! When you congregate with him later today, stare that lunatic right in the eye—let him *fear* you ... no, better yet! Have him fear *us*."

A particularly demanding expression fixes itself across her face.

She retrieves the sign-in sheet with a precise thrust of her pale, slender arm, jams the desk window shut, and turns her back on me, dissatisfied.

When I meet up with Mrs. Hanson just minutes later, it doesn't surprise me that she exhibits the same kind of wariness. She advises me to keep a look out for his "unruliness." To be honest, I think that they've both confused Darren with an altogether different man; these things that they attribute to him don't suit his character at all!

"He's yet to unveil to you what he's *really* like. He's just waiting, he's just playing with your head! Believe the words I speak—when the time is right, Darren will unleash upon you his immeasurable bitterness," Hanson whispers into my ear, all in a single breath.

Bitterness? *What* bitterness? If anything, the poor guy's only trying to *help* me … still, it'd be wise for me to remain alert; there's just *got* to be a reason for the nurses' warnings. Maybe he's up to some trouble and I just can't see it—are they trying to save me from my own naïveté? Ugh, how am I supposed to *know*?

Where am I supposed to turn to help sort things out?

* * *

As if she's foreseen my looming bewilderment, Mrs. Hanson has assigned me a mediator with whom I must engage in a half-hour session before Darren arrives. Her name is Mrs. Johnson; she's tall, thin, well-rounded, in fact a bit *too* attractive for me to retain ahold of any good sense. Just one look at her gives me the shivers … those breasts are far more than "charming." She constantly reminds me to calm down, though her sincere advice only makes me more jittery. Mrs. Johnson offers cold pill tranquilizers, though I immediately decline the offer. Darren probably thinks I'm crazy enough as it is, so the last thing I need is medication that interferes with my sense of judgment.

"You seem even *more* paranoid than usual," she says distrustfully.

Mrs. Johnson is convinced that Darren's negativity has already begun to influence me and I haven't even realized it—*what is she talking about?* First Mrs. Rory, then Mrs. Hanson, and now this mediator of mine—all of them … so *suspicious!* Geez! I'm not saying the guy's necessarily as genuine as I may have perceived him to be, but I certainly don't think he's some ill-willed fool!

Despite my declination of the tranquilizers, she insists that it is in her better judgment that I take them. I suppose I've no right to argue. Ha—I'm not the one running this facility, now am I? If I had good sense to begin with, I wouldn't be locked up here in the first place.

A swig of water helps me down the pill quite easily.

Once I'm calmed (*realllly* calmed), it's much easier to sit still and listen to the soothing words Mrs. Johnson has to speak; her beauty becomes less sexually intriguing and more … *mysterious.*

I can feel every muscle relax as the components of the pill dissolve into my bloodstream. My body becomes wonderfully light, so light that I can nearly feel the air in the room passing right … through … me. Then everything gets thin. And tired and clear. Looks like Mrs. Johnson's taking a tranquilizer as well—or whatever this is … sure doesn't *feel* like an ordinary tranquilizer! Not just one or two or three, but *four!* Wait a second—that's not allowed, that's against the rules! The nurses here aren't supposed to be taking the patients' medication, are they? What's … wrong with her?

Oh, everything's all right, there's no need to worry … is there really … *ever* a need to worry? There is only the need for beauty and to feel it and to understand it and we start laughing together laughing laughing laughing and then I feel our laughs come alive and run all 'round and 'round the room like little mice while everything is naked and stripped down and exposed in a way where I can see every little detail and hear every little sound and the colors oh yes the colors are wonderful too SWIRLING and SWIRLING and … ah, would you look at Mrs. Johnson, just look at her, she's just as free as me, just the two of us here in this room and if I weren't crippled I'd be up and about chasing all the little butterflies around like she is but I can't but it's okay this is just fine the way I am and then there are bright lights everywhere but then they stop so we both settle down for a while and just stare each other down and oh God what's happening to her face turning and turning and melting away and going back together and then and then and then and then and then and then and then we start to talk but you see it's not me talking and it's not her talking so there are just voices coming out of us she says so how shall we begin this session and I say I don't knoowww and then daaa and then daaa and then rennnn and then rennnnn and then daaa … renn? and then daaa … renn?

Darren the Zealot, she declares, Darren the Enemy! Crucify him, crucify him, nail him to the cross!

But this man is innocent! says Pontius Pilate and he shows the Christ to the crowd and he's got a crown of thorns upon his head and the crowd cheers and the crowd mocks him and the voice of the crowd fills the earth so the crowd decides that the Christ will be killed so Darren is flogged and beaten on the ground in front of me and I find myself nailing him down happily with Mrs. Johnson nailing nailing nailing him to the cross as the **Serpent** hisses ecstatically, yes the **Serpent** is victorious, yes the **Serpent** releases its pleasured juices everywhere and—Mr. Fandango, what are *you* doing here? But he's busy slaying Mrs. Johnson slaying so I close my eyes but can still hear her screaming … no, Mr. Fandango, what have you done?! Open my eyes to find her in pieces bloodied on the floor oh no oh no what am I to do? *Shut up and go to sleep,* says Fandango, *shut up and forget any of this has happened* and he starts cleaning up the mess he's made and takes the crown of thorns off the Christ and knocks me across the face so I'm dizzy dizzy dizzy I can feel the weariness in my stomach and head, Fandango is annoyed the world starts spinning everything lets out a nervous cry of defeat and then—

*   *   *

"Do they even know you well enough to make these wild assumptions?" I ask.

Darren sips away at a mug of sweltering black coffee and swallows firmly. He thinks for a moment; I feel as though he can't choose any particular set of words to say what he wants to say. After some while of silence, he answers (somewhat awkwardly): "I don't really know. Maybe the folks here are just ... *scared* of me. Maybe I'm just too ... weird for them or something."

Hmm ... perhaps *that's* it, though Darren's last words don't seem to convince even himself.

Our second meeting has been initiated and is off to what seems like a good start—to be honest, I feel somewhat "comfortable" around him, or at least more comfortable than I'd have expected in this amount of time. The nurses' suspicion has motivated me to find out for myself what's so "wrong" with Darren, though thus far, I've found him innocent of all his alleged accusations! He's unique in a special, indescribable way. This comfort has dawned upon me rather unexpectedly, but it's just sort of *happened*. He's got this way about him, you see, he's got this hypnotic vibe goin' on that just lures you in. In the past hour that we've spent discussing the matters of his "experiment," I've found that I simply can't resist my own sincerity. The nurses have warned me not to tell Darren the things they've said about him, but my words just find themselves slipping out on their own. I feel absolutely terrible (and nearly vomit all over Darren's drab, green shirt), but he says he'll *never* let anyone know that I've allowed myself to "squeal." I'm not sure how it's happened, but our dialogue has begun to guide its own direction. In regard to our conversing, Darren encourages me to be as open as possible—that's the only way that he can get any real results for his "test." Apparently, what goes on between the two of us is no one else's business, not even *Dr. Cohen's*.

Our chitchat continues at a rapid pace. He tells me a bit about his far-out perspectives and abstract theories; I have trouble making any sense of them. Amazingly (might I add *shamefully*, as well), he's gotten me to completely forget about the staff here and all the dogma they've beaten into me. I know that once Darren heads off and I continue on with my day, their firm, authoritative hold upon me will flourish again, but right now in these heated moments that he and I are alone, the existence of Rory, Hanson, and even the Old Man himself seem somewhat meaningless. All of Darren's whimsical musings are overly alluring; a series of foreign and mysterious seeds are being planted into the soil of my brain.

"So have you begun to read what I've given you?" he asks with a tired smile. (*Hmm.* I noticed this detail yesterday as well. Beneath the worn-into flesh upon his face, something deep in Darren's heart is not sitting right. I'd love to know what's really troubling him—I contemplate questioning the matter, but instantly shoo away such a notion. Who am I kidding? I don't have the kind of guts it takes for something like that!)

I inform Darren that I've indeed begun his assignment and have even exceeded his wishes by reading three chapters. His face instantly brightens. It's clear that I've thoroughly impressed him.

We talk about some of the characters and their stances in society, focusing especially on the narrator and Dr. Dawson. Obviously, he shuns the story's antagonist. The worst of all human sins is the perpetration of free will, he explains, and what Dawson has done is a violation of this natural right. The narrator, on the other hand, is brave enough to stand up for what he believes in—according to Darren, it doesn't matter if the way you think is revered, accepted, or even acknowledged at all; all that matters is that you've got enough guts to stand alongside your creed through both the best and worst of times. Everything Darren says makes a whole lot of sense, though as you can probably see, most of his ideals largely contradict those enforced here in my home.

"The story teaches that one is not to fear his or her own

individuality—no matter *what* the circumstances may be," Darren says.

"But who's to say what is right and what is not?"

He smiles and moves his grey, aging hair out of his face. "You've stumbled upon a question that is hundreds—*thousands*—of years old. Our culture, Sid, deems what is accepted and what is not; it's all in the way we are *raised*. You can't tell of what you haven't been told, can you? Very few laws are exclusively embedded into human instinct, instincts of which, might I add, are so terribly polluted that our race no longer exists as nature has intended. We've become de-humanized for the wretched sake of modernization, and look at us! It seems to me that if we haven't been spoon-fed a specific ideal since birth, then that ideal is totally wrong or blasphemous. They say beauty is in the eye of the beholder, but to disrespect a man for his ... possession of a *real* pair of balls is just crazy! Do you understand what I'm trying to say? We are a dually cursed race, or at least I so believe—our evolution, our intelligence, our understanding of the things around us: it's safe to say that any step we've ever taken forward has been just as many painful ones back as well. It's a vicious, unavoidable cycle. At one point in our lives, we all become victims of it. Knowledge, in the long run, is the root of most ignorance, or at least the root of most sorrow. That's just the way things are doomed to work. "

I absorb his words like a sponge—they are insightful and pure, though as I meditate on these things, I find myself feeling unable to relate. "But Darren," I admit humbly, "I don't feel ... 'victimized' in any way at all! Maybe these things apply to your world, the *Outside*, but there are seldom victims of any sort here on the ward!"

"It's impossible!" he says. "It's just impossible. Don't allow yourself to be tricked by your own naïveté. Think hard. Dig into yourself. You mean to tell me that you can't stumble upon one scar, one terribly burning wound that *stings* every now and then?"

I think along terms of the "big picture." Yes, of course I'm plagued with pitiful immobility and apparent insanity, but otherwise, things couldn't be better!

"The very fact that you're here, *isolated* and *trapped* on this ward is enough—don't you understand the way in which you suffer?" He adds forcefully with resentment, "Or have you been programmed just like the idiotic Dawsonites? Have you only been *taught* what happiness is?"

His sudden hostility alarms me. Is this the dangerous side of Darren that the nurses warned against? Is this what he's *really* like? I can *see* the resentfulness in his hard-as-stone glare, I can *feel* it in the way he speaks! How terribly misinformed—he's got it all wrong. I explain to him what it's like to actually live here, to actually be one of *us*. I praise the nurses' love, I praise their dedication and care, I praise their health and vigor ... none of this seems to faze him. There's no getting through—Darren refuses to accept the fact that living here is a *great* thing, a divine *privilege*. Maybe he's *not* as innocent as I'd perceived him to be. What if the nurses were right all along? Oh, I *knew* I should have listened to them, I just *knew it*! A wave of nervousness immediately storms over me, and a horrific burning sensation in my chest makes me nauseous. I lose reality for a moment, but Darren's patient reassurance eventually calms me down.

"You shouldn't get upset like that so easily," he softly advises. Much unlike just seconds ago, his words acquire a sweet, paternal tone. I can't read Darren, I really can't—he's got such a tricky personality! Bitter one moment, angelic the next!

"I honestly can't help my over-reactive nature," I explain. "It's not like I *want* to get ... all *funny* around the slightest bit of conflict. It's just the way this good-for-nothing brain of mine works!"

"*Nonsense!*" Clenching his fists, Darren despairingly shakes his head. "No—*no one* is like that." His voice echoes ominously. The face before me appears to be timeless, filled with infinite wisdom and advice. Solemnly, he confesses: "Believe me; *no one* is quite like *you*."

"But that's why I'm here! That's what makes me *crazy*!"

"Oh, *stop* it. Like I said—you can't *tell* of what you haven't been *told*. You only *think* you're crazy because everyone *else* says you're crazy! Really—do you feel like there's anything wrong with you? Do you feel *insane*? I *know* that you are a victim, I *know* that you suffer; what kind of life *is* this? Can you even *call* this a life at all?"

I try to interject but am cut off.

"If there's one and only one right that every man and every living creature has, it's the right to *live*, it's the right to life itself! And you, my friend, have been cut off from it. Life is *not* behind closed doors, life is *not* contained in any set of rules, life is *not* preprogrammed— life is what you *want* it to be, it's your own to discover. *Your* life is entirely *your* responsibility! Who's to say what you should like or what you shouldn't? Who possibly has enough power to keep your mind in line? The law is one thing, but no one (and I mean *no one*) can stop you from *thinking* about what you want." He leans closer to me. "Do you keep your thoughts under control, Sid? Do you *think* before you *think*?"

"It's only for the better—"

"I don't want reasoning. I'd just like an answer."

He yanks the truth out of me; his hard and unwavering brow is enough to have me crumble. He talks of things I never dare wonder, he ventures into realms of thought that I've always known as sacrilege!

"But how come Mrs. Hanson doesn't think like this? How come every one else here on the ward sees things differently?"

"Well they *have* to!" he exclaims. Something in him lights up like the sparked wick of a dying candle. "How else can they keep folks like you in line? They're just like Dr. Dawson from the story you've read!"

I try to fully comprehend this wide spectrum of ideas he's

thrown upon me, but it's a bit much to digest all at the same time. The codes of life that I've forever known have been contradicted, proved *wrong*; I feel lost for direction and am unsure where to turn.

"But *why*? Why would they bother to *lie* about their love? All the time and money spent … what you say just doesn't make sense! Why, why, why?"

"Why is not a concern of yours … *yet*. All you need to worry about right now is opening up your eyes to things. Manage yourself subtly. Once they find out that you've acquired a *real* head upon your shoulders, it will be the end of the *both* of us." Apprehensively, he adds, "We're sitting on a stick of dynamite, in case you didn't know."

What? *What did he say*?! What is *that* supposed to mean? My gut hurdles, but Darren's strong, comforting hand upon my shoulder helps me remain sane. I share with him my puzzlement—for the first time in my life, I have a sense of *fear*.

"And so you've become human: step one of my little experiment is complete. You've gained knowledge, and only the knowledgeable have things to fear. The key, however, is not to let your fears get the best of you; they must be acknowledged and then *shunned*—a life consumed by panic and alarm is *no* life at all."

I can hear high-heeled footsteps approaching from outside my door—I recognize them as Mrs. Hanson's. Darren ups himself from his seat and we exchange a few heartfelt words of departure. My personal assistant enters and rudely shoos him away.

Hanson throws me a menacing glance. At first, guilt manifests all throughout, but I throw out a rope and lasso onto Darren's words. Fear? I need no fear of her … *right*?

As he is violently shoved out of my room, he reminds me to continue reading the book he's assigned.

"Analyze. Observe. Read intuitively—follow your intuition."

I am to have no fear in dissecting the narrator's thoughts and motives, I am to have no fear in finding pleasure in reading it; I am to fear nothing at all.

I am to become human.

*   *   *

MRS. BURR: *(subsequent a long drawn-out quarrel)* *What do you mean I can't shoot up again today? One fucking shot, Doc, just one fucking shot!*

DR. COHEN: *(irately)* I've told you before and I'll say it once more: we've been abusing our morphine supply, *darling* (obvious sarcasm)—there will suspicion from the corporations if I'm forced to keep ordering such large quantities to feed our needs! What is *with* all of you lately? Did you hear what happened to Mrs. Johnson this morning? She OD'ed on an experimental form of dimethyltryptamine and went absolutely ballistic!

B: *(heavy panting, sweating, eyes bulging)* Oh, I don't give a fuck about her, this is an *emergency*! I can barely *breathe*, Doc, I can barely see things *straightly*! I'm going to die, you bastard, I'm going to drop dead and fucking *die*!

[MRS. BURR FLAILS WILDLY ON THE GROUND, TWISTING, TURNING; SHE FOLLOWS THROUGH WITH A SERIES OF SOMERSAULTS AND MUSCLE CONVULSIONS AS IF POSSESSED.]

C: How despicable! You make it seem like I've never taught you any control—what's gotten into you?

B: *(wailing frantically)* Anything, I'll take *anything*! You don't understand, you fucking cocksucker, *you don't fucking understand*!

C: *(seriously annoyed)* One more thing like that out of your mouth will cost you, you useless experimental bitch!

[MRS. BURR LURCHES FORWARD, SCORES A FORCEFUL BLOW ACROSS THE DOCTOR'S AGING FACE.]

C: *(in awe)* Wasteful *cunt*!

[BREAK OUT INTO SAVAGE FIGHTING; MRS. BURR'S OPIUM WITHDRAWAL CAUSES HER NOSE TO RUN AND EYES TO BLEED. AFTER BEING BEATEN OVER THE HEAD A COUNTLESS NUMBER OF TIMES WITH A GIANT PIECE OF SCIENTIFIC GEAR BY THE DOCTOR, HER BLADDER LOSES CONTROL AND A STREAM OF NERVOUS URINE (FOLLOWED BY AN ONSLAUGHT OF REEKING DIARRHEA) LOOSELY DROPS OUT OF HER. BLOOD STARTS TO FLOW OUT OF A DENT IN HER HEAD. BURR RATTLES UNCONTROLLABLY, VOMITS ALL OVER HERSELF. THE DOC LEAVES HER IN A CRUMBLED MESS ON THE GROUND AS HE SEARCHES FOR SOMETHING SHARP. FINDS A PAIR OF SURGICAL SCISSORS AND RELENTLESSLY BUSIES HIMSELF. ONE STAB, TWO STABS, THREE STABS, NINE STABS, THIRTY STABS, SOME IN THE CHEST, SOME IN THE FACE, SOME FOR THE MERE SAKE OF BRUTALITY.

[BURR IS LEFT LIFELESS ON THE GROUND, SOAKED IN A POOL OF HER OWN FLUIDS AND FLESH. THE DOCTOR KICKS THE CORPSE, SPITS ON IT, DRAWS UP A LOADED HYPOTHERMIC NEEDLE FOR HIMSELF. FINDS THE PULSE, PUSHES THE METAL TOOTH DOWN INTO THE VEIN AND SERVES THE HUNGER OF BILLIONS OF MORPHINE-DEPRIVED CELLS.

[THE DOC REMOVES HIS PANTS, RENDERS HIMSELF ERECT, AND BEGINS TO FUCK MRS. BURR'S DEAD BODY …]

*   *   *

I *can* because I rule this stoop;
I *can* because there's no one to stop me;
I *can* because I say so;
I *can* because I've got a mind of my own;
I *can* because if I didn't, I'd be a fool—and I'm no fool;

I *can* because I'm right; because I *have* the right;

I *can* because I'm as sane as I say I am;

I *can* because I'm no tool;

I *can* because I've been lied to;

I *can* because I've got instincts;

I *can* because no one else can save me, can save this wretched mind of mine;

I *can* because I'm slowly fading away;

I *can* because I'm angry;

I *can* because so much of my life has been wasted …

… yet after a few hours, it's inevitable that I can*not*.

*   *   *

Oh, they *know*—already they've pushed their sights far beyond my weak façade. I haven't even begun acting differently yet, though it's *so* obvious that Hanson and Rory have caught on to my new revelations. They can see right through me, they know *exactly* the kinds of things that are going through my mind! How, just *how* do they know? Darren's assured me that they haven't got the power to inhibit my thoughts, but at times like these, it's impossible for me to believe otherwise. They're wizards, I tell you, malevolent witches with devilish powers right at the tips of their fingers!

This all really isn't like them, though—I'm not accustomed to such *hostility*! When Mrs. Hanson arrived at the lunchroom, she didn't utter a *single* word. As you can imagine, the situation was very (VERY!) bizarre and uncomfortable for me—due to my frantic nerves, I've still got a thick wad of meat from lunch lodged in my throat. I'm not so sure I can handle this for much longer … I just want it to stop, I don't want it to go on! I'd been so confident when it was just Darren and I alone, but as predicted, out here in the open, I've come to realize how *helpless* and *vulnerable* I really am. Who am *I* to defy the ones that love me, the ones that dedicate their entire lives to keeping me up and running? I don't think I've encountered a more belittling feeling than when Mrs. Hanson coldly stomped away from me—*an emotionless stone*—once lunchtime had come to an end. Don't even *remind* me of Mrs. Rory—she won't even look me straight in the eye! I've let down and betrayed my makers; I am unabashedly ashamed. The *worst* part of it all is that I'm not exactly sure how to actually *deal* with this problem. I've led on Darren, I've led on the nurses; I'm caught in a tangled mess. This disaster is without a solution.

What am I to do for redemption? Can I regain everything I once had?

The nurses were right all along—the real world, the one world that Darren has tried introducing me to, *is* one filled with problematic dilemmas. Any world that can't compete with my own perfect little haven here is not a world for me at all.

I'm not sure what I was thinking; some soaring delusional bait must have drawn me in. I pictured Darren's canons helping me here on the ward, releasing some "inner human potential" that I never knew I possessed; he's created nothing more than an emotional *train wreck*! What *right* does that fool have to just stomp his way in through that front door and start screwing around with my head? I'm shocked that Dr. Cohen even *agreed* to this in the first place… I wonder if he even *knows*! I must repent, *that is it*, I must beg for forgiveness from the nurses quickly. I don't want them to give up their hopes *altogether*!

I'm still in here, confined to the chains of this crippled body. It's still *me*—g-good ol' Sid Tate! I've just been tricked like the foolish dupe I am. It's not my fault—really!

Darren: How could I have allowed him to persuade me into discarding the rules of my past? *The rules that have forever kept me in line?* He knows *nothing* of my life here—*our life* here!

Crazy Outsiders…

And that book? Ah, that's just to swindle me as well; what's the point of it, anyhow? The narrator is just some crazy moron looking for trouble. Indeed, Hanson and Rory put it quite well. Ugh, you don't even want to try picturing how *stupid* I feel, how particularly *dumb* and naïve! If it ain't broke, don't fix it … where is my mind when I need it most? Why couldn't I just have had enough guts to stand up to Darren and defended my rights as a *patient*?

Listen world, listen to me closely: I am *not* a human being and do not want to be. I am a product of the glorious splendor of science, and gladly so. I'll take my blissful crippled life in *here* over fame and fortune out *there* any day. I've made the staff look so terrible—I'd portrayed them as miserable, controlling monsters … what foolishness on my part!

With the little energy I have, I attempt to roll myself away from the side of the bed and trudge to my personal bathroom. I clumsily bump into all sorts of things, but the matter's urgent: I'm about to vomit. Uncontrollably, an orange stream of putrid fluids leaps out of my mouth. Oh, it's a mess, I've gotten it everywhere—I can't clean this up on my own! It's hopeless, just *hopeless!* It smells like the inside of a rotting animal's digestive track, and my wheelchair and I are smothered in its stinking brilliance! How great!

This all needs to change, and quickly, too—something must be done. Mrs. Hanson will know what to do, I'm sure she'll know *exactly* how to help me out. I will plead for redemption, I will beg for mercy.

How would I ever manage to survive without her—how could I ever have been so ignorant?

*   *   *

She hasn't spoken a word yet, but it's hard for me to make the first move. Mrs. Hanson is sternly seated beside my bed and consciously daunts me with a silent, wordless lecture. I'm ready to break down, but my fear of igniting the heavily impending fire between us is too great. She feeds me my dinner just as a servant goes about with its mundane tasks; pale, cold, uninterested. It becomes hard to swallow, for a hard, emotional lump has developed in my throat. As my eyes begin to water, I decide that this torment no longer can proceed.

I break down slowly. Each passing second rips another piece of dignity away from me. Luckily, it's just the two of us; no one else gets to watch my desolate shame pour out. After many moments of pensive inertness, Mrs. Hanson eventually comes to me. In spite of my uncontrollable bawling, she cranes down and holds this weeping disaster—*me*—in her arms. My spirits are lifted (for there still is a chance!), but I feel dirty and unworthy; what business does a pristine angel such as herself have caressing slimy filth like me?

At first, we do not speak. In truth, I don't have the courage to spray my perverse breaths upon her. She pushes my plate aside and connects with me through those unmistakable azure eyes of hers. A new entity is born within me, something faint yet significant, something seated amongst the complexities of my inner framework; a new spirit, a new soul, a force that magnetically lures me back into her firm grasp. She wipes my tears with the backside of her hand and allows me some time to pull my sorry self back together.

"There, there," she says gently, just as if I'd never wronged her at all—the unconditional affection she displays makes me feel even *worse* for having been deceived by such silly malice as Darren and his troublesome story.

"You've been swindled, haven't you? Oh, we knew it would happen, we simply *knew* it! We warned you, we tried our best, but I guess—"

"Oh, it's *not my fault!*" I exclaim. I rattle in my wheelchair like a child who's wet his pants. "You don't understand what went on!"

Mrs. Hanson utters softly, "Don't worry, Sid, we *do* understand, and it's all okay! We expected this to happen to you, we knew it from the start; we actually *wanted* this chaos to unfold! We wanted you to learn so for *yourself*."

"Learn … *what* for myself?"

"How grand a life yours is. How much we love you."

"Oh, I've learned that these things are so, *I've learned that these things are so*! You *do* believe me, don't you Mrs. Hanson?"

"Why, of course I do, Sid. I wouldn't give it a second thought.

"You see, between you and me, Darren is a real troublesome fellow, just like that narrator in the story he's having you read. He thinks that just because he has some crazy ideas about 'life' and what it's supposed to be like that he can go around invading other people's *privacy*. We lead a very unique life here, and not many people are familiar with our customs. They think because we're the only people that live like this that we must be *wrong*." She takes my trembling hands and squeezes them sympathetically in her own. "You don't see anything wrong with the way we live, now do you?"

"N-n-no, Mrs. Hanson!"

"I didn't think so. The only reason we allowed you to experience what *pain* and *suffering* and *hardships* are like is so you could get a small taste of what goes on in the *outside* world. All those terrible things you were feeling and thinking are part of Outsiders' everyday lives, you see. Imagine every *second* and every *hour* and every *day* made practically *unlivable* thanks to such troublesome realities. In here, everything's perfect. We've got you, you've got us—we have *everything* we'll ever need to be content."

I take a long, relieved breath. The air that regularly drifts through this facility has never felt so *right*. Love, comfort, safety: they're *irresistible*. I am clueless as to why I'd ever have even imagined stepping foot outside of this luxurious home of mine. I plead in confusion, "Some of the things Darren said ... why did they make so much sense? That's the only thing I don't get: why is it that at the time I felt so happy to break out of these 'chains' of mine, but once he'd left me alone, I was reduced to misery, agony, and others sorts of emotions I've never experienced before?"

"He proposed something new to you, that's all, some daring rebellious idea that you'd never before thought about—which is a *good* thing, by the way. You know that it's your unquestionable acceptance of what we do that *separates* you from the others.

"Our minds like to be adventurous; sometimes they jump to wild conclusions without very much thought. Everybody needs a little bit of guidance. That's what I'm here for, Sid—Mrs. Rory and Dr. Cohen, too. You've needed us on this day like you've never needed us before, and I'm all too happy to be of help. I never want to see you make bad choices or wander down dangerous paths. I treat you as if you are my own; you're like my very own flesh and blood."

Her words are pure sugar, candy for my sensitive soul.

"How about some time in the Game Room? Would having sex make things any better?"

Normally I'd never decline, but I'm just too physically and mentally spent; I'm literally exhausted. There's no way I could withstand all the electricity that sex regularly pumps through you—my brain would be fried to a crisp!

"I think a good night's rest will work most efficiently for you," Mrs. Hanson suggests. "Once you get to bed and fall asleep, you'll be more relaxed; you can reflect on your ideas in the morning. Be sure to tell Darren how you're feeling when he comes in tomorrow. Don't let that creep think he's won over you. Let him know what you felt like after he left and how much you *truly* love it here."

I firmly reassure her of my adherence to the ward's doctrines; never shall I attempt to stray from them again. Her countenance is celestial, flows with golden beauty, and beats in a special rhythm unknown to other earthlings. She is a higher power.

We discuss whether or not I should finish reading the remainder of the book. Thanks to Mrs. Hanson's better judgment, I have instantly developed hatred for the narrator and his friends; rejecting rules, rejecting society! *Despicable!* Only the weak-minded can't handle morality in the real world—fools, dreamers! That's all they really are—just the thought of those radical delinquents *disgusts* me!

"It's up to you," she says. "At least now you've got a better grip on yourself; you're stronger and can understand the ignorance that horrid story represents." Mrs. Hanson strokes my hair, carefully massaging the surface of my scalp in all the right spots. "If anything, let those teenagers' mischief and the troubles they're likely to face reassure you that you're *safe* here. None of those bad things can penetrate *us*."

With a few more comforting words, a kiss on the cheek, and the hauling of my crippled body up into bed, she departs on a fairly bright note. I'm grateful that she's saved me in time. She understands my guilt and weaknesses—I should have expected no less.

I stare into the paper face of this aforementioned work of evil as it sits on the nightstand beside me; I want to destroy it and rid the world of its nuisance! Unlike anything before, it has introduced these foreign trepidations to me and sunken its teeth into my overprotected flesh. It's poisoned me with the *Outside*. I'm quite fortunate that Mrs. Hanson is such a wonderful healer of wounds; I am filled plentifully with her loving antidote.

I don't particularly desire to read on any further—the dialogue of this brash narrator is only to anger me and turn me further cross—but something deep inside my conscience contemplates this. Weakly, I extend my arm outward to snatch up the book. Possessed by its blank, aging covers, I bring it within inches of my face. Somewhat indistinctly, I can make out the image of my face reflected by its cover; its dull, tattered surface is something of a mirror. Impossible, it's just impossible! This is a trick on behalf of the demons amidst these perverse, rebellious pages. Stop it, somebody take this uncanny beast away from me! In a matter of instants, the thought of tearing it to shreds crosses my mind desirably. It may not be my property, but at this point, I really don't care! Witchcraft! The whole thing is *witchcraft*!

Just as I'm about to rip Darren's manuscript right down the center, my door creaks open and Mr. Fandango storms in anxiously.

"Hey, hey, hey! *What are you doing?*" he screeches, tumbling through a series of his signature somersaults. His tiny yet agile hands rob me in a flash.

Mr. Fandango huddles protectively over Darren's story in the far corner of my room. His determined eyes frantically scan each and every page, cover to cover, just to make sure everything is still intact. "Sid, have you gone mad?" he cries. Mr. Fandango hides the book far out of reach and joins me at the foot of my bed.

"What's gotten into you, hmm?" His eyes are drawn open and his head rattles from side to side in nervous fits. Boy, he's more serious about this than I thought! I imagined this act as just another leg of his tomfoolery, but I guess I was mistaken! He starts lecturing me in a clumsy stream of consciousness. After a long while, his onslaught of words starts coming together to form a semi-coherent picture. "It's the Answer!" he cries. "The Answer to ... *huff* ... EVERYTHING!"

The Answer, the Answer, the Answer—that's what this whole debacle is about. Oh, if only I could get out of bed and knock some sense in this lunatic ...

"Don't you see it? Come on, it's *obvious*! Hasn't it *clicked* with you yet?" he sputters.

"What on earth do you mean?" I implore. "How ... how do you even know of my visitor's manuscript in the first place?"

"I've read it, of course!" he barks with a great dose of laughter. "Sped right through it last night while you were asleep. It's a real easy read. I just couldn't put the damn thing down! You've gotta finish it soon, Sid, you've gotta finish it *now*!"

"But why waste my time on such rubbish?" I ask defensively. Nothing in the course of my life has perturbed me more than that devious little narrative, so why in the world should I succumb to it? "It's evil, a work of demons!"

"*What?*" Mr. Fandango is kicked into high gear once again. He begins darting around the room like a ricocheting bullet without sense or direction. "*Sid Tate*! I've always said that aside from *myself* you were the sanest out of us all in here—*and I believed that too!*—but I'm afraid now you've just *crossed* the line! You're *more* than crazy, obviously, *so much more* than that: you don't have a mind at *all*! You're a vegetable, you're no smarter than a pile o' hay! Just listen, just *listen* to what you're saying! Are you an *idiot* or something?"

Fandango continues insulting me in this manner for many minutes more.

"It's a masterpiece—a work of pure genius! Why are you blind? Isn't it *clear* to you?"

My current emotions enter a state too convoluted for words. As my sense of control rapidly starts fading away, I loudly declare, "The only thing that's clear to me now is your stubbornness and inconsideration!" As if on cue, the colors around me start distorting, my insides start hurting, and the regular series of events that occur when I'm provoked inevitably unfold.

"Ah, so you *haven't* read between the lines. It's just as I thought. I thought you were *smarter* than that!"

I try to convince him that I understand the story's meaning, but he does not hold my proposition in esteem. According to Fandango, I've still yet to fully comprehend the power of the storytelling. If I can't read into the narrative's "hidden messages," then I might as well not even read the story at all—and he calls *me* crazy? Much like Darren himself, he mistakes this manuscript as something more than a deceptive trick.

Our quarrelling continues incessantly. He blames my defiance on the nurses, and this starts a whole new argument altogether. You know how personally I take it when my caretakers are disgraced. I feel as if my body is inescapably consumed by a red-hot flame.

"You're brainwashed!" he cries. "Can't you see what you've become? Can't you see what they've turned you into?"

"You're just jealous, *that's* what it is! You secretly mourn for the attention that the staff gives to me and I *know* it!"

"I'd rather win the attention of a dead pig than be lauded by those liars!"

"Now you're starting to sound like *Darren!*"

"Well then maybe he's got some sense!"

"So the book's poisoned you, too! Don't you see what it's done? You need the help of Mrs. Hanson, and *fast!*"

"Oh, stop it! Haven't you learned? Look what happens to you when you're so dependent on other people—haven't you read the story? It's a true account, Sid. Don't you understand? Those characters lived *real* lives!"

"And that's exactly why you should be *grateful* for being nurtured here! Don't you get it? You're saved, you're kept away from all their troubles!"

He shakes his head in dissatisfaction; I've … I've never seen him like this! His anger and fury are wholly genuine. It's not long before he physically wages war upon me. In a speedy flash, this bantam throws himself atop my helpless, good-for-nothing body and latches onto my hair. What is he doing? Ow, ow, ow! He's gone mad, he's insane! *Help me, somebody help!* A brutal backhanded slap wheels itself across my face, followed by another and another and another. There's nothing I can do but vulnerably embrace the pain. Tears uncontrollably cascade from my eyes … for all I know, I'm already dead and have descended into hell.

Mr. Fandango growls mercilessly and looks down upon me with a callous expression that I've never before seen him exploit. Perched upon my weak chest, his appearance is that of a volatile imp. "Get some *sense*, get some *goddamned sense* while you can! Now is your chance—read; *learn!* Don't be a fool! If there's anyone here on this ward who wants to save you, it's *me*. To hell with the nurses and to hell with Dr. Cohen! You listen to me, and listen closely. If you *ever* want to see my face again, I better find out that you've read that book. Read it once, read it twice, read it three fucking times, do whatever *the hell* you need to do to get the message through your

head! Time's running short: *now is your chance!* Don't you see it?
Can't you feel it in your heart?

"If not for me, you'd be the mindless scapegoat they *want* you
to be!"

I shut my eyes in bleak confusion, only to find that instantly,
all the pain has disappeared. I reopen them and discover that Mr.
Fandango is gone and nowhere to be found. Everything is as it
was: the mess has tidied itself up, the door is shut, and Darren's
manuscript has relocated itself beside my bed.

I feel like an apparition traveling through an unknown world,
a stranger in a strange land. I'm having trouble understanding very
much of anything lately. What in the world has just happened?
More so than ever before, I feel like I'm losing my mind. I'm slowly
falling apart on the *inside*: someone needs to help me.

Weakly, I take the book into my hands. I bury my distraught
face in the manuscript's covers and am left alone with my boggling
puzzlement.

And my mind whirs with thoughts.

And my body aches with fatigue.

And my conscience boils with anger.

And for the first time in my life, I've become angry, *really* angry,
and I sure as hell don't like it.

Someone's going to pay, *big time*, though I'm not yet sure who
it'll be.

*   *   *

I have trouble sleeping. I've been glued to my bed idly for quite some
time now, staring mindlessly into the nothingness that is in fact my
home. It's hard to get any decent rest when you're at such unease …

The sound of utter silence makes me feel stranded. I'm starting
to believe that I *am* alone and that *no one* can understand or rescue
my tired, wandering soul.

I'm stared down coolly by the mocking eyes of that tempting

work of literature: it attracts me exotically. I'm a Serpent summoned by a charmer, curiously lured toward the supernatural essence the book suggests. It's set a trap and I've fallen into it—despite Mrs. Hanson's judgment (as well as my own), a faint yet sinister urge has conjured me; it's just so immense that I *can't* ignore it; the story finds its way into my quivering hands on its own.

I know I'm going to regret this later, but a more powerful animal instinct forces me to open up to where I've left off.

CHAPTER 4

Once Allan managed to get his act back together, he underwent a completely perceptible transformation; the butterfly had at last spread its wings and was leaving its tattered cocoon behind. He was more focused, more fearless, and had improved upon his character overall. I'm trying to explain things in an orderly fashion here, so I won't spoil the story for you by *completely* getting into Allan's new ways of life just yet. Be sure to keep in mind, however, that he's inching his way toward "personal enlightenment" throughout the entire next part of my tale. This gradual metamorphosis was nonchalant and unspoken of, but believe me, the gears in his brain had really begun to turn. The whole process was an unplanned, organic sort of thing. He was never able to explain what these sudden revelations exactly meant to him per se, but one thing is for certain—life, as a whole, started making sense to poor, perpetually tortured Allan.

Both he and I had been away from the Cage Breakers' affairs for about a month now, so neither of us knew exactly what to expect once we'd returned.

Things were different, *waaay* different.

We'd literally created a new youth culture altogether; all the hard work that we had put into appropriately cultivating our high school classmates had finally paid off. I imagined that our efforts would sooner or later lose steam and eventually become futile, but my pessimistic estimations were wrong, *dead* wrong. More than a hundred of our peers, all of different ages and races, had begun to immerse themselves in our little sub-society in the middle of Dawson's social zenith. We were seen as prophets, *all* of us, even Allie! In less than two months—just two short months!—we'd re-humanized nearly half of our school's student body. So far, things proved to be easy. Most miraculously of all, the school system had remained totally uninvolved. If they knew about the Cage Breaker's affairs at this point in time, they sure did a good job of keeping their insights a secret.

In spite of our demands for them to do so, our followers were at first reluctant to rebel in the real world; their rebellious natures were nothing more than imaginary, pretentious delusions. We frequently advocated our devotees to take their rebellion to the "next level"—and how stupid we'd been. In order to prove their defiance to us, our followers suddenly transformed into savage, schoolyard beasts. Massive anarchy exploded throughout the student body overnight, and this caused the teachers and principals to grow suspicious. Where had these once docile, tamed, and robotic children derived their anger from? Unfortunately, the school authorities at last had a rightfully valid accusation to make against us. Had we just accepted the matter and left the peace as it was, perhaps the disaster that tore us apart would never have gone down. But what's done is done, end of story. There's a greater purpose to it all, I *just know it*.

This dissonance wasn't as immediate as you'd imagine, though. Halfway through the school year, things started getting rough, but before our lives elevated into an uncontrollable mess, there were *plenty* of great times; I'm sure that *anyone* who was part of 'em would say they were some of the most exhilarating moments of their lives.

Allow me to explain to you how we'd come to be known as the "Cage Breakers".

The titling of our group was totally unintentional. We'd gone on namelessly for quite some time. We were in the middle of a huge group meeting on one random afternoon. At this point, the abandoned house that we'd discovered was fixed up pretty nicely: Allan and I took particular interest in converting it into completely livable quarters. There were a few things that needed patching up, but we were all just so anxious to have a giant celebration; it was time for a fucking *party*. A big party. The biggest goddamned party the world had ever seen.

We were totally up for it but were scared out of our minds; not once had we attempted anything of such grandeur—for that matter, neither had anyone else in the entire fucking town for the past fifteen years! After overcoming our initial fears, we finally managed to set a party date in stone.

We conducted a meeting that concerned all its attendees on the day before our momentous gathering. Basically, we invited everyone that was willing to go—our mentality was simple: the more, the merrier. At this point, our followers had come to be known as the Disciples. About halfway through the meeting, we decided to run over some precautions that needed to be taken in regards to our get-together; because of his overt and intimidating persuasiveness, we assigned this duty to Juan. Our simple yet plausible idea was to firmly block off all entrances but one, which in reality was a decoy—just in case we *did* get caught, we'd have time to escape before our fortress was to be penetrated.

"And who are going to be the weight-layers?" Juan asked, in reference to a heavy load of cinderblocks we planned to seal off the main entrance with. He's got this real funny Spanish accent, in case you didn't know, so a bunch of people misunderstood him. Someone in the crowd yelled: "Cage breakers? What the hell is a Cage Breaker?" The result of this dimwitted remark was nothing short of chaos. Everyone began to bicker and misunderstand each other. Some loser got the bright idea to shout out, "Cage Breakers? We *are* the Cage Breakers!", and instantly, everyone just fell in love with it—the name unfortunately stuck and the rest is fucking history.

Afterwards I was introduced to Devin, who (just like Allan) became one of "us"—he made sure he was always trying to make a difference. While I was away, he managed to weasel himself into Seth's, Greg's, and Juan's personal affairs, so he just started fitting in naturally. He was soft-spoken, calm, and fueled by his newly awakened craving for absolute freedom. I always had trouble deciding whether or not I REALLY liked him. I never got quite as close with Devin as I did with the others, but we rightfully accepted and respected each other. For someone so quiet and reserved (who'd spent their entire life as a Dawsonite, as well), he was a surprisingly weird dude. Way out there, perhaps *too* out there.

That night, we all hung out together, so before the Cage Breaker's first "official" party, Devin and I got a little better acquainted. Later, we snuck out of our homes well past midnight and met back up for some good ol' night prowling.

We smoked a few rounds and just felt *great.*

There's nothing quite like carelessly strolling 'round town when you're totally stoned; reality crumbles, melts away, and all the colors and sounds and smells around you melt into one giant sensation that you can feel pulsing throughout your entire body ... like you're in a dream ... like the reality outside of your mind is just a joke in the first place. I sort of drift into this world of my own where everything makes perfect sense, where I can see so much *deeper* into the meaning of things, where every atom of every molecule of every piece of matter is reduced to pure consciousness. You take a step outside your false state of being and realize what the hell everything's actually about: there's a spirit in nature that secretly joins us all, and on that night—more *than ever before*—I felt connected to this divine entity. It was on this night that I realized our original intentions had somewhat been forgotten. Dawson had managed to slip between the cracks. Who the fuck cared about *him* anymore? We'd ignored his laws so greatly that we'd taken him out of the picture altogether. At this point, he'd done unto us more good than harm—he's the one that catalyzed our crazy sort of life, no?

After spending some quality time together intoxicated and out in nature, we headed back to Devin's place. Man, he had the best fucking room ever; the whole top floor of his home was his own private haven! It was perfectly designed to accommodate our needs; there was a bathroom to secretly smoke pot in, a small kitchen, a fridge to feed us, a widescreen TV, and a whole load of strange books about obscure occultist myths and legends. Devin's room was without doubt the coolest place to be, second only to The Cage—don't ask how our hangout acquired its name, 'cause I myself don't even know at this point.

Halfway through the night, I found myself relocated over at The Cage with Allan Burns. It wasn't long before he and I sought tranquility that was unable to be found with the others. I remember us both collapsing exhaustedly onto the floor. Once we'd sobered up a bit, he said that he had something to show me. Anxiously, he guided me upstairs into a room that looked like it at one point had been a kitchen of sorts. I honestly had no idea what to anticipate, but a *wonderfully painted piece of abstract art* was far from my range of expectations—Allan had made an artist out of himself. His work consisted of surreal shapes and designs swirling in and out of one another, all achieved with impeccable precision and passion. Something about the mood of his painting cannot be conveyed in words alone—it in some way perfectly captured the transition from his painful past into our own chaotic lifestyle. I perceived the artistic depiction of the two ideals as nothing short of genius. Each stroke of his painting was given such detail, such fucking *commitment*. Jesus Christ … the whole thing was just perfect!

"It's for you," Allan said. "I've been working on it for a while."

Instantly, I almost broke down in tears. You, reader, might mistake this affair as a figurative allusion to a more intimate relationship between Allan and me, but this is not at all the case. Ha—what a hysterical notion! It's just that he and I understood each other unlike two men have ever understood each other before. When one man saves another's life, the relationship between them is forever changed. There exists something unique, something unexplainable, something attainable only through likewise means.

I remember telling him that I'd never be able to repay him for this; how could I possibly reciprocate something so beautiful, so pure? I was so terribly grateful, but he just incessantly went on and on about how much *he* owed *me*. To quote him: "If I could, I'd give the world to you and more." That really meant something to me, and it still sure as hell does. Few people have friends that say such things and actually mean them, but I can assure you that Allan spoke unto me nothing but the truth.

"One day," I said, "you'll have your chance to pay me back. It may not be any time soon, but trust me, the time will come."

I'm afraid that with the way things are looking now as I write this, Allan may never have that one last chance; this is the one instance that my faith in things has … failed.

But that's just personal fluff. On with story.

In order to avoid going back home to his foster parents, he spent the night over at The Cage as usual. I headed home anticipating what I imagined would be the greatest day of my life—the first official celebration of our short-lived cult, The Cage Breakers.

.   .   .

Despite his recent entry into our lives, it was inevitable that Devin was becoming an integral part of our affairs. When we all met up at The Cage at around noon the next day, we invited him over to help with our plan making. We contacted Allie too, but she unfortunately was drifting away from us—not from our culture, but *us* in particular. I don't know what had gotten into her. She'd become obsessed with a buff retard from a few towns over who'd just become a Disciple a few weeks back. We still talked and all, but nothing was ever the same—our break-up *still* hurts me, *still* haunts me, and *still* makes me feel like the biggest failure ever, but back then, I just shrugged it off. My attitude was basically "fuck it," and rightfully so—I was part of this great phenomenon, this wonderful, rebellious success! Every day I was fucking somebody new, and though at that time I thought *I was the man*, I can honestly say that no one quite satisfied me like my Allie. No one quite had that magic touch. I miss that girl every fucking day and just wish I had a chance to tell her I love her again. Maybe in another life, but in this world, we truly fucked up. *Big time*. Ugh ... my apologies for the negative vibes—I don't want you to get the wrong impression; tonight and the many others that followed were filled with nothing but wild, undomesticated fun. There's an old saying, something about things "never being quite as good as the first time," and it sure as hell is true. The night of the Cage Breakers' first party was unarguably the best and is, to me, the greatest achievement of my life thus far.

Here's how it all sort of went down: we spent the entire day over at The Cage—cleaning, organizing, securing, preparing. By the time dinner rolled along, we returned to our homes contently; everything was set and ready to go. At this point, all we had to do was wait. We were about to unveil to our peers a long forgotten and taboo pastime—the art of teenage partying, the art of having *fun*.

Here are the tactics that led to the greatest success of our lives: we organized a phone chain with us at the top. We called all the shots and told everyone when their moves were safe to be made. We agreed upon 2:00 A.M. as the official "break-out" time, and if anyone arrived later than a quarter after, they were not permitted to enter.

Seth and Greg were the first to sneak in. They made sure the coast was clear for Allan and I, and Allan and I then gave the green light to Devin and Juan. Since we had tidied everything up earlier in the day, The Cage was completely prepared for savage, party madness. You don't even know how *crazy* this felt for all of us. Take the simple joys that filled the days of our early stints and multiply them by the stretch of *infinity*.

We'd won the battle—we had finally achieved everything we ever wanted.

The rest of the night passed by in a sporadic blur. Kids started flooding in like there was no tomorrow, and I mean *way* more people than any of us had expected. The place was fucking packed in what seemed like an instant. There was a constant tide of bodies crammed into every space that The Cage could handle. Before things got crazy (oh, and they sure as hell *did* get crazy), we quieted things down for a small ceremony that Seth and Juan organized. They gave a speech about why we were all there in the first place (that being vengeance against Dawson), and babbled on and on about all this stuff that I'm sure no one really wanted to hear—most of 'em just wanted to party. Seriously. Not that we even thought about it then (or cared, really), but I bet you that half of those dim-witted fuckers truly could've cared less about Dr. Dawson or our philosophies in the first place; we—as the Cage Breakers—had opened up our peers' eyes, and they sure as hell didn't plan on shutting them anytime soon, even if they weren't seeing what we as their masters wanted them to see.

Regardless, we were merely happy to see kids our age having fun, *real fun*, and sure as hell didn't give a damn about the collective motivation fueling the matter—we wanted to party *just as* mindlessly and *just as hard* as they did.

There were a few great points that Seth and Juan brought up in that speech of theirs, but it was just too damn long; a wave of relief spread over the crowd once it was over. The tension in the room exploded, and everyone just went all out. And it was fucking *great*. From watching these same faces live the programmed lives of Dawsonite robots transform into full-blown anarchists wreaking the havoc we loved so dearly was really quite something. It gave us all a great sense of accomplishment, purpose, and power.

And there you have it. There were drugs, liquor, good music, sex—all the constituents of a great time. For me, the most memorable moment of the night involves Greg munching away at the clitoris of some random Asian chick on the second floor of The Cage. Just picture this: he sees me, gets real surprised, tosses the naked girl that's on top of him off to the side, does this crazy flip coupled with an intoxicated war cry, hurdles down a set of stairs, and just conks right the fuck out as he crashes to the ground. Ah, now that's *classic*. There were threesomes, foursomes, fivesomes, fifteensomes, thirtysomes, the bodies just piled up and up; there really was no end. No one was there to stop any of this madness, and that was the way we liked it.

You get the picture of how things were—in short: *fucking awesome.*

The Cage wasn't really adjacent to any other homes; to our own amazement, no one *ever* complained of the noise. Before the party took off, we warned everyone to try to keep things down as much as they possibly could, but of course, amidst our orchestrated chaos, that was really impossible. We were loud as hell, I'll say that much, but apparently never loud enough to bother anyone else. That was always a real mystery, but it's all about faith. Things always worked out one way or another for us, which is why as I write this, I look to the future semi-optimistically—one day we'll all be liberated and free.

I sure as hell know that I won't be stuck in this hellhole forever.

Anyway, things raged on wonderfully. It's unfortunate that I was introduced to the lowliest bastard that I've ever known on this same great night.

Cali, or so we called him. Originally from California (hence the nickname), he moved into the area not so long before the Cage Breakers' formation. In just a few short months, Cali had literally become our sworn enemy—I can still picture that deceitful twinkle in those big bug-eyes of his. Why we'd ever let him become a Disciple in the first place is beyond me.

Ever since we'd begun to gather a following, Cali wanted in—the *totally in* sort of in, not just the *in* like everyone else had ... you get me? We incessantly denied him entry into the heart of our group, but this, of course, never managed to faze him. He was never able to get the hint, you know? He was never able to accept the truth. Cali was as persistent as a starving rat in a maze; in his case, the cheese—*entry into our group*—was completely unattainable. He knew damn well that nobody really liked him, and that just drove him mad.

He was quick to get over on people and always had something rotten to say; he'd truly perfected the art of *bitching*. Neither Juan's furiously open attitude nor Allan's physical aggressiveness were enough to ward Cali away. Why in the world did he keep coming back to us? Our intolerance of his insolence was never a secret, and I think we certainly did a good job of conveying our indifference. He'd always openly whine about how unfairly he was treated and all sorts of likewise bullshit; what I don't get is that if we treated him so goddamn badly, why didn't he just get up and leave us alone?

So halfway through the night, out of the blue, he starts some wild protest in the middle of everyone else's fun, winds up making a laughing fool of himself, and angrily stomps away from the party in dismay. Seth had almost drunkenly clobbered him to death, but Cali luckily managed to get away in time.

Okay ... enough of him.

For now.

I try to remove his existence from my memory altogether, I try to pretend that he's just a figment of my imagination, but sometimes, you just *can't* escape reality. From here on in, his unwanted presence just starts popping up *everywhere*; I may fail to mention his being around, but DO NOT forget about this guy—he plays a crucial role later on in our demise, in our destruction, in the fall of our band of brothers.

CHAPTER 5

I'd go into further detail about that night and the others like it, but there's really no point; time is of the essence. Just know that for almost an entire year, the Cage Breakers functioned flawlessly. Our parents (lost in their own robotic obsessions with Dr. Dawson) never caught on, authorities never gathered enough concrete evidence against us, and the few peers whom we never managed to convert simply stayed out of the way.

Things, for the most part, went smoothly. Aside from Cali's audacious attempts to override our power, we hadn't a thing to be worried with.

Before I fast-forward the story, I think it's appropriate to change the direction of things for a bit. I went back and read what I've written so far and realized that I've not yet elaborated on anyone else's life but my own. There are plenty of interesting things to learn about the others who operated this rebellious faction, and it's only fair (with all due respect to them) that I share with you a deeper analysis of their characters. I'll step myself out of the plot for a moment and give you a more in-depth look into the lives of my subversive brothers.

I'll firstly introduce you to Seth. Though I've got nothing in my heart but love for the guy, I'm aware of the fact that he'd always been the most ... distant from me. I attribute this primarily to the age difference between us, but don't take what I say the wrong way. Seth, as you know, was the oldest of the bunch, and just for allowing us to be a part of his regular life grants him, or at least in my opinion, the right to the isolation he so exploited. He always needed to feel like he was the one running the show, but somehow, this quality of his never managed to create problems. No one was bothered by his ego, in fact his very cockiness was one of the major driving forces behind the actual formation of The Cage Breakers. His initial rebellion against the Dawsonites was not fueled by the deprivation of any political or artistic rights ... *hell no*. He just wanted to have fun. That's just the kind of guy he is. Out of all of us, he had the *least* amount of faith in things. Again, I think that had to do with the age difference as well. The rest of our dreamy fantasies seemed childish to him; he said we'd all realize how stupid we were once we grew up. (I always used to disagree with him in the past, but now that I'm older, lost, defeated, and forevermore *fucked*, I'm starting to wonder if he was right ...)

The interesting thing about Seth is that despite his carefree attitude, his mind worked like a complex network of confused thoughts and ideas. There was this slight arrogant air that he carried around with him and at times he was condescending, but overall, Seth was a rational guy. His flaws were pure and unwilling to be fixed by anything but nature's own path, which to me is just the way life should be lived. His hedonism inspired me to take things less seriously than they ought to be taken (whether or not this has been for better or for worse I've not yet decided), and I can say that it was indirectly through Seth that I've learned the meaning of life: indestructible happiness. There's just something you gotta adore 'bout the guy. He set a good role model for the Disciples; stubbornness aside, no one better represents the Cage Breakers for what we really were—he was the epitome of what we stood for.

Much unlike his abovementioned brother, Greg hated being the center of attention. He simply stepped to the side and let things happen as they were. Life's insightful little secrets never managed to faze him, and for the most part, he was unconcerned with merging far-out fantasies with the real world. In a strange way, Greg is the embodiment of average. He's so plain and easy to relate to, yet his inner thoughts are so miles-deep and valid. Despite their differences, he looked up to his brother Seth with admiration; the latter inspired Greg to rebel for his freedom. It's in hands like Greg's that the power to change the world resides. It's the culmination of many tiny things that make Greg the wonderful gem that he is. He's taught me one of life's most valuable lessons, and that is the importance of being *real*. Nothing about that kid is phony or bogus, and that's just why I love him so much. That's the quality that makes *all* of us so special: we're all *real*, we're all organic. We're sometimes flawed and we know it, we're sometimes wrong and we know it, but there's nothing pretentious about us. We refuse to wear the mask of the Dawsonites, the mask of lies, the mask of loss, the mask of idiocy. Not once have I heard Greg utter a word that he didn't truly believe in.

And of course the same goes for Juan. Just to let you know, Juan is probably the most naturally sarcastic person the world has ever known. That bastard could fool just about *anyone*. His character drew from the best of all us; without a doubt, he was the most well rounded. His rude and abrasive sense of humor sometimes was borderline insulting, but it's through people like Juan that you learn how to take a punch. Despite his absurdities, he managed to retain a good head on his shoulders. Without him, we'd all be nothing more than a bunch of aimless lunatics. Using his nonsense as a foolproof medium, he managed to always keep us in line. He was the most irrational voice of reason there ever was. If I only I could really explain him to you ... truly, his ways are beyond words.

Juan's rebellion had come in similar fashion as my own; he's not interested in spirits and nature and art the way I am, but we undoubtedly have a definite common denominator— our uncomfortable niches in society were rooted in likewise soil. If not for his faith in things, I'd call Juan an absolute realist; he never got caught up in personal pipe dreams like I so often did. The point at which we ideologically diverge is the fine line between the spirit and the flesh.

So you can see what a diverse set of friends we were, and I strongly believe that it was our isolated individualities amongst our own unity that kept things going. We fought like cats and dogs 'round the clock, but the very fact that we were fighting in the first place in the midst of our Dawsonite world is the main point I'm trying to make. What I'm getting at is that my life would be truly incomplete had I not crossed paths with any of my great rebellious brothers, Juan particularly. Whether he's busting on every wrong thing you've done or carrying on about some cute girl that you're too shy to approach, Juan's prattling somehow makes you feel good about yourself, no, *great* about yourself. He reminds you to thank whatever god is out there for creating people as genuine as himself.

Ah. How dare I almost forget to mention Allan Burns—now he's a character indeed. Much like Juan, his greatest attributes are inexpressible; you've just gotta meet him. He lived like no other, in a way that the Dawsonites saw as totally blasphemous. He was a maverick, an oddball; I'm sure you know of the sort. He's the kind of guy you see on the streets that immediately grabs your attention thanks to long, messy hair and purposely uncoordinated clothes. Like he cared! You might call him a loser, you might call him a fool, but I call him a damn-straight genius.

Had I not intervened with his tragic path, maybe things would have turned out differently, but oh, how *faith* has its ways.

There's nothing really relevant about the last of our friends, Devin, that you don't already know about—aside from always being part of the fun, Devin never seemed to directly influence our "internal affairs." Always was looking to get stoned, always looking to party; sometimes he'd get real bossy and we'd all get pissed at him, but things always positively resolved. See, that's the thing, *that's* what kept our relationships so strong; we knew how to *handle* our problems. Sure, each and every one of us had major flaws, but we knew how to deal with them: that, I really believe, was the key to our own success *away* from the Cage Breakers—our interactions as regular people were just as organic and pragmatic as we so preached they were. With that in mind, you can see *why* our friendship's disastrous collapse came as such a shock. No one expected it; no one even imagined that it was *possible*.

I suppose that now is a good time to move on to the darker side of my story; the end of it all draws near.

The end? You mean to tell me that these guys' power comes to an *end*? So the narrator *hasn't* been leading me on the whole time after all—there really *is* some horrible catastrophe that wrecks the Cage Breakers' lives and destroys them for good! I can't even imagine the likes of *Dr. Cohen* penetrating the rock-hard will of these insistent teens—it's got to be something big, *real* big, that destroys their lives and changes them forever.

*   *   *

[FADE IN, MID-CONVERSATION]

MRS. RORY: It's just that I don't see the point it in all, Doc. Can you even fathom the expenses of such futuristic killing machines as the ones you're concocting?

DOCTOR COHEN: My dear Mrs. Rory, the essence of what it means to be human is growing passé! If you believe that our world is not going to transform into an empire of super-intelligent androids, then you are *sadly* mistaken—any day now, the dust of the earth will in fact *know* that it is the dust of the earth; that day will be the end of humanity as we know it, that day will be our step into the future!

C: The power to instill life into inertness is on its way. Our own ways of life will be devoured in instants by this mechanical, impregnable beast. The last war of the world will come and go in the blink of an eye. Mrs. Rory, it is *inevitable!* People like me will make the *difference*, people like me will guide the world into this new, glorified direction … just think! The very government that funds us with millions of dollars each year will eventually crumble *powerlessly* in the wake of what minds like my own have in store.

[EXTENDED SILENCE, FOLLOWED BY A CHUCKLE FROM THE DOC.]

C: Mrs. Rory, why don't you *hang yourself* upside down from the ropes I've got set up in front of my desk? I want something nice to look at while I sort through my paperwork. I've been quite lazy lately … tsk, tsk, tsk … you're likely to be hanging there for hours!

R: (*robotically, in a way that seems overly grateful*) Really? D-d-do you *mean* it, Doc?

C: Why of course I do! Hurry now. I haven't got all night!

[RORY RUSHES OVER TO A SERIES OF PREARRANGED ROPES THAT ALLOW HER TO HANG UPSIDE DOWN.]

C: Do you need help, sweetheart?

R: *(trying to hurriedly tie herself up on her own; sounding as if she wants to make the Doctor proud)* Oh, no, I'm just fine, Doc. I can do it all by myself!

C: *(to himself, laughing)* Suit yourself, my dear.

*   *   *

The world around me is cloudy and thick, as if everything has condensed into a single, immense, solid block of matter. I've awakened at some strange hour (my digital clock seems distorted—the white fog that envelops the room has it masked); I feel light, disconnected, and incongruous to myself. The man in the white silky robe is silent and faceless, though his skin glistens like the gently wavering face of a serene pond. There's a particular glow to him, a shining aura that softly encircles his being. A warm, angelic voice assures me that there is nothing to fear; I am to take the phantom's pristine hand and have him guide me away. I tell the specter softly that I am crippled and tired, but he pays no mind to my excuses. There is an undulating force that shoves me up and out of my bed—I am left suspended *midair*.

Rationality is exchanged with pure adrenaline. Every inch of my drifting being surges with a confident flow of electricity. The external world moves by rapidly, and everything seems to be happening all at once. With what seems like much ease, the ghost pulls me along with its magnetic leash.

My body begins to whirl through space in what feels like most perfect of geometric patterns. The spins are consistent and prearranged, defined with such alien precision that I'm beginning to feel overwhelmed. Everything is so *glorious*, everything is so *great*, and everything is so *unbelievably wonderful* that once the hooded angel dissolves into nothingness and drops me out of its aerial grasp, I nearly vomit from the uncontrolled daze I'm thrown into.

I'm left alone in a disheveled mess near the entrance to the cafeteria. I feel like I've somehow experienced this episode before. *Eerie.* The presence of my euphoric trip still lingers in my bones, however its company is greatly overshadowed by a horrid plague that's got me twisting and turning. In just the blink of an eye, I've grown worn, as sore as a fighting warrior—I can barely *move.*

My heart twinges; I feel the foreboding power of some evil force approaching. It manifests like a dark beast deep within me, a surprisingly *familiar* dark beast. I've seen the face of this sin, I've tasted the bitterness of its fright—I've surely heard that twisted scream before.

An obscene travesty of myself slowly materializes out of nothingness. Indeed, this make-believe charade is perverse and gross. It silently and incessantly lays the weight of its gaze upon me for a long while. Its exposed brain—(the upper portion of the skull has been removed)—is littered with a variety of blasphemies: fat, erect penises, fluid-filled needles, baby rats gnawing away.

The expression it displays is bleak and distant, lost in a realm of perpetual darkness. Slowly, the hunk of pulsing crimson seated in the bowl of its severed head begins to corrode. Blood starts oozing out the sides of its brain—the ghoul collects some with a single finger and tastes it gratifyingly, in awe of its magnificent flavor. What is *wrong* with him? What kind of foolish impression of me *is this?*

This furious, macabre replica of myself retrieves a sharp-edged knife from seemingly out of nowhere and has begun stabbing itself severely. In a matter of instants, it collapses into a disheveled wreck upon the ground, soaking in a deluge of its own fluids.

I turn away in despair, though the geometric euphoria has now returned; my sight is clouded by the swirling together of countless neon shapes. From behind this colorfully deceitful wall, I can hear something—some*one*—else approaching, someone small, someone agile, someone who breaks into complete hysteria upon arriving at the foot of the corpse.

"Godammit!" Mr. Fandango barks. "Stupid motherfucker! Goddamned stupid motherfucker!" He lands a hard blow across my fallen counterpart's face. He scurries over to the corpse's encroached brain and begins tearing out the wicked oddities jammed into the soft, pink tissue. "What a mess, what a mess, what a mess!" he shouts, hurling over his shoulder one of three rigid penises. "Look what you allow yourself to get into—do you *see this*? Do you see this wreck? For cryin' out loud, do I have to keep a watch on you *all the time*? I thought you had more sense than *this*! You're beginning to frustrate me!"

He leaps forward like a frog, grasps my arms tightly, and shakes me like a rag-doll. "You worthless piece of shit!" The quick flurry of punches he exerts (which of course send me brutally the ground) knock a sense of reality back into my dreamy state of mind—I am reminded of how just hours ago we'd undergone a similar fanfare. I'd nearly forgotten . . . the book—*Darren's* book was the root of the cause.

"*You are killing yourself, fool*," Mr. Fandango wails, "and for Chrissakes, you're no fool, right?"

A burning flame arises in my gut.

"This is no *illusion*, you blind rat." He points to the bloodied corpse—*my* corpse. "This is *you*."

*　　　　*　　　　*

I awake beneath the comfort of a bunch of warm blankets.

I gasp at Dr. Cohen's sudden presence at my bedside. His expression is silly—*drugged*.

He says, "Years ago, I spoke these words unto you:

"'Your reposed body cannot hear me, dear child, but you will learn in time that you've been brought into good hands. The hard and troublesome days of your past are long over and will eventually be completely forgotten—I will reintroduce you to a new kind of world, a better world than you have ever known.

"'You will be the center of my personal little empire, an empire that will be mine to rule as I choose. I shall be *Kratos*, the ancient god of power, and you shall be reborn as *Oizys*, the ancient goddess of pain and misfortune.

"'You will not feel the pain I am to drive into you, but that's because you will be blinded, blinded by the sheer purity of my *love* for you. Your flesh and bones are now futile: I need only your fiery mind, the mind that has landed you here in the first place. Our life together, as you will learn, shall be symbiotic. I will live off of *you*, and you will live off of *me*. I will create an intimate bond for us to share, a bond so great that it will be *impossible* for you to resist.

"'This empire will develop around the two of us—the greater our union, the greater my kingdom, and I *assure* you that my pursuit will not end in vain. As it is believed that Jehovah took the very dust of the earth and breathed into it consciousness, I will do the same: it is in my power to become God, *your* God, the deceptive, malicious, and evil God that I so desire to be. By the time I'm done with you, *vile rat*, you'll be utterly obsessed with *me*, just as I am presently obsessed with *you*; from there, the tables will turn, and it will be a great pleasure to watch you perish slowly from the inside out. You will pay for your ambitions, but not until I have watched you pave the road to your own madness.

"'Now you keep resting, young Oizys, as I get to work. Soon, the rudiments of my empire will be complete; in time, I will bring you up out of this icy tomb and into my rule. Until then, sit tight.

"*I know that's always been a problem for you, hasn't it?*"

The beast roars in laughter.

"Some things *never* change … now you listen here," he says with a silly inebriated inflection, "you're *crazy*, kid. You're *crazy* and don't you *ever* forget it."

part 3

The black of sleep slowly wanes away.

Perhaps even more frightening than the grotesque imagery that'd confronted me last night is my very exit from the nightmare *itself*—as if only a second has passed, I reopen my eyes to find the morning sun's bright light inching its way through my window. It takes a while for me to affirm my oneness with reality. I scan my surroundings and find that everything seems slightly ... *different.* The colors that make up the room are curiously drabber, more mundane; things have acquired a dull, bluish tint. I stop to think for a moment and reevaluate my observations.

What the hell?

The three-dimensional qualities of my world seem to have disappeared, seem to have faded into the background to form one seamless mess of blotchy colors! The sobriety the morning brings ignores all sense; I still feel dazed, I still feel confused, I still feel absolutely horrified!

Just as I'm about to submissively call for Mrs. Hanson, I wisely stop myself; I need some time *alone* before I proceed into the day. This perpetual anxiety and stress must stop. I feel like I'm losing the little sanity I have left; I think I've finally lost my mind *altogether.*

A lifetime of agony that I've never known has suddenly reared its ugly head. It seethes in my blood furiously; consciously ... it is a second life form on the *inside.* This strain feeds like a hungry parasite, munching and munching away. I just want to be free, I just want to break out and run away from it all! How—*why?* In a matter of days, the life I've always loved—(the life that's allowed me all the glory and affection I need to survive)—has begun to crumble! I've battled with these marauding thoughts before, but the struggle is useless; the fight is one-sided

I can *feel* the world around me deteriorating, I can even *see* it in the colors!

Who is the perpetrator of this emotional mess—is it the staff? Is

RAYMOND

it Darren? Is it a combination of both of them? Is it Mr. Fandango? Is it my very self? Nothing appears convincing enough to end this feud, and *that's* what's driving me mad. To be left in solitude is all I *really* want!

If I am to decay and die, then so be it, but I'd rather decay and die in peace—*alone*.

My naïve seclusion: that's all that's ever been, that's all there ever was. Now that I need it most, this solace remorselessly evades me. Emptiness is my eternity, though I feel like I've stepped out of the void; minus the love, minus the attention, minus the care and good intentions, my life here on the ward is a drained vacuum, a bleak, rotting consciousness in the middle of empty space.

I stare down into my battered palms, and the bruises upon them start stinging like crazy; have they come from the roots of my deep confusion?

I don't understand why everyone wants so much out of me ...

A wave of grogginess storms my belly, and it suddenly occurs to me how severely I've *physically* suffered from this torment as well. The past few nights have been filled with terrible pains throughout my body and ominous, indecipherable hallucinations—things simply *can't* go on like this!

I want to ricochet back into the grasp of the staff's judgment, I want them to bring things back to the way they used to be; on the other hand, my reasons for wishing so are *unclear* and frighteningly robotic. This urge is preprogrammed into my database, I feel *forced* into my thoughts—and *why*, I ask myself, why? I am no *machine*! I futilely attempt to fight these irrational judgments of mine. The shifting of my ideas is combated easily by haunting biological powers. Ugh, something isn't *right*.

Everything explodes in a gentle stream of tears; I can't hold it in any longer. As I weakly attempt to dry my dampened cheeks, I hear the approaching of Mrs. Hanson's clacking heels. My heart rivets—I try to hide that I've just begun to weep, but my great assistant's resolute stride is far too quick.

She comes to me anxiously. The gaze I'm assaulted with is familiar, yet *changed* in a way I can't explain. Mrs. Hanson begins to speak, though what she says is undecipherable. Sounds like I've never heard before pour out of her determinedly, sounds like those of a malfunctioning computer; she's activated the breakdown of some digital program inside of my brain! I offer a distorted expression of fear and confusion as these jarring bleeps go on rampantly. She receives this curiously. I don't think she knows what's going on ... and for Chrissakes, neither do *I*!

My skull fills up with the chirping of this futuristic network, but eventually—thanks to the joined efforts of Hanson *and* Rory (whose assistance I suppose has been called upon)—things settle down.

The sensation passes, reluctantly and contemptuously.

Once I'm back to normal (how oxymoronic!), I regain ahold of myself. Once the nurses discover my reawakening, I am plunged into a series of invasive questions.

They come to me as if they *care*, as if I am their *only* worry in the world. They hover over my bedside compassionately, brows ruffled in concern; they place their tender, maternal hands all over me gently, trying to "ease" whatever "trouble" I am going through— can't they see that this is *no cure*? Their *sciences* can't save me, and neither can the shallowness of their words!

"Are you feeling well?"

"What's gone wrong?"

"Do you need another dose of medication?"

"Do we need to call Dr. Cohen down here?"

"*Your dreams*. Tell us about *your dreams*."

"Don't forget that we're *here for you*. Things can't get any better unless you open yourself up to us."

"Would skipping your session today with that weirdo Darren make things better?"

"Just tell us … whatever is on your mind."

"We know the answers … to *everything*!"

These (amongst other flimsy ploys) are used in attempt to comfort me, yet their effect is merely that of anxiety. The nonstop onslaught of their concerns has buried me alive, and I've barely any air left to breathe.

My robotic instincts ward away these negative thoughts and replace my anger with *affinity* toward the nurses—I have no choice but to adhere. I am weak and powerless against this brewing force; I'm discontented, yet my mind believes it is *satisfied*! How? How is the inhumane witchery even *possible*?

While Mrs. Hanson is out retrieving a jug of water that I've requested, I'm left alone with Mrs. Rory and all her psychotic powers. We are speechless for quite some time. The mask I try to hide behind is thin and transparent as cellophane, but I try to keep my cool.

Mrs. Rory's stature has begun to change. She shrinks, expands, shrinks again, expands again, and is elongated and adorned with the skin of a reptile.

The Serpent watches me with a cold-as-ice stare, rhythmically swaying in place. Its scales are arranged in such a design that I can't help but to quiver in fear.

"Talk to me," It says perversely; the Serpent silently communicates with my conscience. Sweat soaks my flesh, but I *need* to give in to the questioning of this Evil—if I don't, surely It will snap out and devour me alive.

I catch my breath and speak. Sincerely, I plead, "What the hell is *wrong* with me?"

There's a twinge in the back of my brain—that's where It lingers and haunts me: something makes me feel like Its presence has been there for*ever*.

"It is your own foolishness, of course! Why do you *bite* the hand that *feeds*? Why do you blaspheme your God?" It rattles Its coils frantically. "Why have you gone and befriended the *Outside*?"

"The Outside ... what do you *mean*?" I cry. "I *have* no friends—I am hopeless! I am nothing! I have no relief but my own, and certainly there is none to be found within my*self*!"

"It is what you have *chosen*!"

"But it *isn't*! It's just what has come to be! I'm crazier than ever before with Darren in *or* out of the picture—it really makes no difference! Sane one day, mad the next!"

"So you go as low as to blame your *home*, the ones that have raised and aided you?"

I moan in agony. "I ... I don't know, I don't know, *I don't know*!"

The Serpent cocks Its head. "Why are you so at one with Darren's stance in all this? Why is *he* vindicated of blame?"

"It's because ... because my *heart* says so!"

The creature cackles. "Heart? What kind of heart can filth such as you possess?"

"A heart just like anyone else's, one just like any other *human* has—*that's* why I defend *Darren*, that's how I know he's not to blame! He's teaching me to be *human*!"

The Serpent growls angrily. Its disgusting countenance distorts into the face of the Devil's own.

I continue bravely: "He knows the rights that every human possesses, he knows the decisions I should be making, he knows that I should have a mind of my *own*! I'm not allowed to be *myself* here on the ward, I'm forbidden from my own thoughts! I've been robbed and raped—the workers here are *thieves*!"

Though my words are valiant and my will is strong, I'm suddenly overcome by an unbeatable force.

There is a sense of erosion in my chest's cavern—rocks which have forever been in place begin tumbling away. My inners are tarnished, worn away by, quite literally, a slew of malignant chemicals. I close my eyes, but the Serpent remains; It is present and everlasting.

I can no longer speak—I am overridden by the control of a new voice: a *Savior.* I've torn through my own dimensions and ripped a stark, bleeding hole into my madness—a powerful force has escaped and possessed me.

Using my terrified self as a communicative medium, it speaks directly to the Serpent. "*I know you,*" it says. " ... I've known you *all my life!*" A devil scorched with Holy Water, the reptilian beast wails in horror.

I am shown something of a slideshow by this newly awakened entity. Blurry, unreadable images flash before my eyes. Though difficult to make sense of, I deem that they are images of my life. "Look deeper," the voice urges. "Look *deeper.*" And amidst the distorted snippets of light that blaze past me, *Its* presence is there—the face of the sick and twisted Serpent is *there.* It has watched over me like an ill-willed guardian angel, It has had me choked in its tight, vice-like grip for eternity. I've been confined by its power all along! I've been Its servant, sucker, and scapegoat. The revelation that beats within me tells me to go *back,* as far back as I can go—I am transported to a memory of birth. The recollection is a screaming blast of pain, a horrid vision of blood and gore.

I look into the womb from which I've come. Wriggling in all its nascent madness, the Beast grows simultaneously beside me. It has been with me since the beginning of time—we've grown up and lived together, side by side, day by day. I have been Its fuel, Its source of life: in an unexplainable (and unbelievable) way, it all makes terrifyingly obvious sense.

My brief moment of realization is useless: there is a sudden electric charge that surges through my body and wipes my memory clear. The Evil has returned and I am forced into Its unyielding grip. The other dimension I'd momentarily tapped into has shut its doors, and the hell of reality returns.

The Serpent's hoarse shriek fills up my head once more—for a moment it seemed like It had lost Its power! "How dare you! The love, the time, the *research*! You ungrateful *fuck* … who in the hell do you think you are?"

I suddenly become shrouded in a green and poisonous mist. This smog devours everything in sight with the exception of the beast's fiery, magnetic eyes. I'm pulled into Its zone, the Serpent's Zone, right where It wants me to be …

… be

… be

… be

… and every cell in my body has become alert and drawn to the pure beauty of the Serpent. Its detailed flesh suggests nothing short of perfection, in fact I don't believe I've ever witnessed anything so … *beautiful*! An aura has developed around its pulsing, muscular body; I am weakened and in love. It slithers down the side of the seat and crawls into my bed sheets. I can't resist the allure—why would I *want* to resist it in the first place?

I reach out merrily to play with the Serpent beside me (my weak, paralyzed hands are suddenly surging with strength!), but it erupts into thin air with an apprehensive squeal. I jerk back—where? Where has it gone?

I glance up at Mrs. Rory; she sits firmly in her seat, observing and accounting for each and every of my moves. A recording device of sorts is slyly hidden beneath the folded hands in her lap … it's only so I'm protected, though; it's their *job* here to keep a close watch on me! Her smile is warm, divine; in just an instant, everything feels right again. Along with the severing of my chains to insanity, that familiar coziness has returned—I feel *normal*, I feel the way I *used to*. She tucks the recorder away into her uniform and comes to me slowly. Rory crouches at my bedside so our eyes meet directly. For just an instant, her face morphs into that of the brilliant Serpent.

"Where did it go?" I ask her. "I'd only wanted to *play* with It!"

Through means of her inhuman powers, Rory wordlessly urges me to examine my flesh.

At first I notice nothing strange in the makeup of my skin, though once I'm ordered to observe more carefully, there appears to be a slight change—scattered abundantly are the marks of budding reptilian scales. At first, I can't believe this; immediately, Mrs. Rory stops me from second-guessing myself. "Everything is fine," she says. "Everything is moving *back into place*." She strokes my scalp gently with a smile. "Go back to bed. We'll delay your meeting with Darren to later this afternoon. I'm sure you're feeling a bit off; some rest will make a world of difference." The look on her face is satisfied, perhaps *too* satisfied.

Mrs. Hanson eventually returns with a giant jug of water and places it beside my bed. The two nurses drift out of my room like ghosts and leave me to myself. I examine my flesh again, still appalled at this sudden transformation. Scales—what kind of human is dressed up in *scales*? First, there's the arrival of those mysterious scabs in the palms of my hands, and now *this*! I suppose it's all right, though—Mrs. Rory has assured me that everything's just fine, and she and Hanson, of course, always know what's best.

It's not that my troubles have been washed away … it's like they don't *matter* anymore. It's like they've never mattered at all—my newly acquired reptilian flesh lights up delightfully at the passing of such a thought.

What a strange start this morning's been off to!

With many weighty burdens now relieved, I can sleep clear-headedly once again.

Just as I'm ready to doze off, though, some wary instinct prevails.

Standing in the doorway is a furious Mr. Fandango—he seems

tired and defeated. His stern look instills fear into me ... what's gotten into him?

He shrugs his shoulders, sighs, and leaves me alone to myself ... or *does* he?

*   *   *

"You are asleep and dreaming."

I sit cross-legged in a cavernous indentation in the side of some mountain. I have no reason to disbelieve Mr. Fandango (who presently is busy collecting odds and ends for the use of a campfire)—this is not some wide-awake hallucination where reality has just run amuck; no, I'm positive that this is actually a *dream*.

I scan the vast space that stretches out around us and am overwhelmed. The vast distances that I behold are simply beyond words alone. The mountain itself is equally baffling. I look *up* and estimate that we're not even halfway to the top; I look *down* and am faced with immeasurable nothingness—from here, the ground is invisible, shielded over in a thick blanket of clouds. Something about being all the way up here makes me feel at rest, at peace, almost as if I'm—

"No, you're not *dead*." Mr. Fandango interrupts my thoughts. "... or at least not *yet*." His stark honesty is as alarming as it is confusing. He chuckles and playfully shoos away my fright. "Up here, we are *safe*," says the little dwarf as he fixes the two of us a small pile of rubble and twigs. To himself subtly: "*This should be enough to get things cookin'.*" He obsessively straightens up his little mound of gatherings. Once he's done, Mr. Fandango lightheartedly parks himself down next to me and pats my shoulder jovially.

"*Weee-hooo*, have we got *lots* to talk about," he says with a great big smirk—it seems like it's been *ages* since I've seen my fellow gnome-of-a-friend smile the way he used to. Oh, he's *certainly* up to something, that much is for sure.

"First, let's eat and drink up." He downs a mouthful of liquor—

out of thin air, he's conjured a frying pan, a plate full of raw fish, and jug of red wine.

I'm passed the ceramic pitcher and am told to take some as well. The nurses generally don't allow me to consume alcohol, but this *is* just a dream, after all.

"Cheers to the beginning, cheers to the end!" Fandango declares.

As he turns his back and begins kindling his fire, I stretch out my legs and remember the beauty of dreaming:

That you are invincible.

That you are everything and anything you want to be.

That I am able to *walk*.

*   *   *

"Oh *puh-lease*, this is nothing," Mr. Fandango insists when I compliment his cooking—really, this fish is perfection! "Just whipped a lil' something together real quick. Maybe when we come back and visit this place again, I'll come more prepared with some better grub!"

Again? I think to myself.

The natural beauty all around us compels me; everything just seems so ... *endless!* "Where ... exactly *are we?*" I implore, genuinely intrigued by our surreal backdrop.

Mr. Fandango lights up excitedly. He takes a hungry bite out of his impaled fish-kabobs, swallows energetically, and offers a sincerely deep gaze. "Well! 'Bout time you asked! Always too busy killin' yourself with them useless questions all the time that you've forgotten 'bout the *important* sorts of things!" He tosses his half-eaten meal aside and waves me over to follow him up a long, winding path. I take a moment to examine the ascending trail along the mountainside, but of course, Mr. Fandango interjects. "Now come on! I ain't out to *hurt* ya for Chrissakes! We haven't got all morning! I said we've got lots to talk about—*lots*. You're likely to wake up in another hour or so—my *God*, have we got to get a move on things. Time's a wastin'! Hurry! *Hurry!*"

So I follow him (somewhat suspiciously) farther up to our destination.

*   *   *

He's asked me to explain where I think we are.

"A dream, you say … that we're in a *dream*—bah! What kind of answer is *that?*" Mr. Fandango grimaces playfully. "My dear friend, have you any idea what a '*dream*' really is?"

I think for a moment; what do my dreams *honestly* mean to me? I start expressing myself slowly, but eventually find it difficult to hold back my constant wave of thoughts.

"Dreams … are where we are all able to live through the eyes of the immortal, where our fantasies are able to become truths. When we fall asleep at night, we escape reality in a way that's intimate and personal … you know, in a way that's especially our own. We enter a mode where sense is in fact *nonsense* and nonsense is in fact *sense*. We are undistracted, we are able to appreciate things for much more than what they are. We *hear* things differently, we *see* things differently, we *feel* things differently—yet are we really feeling or seeing or hearing anything *at all*, Mr. Fandango?"

The question is unintentionally rhetorical.

For inspiration, I look out into the immense space that so greatly dwarfs us. Though we're not much higher up than before, the world seems to have … *expanded*. I turn back to Fandango and continue; he seems pleased with my intuitiveness.

"Go on!" he urges. "Talk, talk—I know you've got more to say!"

"Unless you've been *trained* to behave your thoughts like I have, I suppose dreams can really be … *anything!*"

I stop and ponder—I realize that I've never dreamt quite like this before. Never in my life have I ever felt so free!

"My dreams are usually filled with pain and torture, with dismay and gross illusions!" As I try to continue, my stomach instantly grows weak; my brain and muscles tire. A deep affection toward the staff wells within me—just as always, the love is governed by a concoction of undefeatable chemicals. The struggle to alleviate my torture is, as usual, useless.

"Ignore it!" Fandango commands. His words resonate like thunder. "There's no use in fighting battles you can't win; don't you know that much by now? You've got to learn to let things come and go." He claps his hands powerfully, and the discomforting sensation is driven away.

The newly formed scales along my flesh sting angrily, but I'm told to withstand the pain.

Suddenly, I feel the looming presence of my captors. "It's them—the nurses and Dr. Cohen! They know about us, they all know where we are! Isn't there something we could do to hide from them?" I crumble to the ground at Fandango's feet, pleading for some form of help; instead of comfort, I'm given a brash kick to the jaw.

"And for a second I thought you'd toughened up or somethin'! C'mon, don't make me feel like I'm wastin' my time here!" His legitimate interest in my well-being overpowers his rising frustration. "Get yourself together now, up, up, up. Up on your feet. What kind of bullshit are you talking about? I told you—we're *safe* up here. Nobody can get us, I *promised*. What's the matter? Don't you *trust* me?"

He tells me to settle down, though I can't help but let the fury pour out of me. "*See*? Do you *see* what I mean? How my thoughts are *inhibited*? How I'm such a prisoner? What do you expect me to *do* about all this?" The buzzing feeling arrives in my gut once again, but with deep concentration, I successfully drive away the presence of the deadly **Serpent**. Losing patience, I grumble: "Why can't I be free like everyone else, Mr. Fandango? Why the hell can't I even enjoy my *dreams*?"

Mr. Fandango laughs and waves his arms in the air. "All right, all right, all right already. Enough of you and your 'dreaming' nonsense—you wanna know what it *really* means to dream?"

I suppose I've no right to object.

"To dream," he begins after clearing his throat sarcastically, "is to temporary delve into *insanity*. There is no 'intimacy' in dreaming, for there are only enzymes at work, networks of data rearranging themselves, and bodily chemicals flowing in and out of your brain like mad! I know a lot of this probably sounds like nonsense to you, but just listen to me, listen closely.

"Our presence here right *now* as we speak is a façade—we are intangible and invisible; we linger in the existence of a few buzzing microscopic particles. We are literally unconscious consciousness! We are literally nonexistent! You, my friend, are dormant in the real world. You are likely to forget that any of this has ever happened in the *first place*. I, however, have got a *job*, and that job is mine to fulfill." With a passionate sparkle, he adds, "It's not like *I'm* the one calling the shots around here, if *you know what I mean*."

He stares into me so powerfully that I can nearly feel the weight of his crushing gaze. Something is familiar in his troll-like face; something in the two of us is joined in a non-physical way.

"You *still* don't get it?" he asks—and *no*, I truly don't. What is this lunatic talking about? "*You haven't figured out what I'm all about?*" He laughs. "Well I s'ppose there're more important things concernin' us right *now*." He ignores my confusion and continues raving. "Anyhow …!"

He now conducts a thought-provoking explanation regarding the impossibility of the staff's control over my thoughts. I listen to what he says, though I'm more boggled by the nature of this fanfare in the first place. What the—? Mr. Fandango? Taking things *seriously*? What kind of nonsense *is* this?

"You *are* aware of what they do to you, right?" he concludes after a minutes-long rant. "You're not *that* brain-dead, are you? Come on, you *must* know, you *must*!"

An awkward lapse of silence precedes my realization, but I *do* know these horrors to be true ... and have *always* known these horrors to be true.

The thought has been there forever, though until now, it has remained ungraspable. With my own refusal to accept the truth and the evil molecules throughout my body combined, imagining such terrible things as more than just delusions has (for all of eternity) been impossible.

They'd had me brainwashed! Those bastards have had me *brainwashed*!

I've been a tool, a science experiment, a mere toy for those jackasses to play with—God only knows who I *really* am or what I'm *really* supposed to be! And how, I ask, how and *why* have I ended up with such a fate? Me, *why me*?

The force of this riveting insightfulness has winded my gut. Looking down the side of the mountain is nauseating, though I might as well jump off and die right now—there's no reason left for me to live. Truly, I am *lifeless*. I stare into Mr. Fandango, trying to understand who he really is and what he represents, though my mind draws a blank; he instead allows me time to reflect on myself so I can better understand my polluted existence.

When does a singular man in fact cease to be that same man? Our identity surely is more than just a name; is it in the flesh, in the mind; is it in neither at all? Is it something on the inside that no modern science can penetrate? Or are we innately purposeless, inferior to ourselves and the better judgment of nature around us? If we as humanity are granted freedom—(if such a thing can possibly exist)—then why have I been excluded from this privilege, this natural right? *Why, why, why?*

Everything disappears for a moment; I become immersed in a

blank vacuum, a stark void of purely white space. From head to toe, everything inside of me collapses. Like the fall of a great ancient monument, I meet my structural demise.

It all makes sense now, and knowing that it *always* has made sense is in no way comforting. Minute after minute, hour after hour, day after day, month after month, year after year, I'd allowed this to go on (and gratefully so!). It'd been the work of my own ignorant hypnotism! And now, it's all too late—the damage is done and irreversible. I cannot be saved ... can you imagine me cured of this sickness? *Can* you? Things like this are *incurable*!

Through the dense white block of solid mass that encloses me, Mr. Fandango calls out just as I'm ready to explode. "It's all right!" he exclaims in effort to save me. "Everything's fine! Just calm yourself down now! 'Member—we're in a *dream*. *You* make up the rules here, my boy. Ain't nobody gonna get you when you're here—'specially when you got me around to protect ya! I'll be *sure* of it!"

I battle off my wrenching dizziness, and all that is covered in milk-white fades away. We've relocated, it seems, to a completely new region of the mountain—we're inside a faintly lit alcove now. The weather on the outside has changed. It's dark out there; *hazy*—the pitter-patter of moderate rainfall sings a melancholy tune. I'm still sickened, though the sound of the brooding drizzle is paradoxically calm and mesmerizing. Miles away, I can hear the rumbling of swelling thunder. I glance outside this small cave and am greatly surprised at how dark the vast space (which just moments ago had triggered a flow of breathtaking emotions) has become; its beauty has been devoured by the pitch-black of night.

"And even *still* in the middle of this ragin' storm, we are completely *safe*," Mr. Fandango confirms. We are both uncomfortably seated in the confines of this small recess. He spanks my thigh optimistically and whispers into my ear: "You listen to me, listen to me *real* good, 'cause I've got something that I need you to know.

"At this point, your very own insanity has overridden all the nasty things that've polluted your brain over the years—you're *freed* from the control of your very thoughts! *Now* is the time to reap the benefits of your madness, *now* is the time to let your insanity play its part! Your vivid hallucinations are only nightmares because of your predisposition to *fear*! You are finally able to rule yourself—you just need to *allow* yourself this power!"

"But how?" I ask. "How can what's driving me mad wind up saving me in the end?"

Mr. Fandango pounds his chest and the whole earth beneath us rumbles. The impending rainstorm reaches its end, and the dreary grey clouds dissolve into a bright blue sky. A grin precipitates from under his thick ebony beard. "I suppose there's no reason hiding from you anymore. Do you want to know who I *really* am?" he asks matter-of-factly.

Before he reveals his "true identity" to me, he wants me to guess on my own first. I wrack my brain for a logical answer, but there is none. He's something of a frenzied bantam with a particular interest in myself, a rebel, a fellow of many words and mannerisms, a chock full of energy, a powerhouse of mischief and mayhem—is there anything *more* to say? He's not been here on the ward for very long, but it certainly doesn't feel that way. It feels like I've known him all my life.

"And that's because you *have* known me all your life!" he cries victoriously. Mr. Fandango leaps into a series of somersaults and shouts wonderful cries of triumph. He takes my hands and swings me into a dance. My paralysis washes away and I am swept to my feet. He waltzes me around the mountainside with much confidence and pride. "I have been with you since the beginning of *time*!"

Since … *what*?

I stop the rhythmic beat that our dance has conjured and crouch down to Fandango's height. I study each and every line of his face carefully, trying to decipher whatever riddle he's just presented me with. I examine his eyes, I examine his hair, I examine his flesh—I don't see anything different in him that I haven't seen before, though a more intriguing realization dawns upon me. Mr. Fandango is not human—he is from a different world.

"Who *are* you?" I ask, wrapped up in my fascination. "No—better yet: *what* are you?"

Mr. Fandango performs one last glorified flip and lands masterfully on a single limb. "Now *those're* the kinds of questions I like to hear! Usin' your head now, I see." He poses sarcastically and clears his throat yet again. "Why, I am nothing more than a *reaction of chemicals in your brain!* I am nothing more than your own body's answer to *fear!*" He claps his hands together excitedly. "Take it in, take it in, take it *allll* in!" He jolts around in frantic circles—he cannot contain his joy. "Whooo-weee! Doesn't the truth feel *greeeaaat?*"

The walls of this small cavern have broadened—there is more legroom, and I am now able to stand. I bolt up and look down into the troll's bright blue eyes in disbelief. If I could express the complex rush of emotions running through my mind, I certainly would, but this feeling is untranslatable! Dear listener of my crazed and wild account, it is now in this dreamy moment that I've realized how poorly I've narrated my tale thus far—these emotions, these visions, these feelings of mine are all *incommunicable.* I am of another universe, you see, I am a completely different *life form*: how can someone like you *ever* understand my experiences? I can speak, but not enlighten. I can babble, but not inform. I can give folks like you only a mere *glimpse* into a much-distorted world such as my own!

After a few moments of thought, I manage to stammer in astonishment, "You … you mean you're not … *real?*"

The cavernous boundaries spread even *farther* apart now, so far that the cave itself has crumbled. I scan the area to find the familiar stretch of sky-blue infinity within reach once again; we are higher than before. Still in awe of this nonsense, I watch in amazement as

Mr. Fandango teleports gleefully around the mountain. Now he is here, now he is there—he's everywhere! He's not only a four-foot gnome, but a body builder, too! And a little boy, and a little girl, and a full-blown woman, and a full-blown man, and a clown, and a mime, and a lion or tiger or bear!

"Alrighty, now that *that much* has been taken care of …!" He returns to his original shape and scurries up a new trail. "By the end of this dream, my friend, the two of us are going to reach the *top*!"

*   *   *

"Yes, it is as you've concluded: I am only present in your mind—no one knows of my existence but *you*! Not Rory, not Hanson … not even the Doctor himself!

"I am the one thing that the ward was never able to take away from you;

"I am what keeps you *alive*;

"I am everything that you are *not*—I am *bold and daring, loud and obnoxious*!

"I am your fantasies *personified*.

"My very *life* feeds on all that you cannot be. I'm like a horror movie that gives you your kicks, that gives you a rollercoaster ride of third-person thrills. You live your utmost desires through my manic ways; if not for my perseverance, who *knows* what would have become of you! I'm sure that you are unaware of just how dangerous your own insecurities can be.

"I've *always* been around, but it's just that you've never been *crazy* enough to realize it! Now that your sanity has *completely* been lost, I've been able to materialize and converse with you; most importantly, I'm able to finally *save* you!"

He takes a breath and continues. "My friend, you are being eaten *alive* from the inside out, and *that's* what my main concern is. When you die, *I will die* with you, and I sure as hell don't wanna die just yet; are you forgetting? It's like I said … we're *together* in this *fucked-up* game of this *so-called* life. You've gotta save yourself quick because Rory, Hanson, and the Doc *all* know how you feel. They don't live inside your mind, but they sure as hell have got the power to manipulate you with just a solemn stare!"

"Then let's get to work!" I anxiously exclaim. "Let's get busy! I'm ready, I'm *ready* to be saved! What are we waiting for?" I rise to my feet and begin pacing around frantically. "What am I to do? Who am I to see? Oh, Mr. Fandango—(or whomever or whatever you *really* are)—just *save* me!"

He sobers me up and gently brings me to my knees.

"If you *really* want to be saved," Mr. Fandango whispers, "then listen to Darren. Yes, *listen* to every last word he has to say, *believe* every last bit of advice he has to offer, *understand* every last thing he tries to explain to you about life … when I say time is short, I *mean* it—we've got hours left to succeed in this fight, mere *hours*, and we're either winning this battle altogether or failing like valiant fools; there's *no* in-between.

"Are you willing to accept Darren as—quite literally—your savior?" Mr. Fandango asks.

I give the matter some thought, though I realize that my overanalyzing of everything (the *wrong* things, of course) has in fact played a large role in my destruction. With every ounce of faith this dream-body can summon, I wholly surrender myself to Darren and Mr. Fandango.

"*Yes.*"

"Excellent. This trail right here will lead us straight to the top. Be careful now. This path's rockiest of all, so you've constantly got to be on your toes. You don't want to have come this far only to find yourself disappointed in the end, do you?"

No, I most certainly do *not*.

I follow Mr. Fandango hurriedly, fueled by the rush of adrenaline coursing through my veins. As I ascend the jagged pathway, I catch sight of a pit filled with three menacing **Serpents**: Hanson, Rory, and Dr. Cohen.

To overcome their might is all that stands between me and finally being cured!

*   *   *

The walk is long and tiresome. By the time we reach the top, nearly all my energy is sapped. Mr. Fandango has remained silent—this is the trial, or so he says, and only if I can overcome the incline will I be worthy of what he needs to say. When the rugged upward slope levels out into a long stretch of flat ground, he finally stops and parks himself contently on a patch of soft grass. My legs are sore now, though in some strange way, they feel lighter than they ever have before; my stride has become so burden-free that I'm nearly floating around! As Mr. Fandango's kicking off his hiking boots and fixing himself up a place to rest, he orders me to take a look down off the mountainside just to see how far up we've come. I take a peek below and am overwhelmed: from here, not only is the whole world visible, but the rivers, seas, forests, and every last creature from the largest whale to the smallest insect are amazingly distinct; the clouds have parted entirely. The feeling is wonderfully powerful, a feeling I've never quite felt before. Once I'm done with my marveling, I notice Fandango's begun to cook another meal. He calls me down next to him and insists that I listen to his tale.

"Now I can't tell you *everything*," he says. "I don't want to steal all of Darren's much-deserved spotlight. He's the fella that should *really* be telling you 'bout all of this, but circumstances have gone awry. I ain't ever actually *met* this Darren fella in person, so why don't you tell me what you know about him—or what you *think* you know about him, at least." He nonchalantly pulls a pair of meaty steaks out of nothingness and begins seasoning them gaily.

I'm a bit confused—how can he never have met Darren if he talks of him so intimately? How can Mr. Fandango meet anyone in the first place if he's *not even real*? These questions are futile, I'm sure, with answers that are probably beyond my capacity to understand. I find myself transfixed upon this unexplainable gnome, still in awe of everything that he's shared with me thus far. Though I've never thought about it (because my mind has always been trained otherwise), it is as he's said: all my innermost desires are carried out in the form of his devilish abrasiveness. Even when his presence was unknown to me, I *still* knew of him—amidst the network of my mind's erroneous perceptions, his voice has always rung most truly.

Lost in my thoughts, Mr. Fandango makes me snap out of it and focus again. Right. *Darren*. "Well he's a nice guy," I begin. "He's tall, rugged, blue-eyed …"

"I don't mean *those* sorts of things! *Ya know*, I'm talking about his beliefs, *man*, I'm talking about what he thinks of the world and of you and of your pitiful situation!"

Despite my deep enigmatic attraction to Darren, I've still plenty to learn about him—now that I think about it, I barely even know the guy at all! I contemplate what he's said about freedom, art, and the impurity of Dr. Dawson (whose actuality in the real world I'm still unsure of), but Mr. Fandango stops me before long.

"Okay, okay, *enoouugh*." He waves my thoughts away sourly. "It is as I've assumed."

Before he reveals to me Darren's "true identity," something heavy falls out of the great sky above us. In unity, we gaze upward— alas, the heavens are crumbling away! At first there is just one small crack in the atmosphere, though it eventually branches out and begins devouring the sky in its entirety. "Your dream!" Mr. Fandango cries. "Your dream is drawing to an end! Quick! Let's run for cover!"

And so we dart quickly around a rugged path of stones to find an alcove just large enough for us to squeeze into. The ruckus outside becomes deafeningly loud—I've nearly got to jam my fists into my ears to block out the chaotic cry of the sky's demise!

Mr. Fandango speaks passionately at a rapid-fire pace; he's pulled me in real closely and has got me by the neck. "Wipe your mind clear of *everything* you think you know about Darren. He's not part of some university, he's not come to you to administer any 'test'—the *TRUTH* is that the government is now suspecting the cruelties of this madhouse, *your home*, more so than ever, and *he* is the only key to your redemption!

"Tell him that we've met here in your dreams; tell him that you know who I am. You need to finish reading that book *immediately*, the very second you return to consciousness. That's just not any old story—" He takes a deep breath and robustly exclaims: "—*it's the key to your past!* It *is* your past! For all these years, how could you ever have believed that you were just some crazy goon locked away for *insanity*? You're a revolutionary, a rebel, an angered soul banned from society! If there's one thing I know for *sure*, it is that your fiery, deprived ambitions have not gone completely to waste just *yet!*"

In just an instant, everything begins melting away. I feel consciousness slowly returning, but I'm not yet ready to leave this land of purity, this land of truth and hope. Though his body has disintegrated into a wave of shimmering light, I desperately cry out to Mr. Fandango, "How will I remember any of this? How can I be sure that all this time hasn't been wasted?"

"I've already dealt with the other domains of your mind—our conversation has been preserved in its entirety across walls and floors of your room! When you awaken in the real world, you'll see what I mean. Ha—do you think I'm the only one of your little minions? There are hundreds of us, *thousands* of us, and I've sent them all busily off to work! They write in a language that only *you* can understand, they paint with colors only *you* can see; our little meeting has been secure as always. *You'll see.*"

This bright light flashes more brilliantly than before.

"Quick. Get back into the real world and do what needs to be done. Learn of your *past*, learn of why you're *stuck* here, and learn of why you need to escape!"

*   *   *

[DR. COHEN'S MAIN OFFICE. THE DOC—INEVITABLY UNDER THE INFLUENCE OF A HEAVY DOSE OF MORPHINE—READS THROUGH A SCIENCE JOURNAL, STUMBLES UPON A PERTURBING QUOTE.]

DR. COHEN: **(to a chained-down, unnamed nurse)** Ha—you want to hear something funny that I've just read?

[NURSE TURNS, REVEALS DEFORMED FACE, MISSING EYEBALL, ABNORMALLY OBTUSE CHIN.]

NURSE: What, Doc?

C: **(clears throat sarcastically)** "*The release of atom power has changed everything except our way of thinking ... the solution to this problem lies in the heart of mankind. If only I had known, I should have become a watchmaker.*" You know who said that?

N: Who, Doctor?

C: Einstein. Albert fucking *Einstein*. Doesn't that just ... *get to you?*

N: Um ... no? Should it, Doc?

C: Well, of *course* it should! That's some *pussy* shit right there! *Pussy shit! Sigh* ... just another waste of a brilliant mind ...

*   *   *

Reality returns slowly—*very* slowly—but surely, nonetheless.

The image of the real world is initially blank, but my vision eventually clears up and a single, cohesive picture is formed; indeed, what a remarkable picture it is.

This awe-inspiring vision is not a regular human experience, dear listener, so I won't waste time trying to describe it. Maybe it was meant to be that way. Something tells me that this work of art is for my eyes and my eyes *alone*. Despite it being a giant mess of sloppy, unreadable graffiti sketched across every last inch of my room, I understand it immediately. I can't comprehend what every individual symbol means, but I absorb this as a whole, digest it, and at once am able to comprehend the things being expressed. I don't question myself or chalk it off to my insanity—the knowledge effortlessly falls into place where it belongs.

Under normal circumstances, I'd take the time out to inform you of the mind-blowing truths I've just uncovered, but something leads me to believe that you're already "in the know."

Aided by a slew of miniature cleaning devices, a squadron of elfish creatures comes stampeding in from out of nowhere. Hurriedly, they begin brushing, scrubbing, and polishing up their abundant tagging. Mr. Fandango, who leads this comical troupe around, shouts out orders in a gnomish language of his own. He doesn't speak to me in words—that proud, reassuring gaze of his is communicative enough. When Mrs. Hanson comes back in to check up on me, she passes right through these playful goblins like the transparent illusions they are. My first impulse is to nervously surrender myself in guilt, but I maintain a firm grip on myself and dare to withhold the falsities my mind perceives.

Mrs. Hanson comes to my side. I know what she thinks—so at last, the tables have *turned*! She believes that I see her in some mystical fashion, that she is still worthy of my respect. I am no longer in need of her false love! Which of the two of us is so foolish *now*, hmm? I look upon her vibrant smile with disgust; I no longer see her as my devoted assistant—I see a disheveled demon, clad with a jackal's snout and a set of ebony horns. She will try to deceive as *any* devil does (in fact she tries to deceive me right now with that repulsive smirk of hers), but I've got the power to resist. There's an army in my favor, an entire army of whatever or whomever I choose to make it up of, for my insanity has become a friend, my *best* friend, the only friend that is true to myself at all times.

She greets me in her regular manner. "Here, Sid. Have some tea," she suggests.

I would like to respond to her with bitter obscenities, I would like to get up right now and rip her flesh, I would like to proclaim my thirst for freedom to the world, but I refrain from such actions. My thoughts are one thing, but what I carry out in the real world is another—*restraint, Sid, restraint!* I simply thank her for the tea she's offered and request it to be placed at my bedside. Normally, Mrs. Hanson feeds me and helps me with my drinks, but isn't that just *nonsense?* I am no child! I'm a grown man, a full-fledged, fucking *man!*

"My appetite is slim right now, Mrs. Hanson," I tell her. There is a clumsy pause, but I try to persuasively fabricate some reasoning. "I'd … just like some time *alone* before Darren comes; if I can organize my thoughts together, it will be easier for me … to express to him what I'm really feeling." Phew—that was rough, but I think I managed to successfully pull off the lie.

With a spark of intrigue, she asks, "And what kind of feeling is that?"

The words slip out on their own: "*Pure hatred.*" Yes, pure hatred, indeed—of those that have betrayed me!

"Oh, just *wonderful!*" she rejoices—the menace has not seen through my lies. Her days of power are over, her tricks can no longer swindle me! At last has come the end of her reign!

"I suppose just this *once* I'll leave you to yourself. Now you think, Sid, you think *real* hard now about all the nasty things you'd like to say to Darren! It's such a wonder to know that you've finally begun to think for yourself! How joyous!"

Ha … *indeed.*

Mrs. Hanson floats out of the room, conversing with herself until she is completely out of range. The dutiful pack of elves which my mind has deployed laughs in unison, a victorious laughter that I gladly share with them.

So I have attained the courage to both lie and face the truth. To hell with these masters, to hell with all they stand for! Along with Mr. Fandango, my team of gnomes cheers in triumph. "Smash that cup!" their leader orders. "Smash it! Break it to *bits*!"

He motions over to the ceramic cup of tea that Mrs. Hanson just brought over. I try to grasp it, but it is out of reach. I stretch even harder, but the effort is useless; my paralysis keeps me from moving.

"Oh, what hogwash!" Fandango scowls. "You don't *actually* think you're *crippled* now, do you? Come on! Just get up and smash that damn thing!"

"But I can't *walk*!" I declare. Mr. Fandango knows this all too well—what is talking about? "I can't possibly—"

"Would you just *stop* your doubtin' and just give it a try?" he urges.

Mr. Fandango has helped me so greatly already, so I'm not about to underestimate his all-powerful wisdom. I try to move one leg, though it doesn't budge. I try to move the other, but the brain signal is interrupted. As hard as I can, I try shifting them in unison, but the effort has me awfully winded. "Don't you see? It's useless!"

"Focus, my friend, *focus*! If you'd only known yourself in the *past*—a fighter like you never gives up after one measly try! Come on now!"

His words empower me with a foreign strength, a burning curiosity that flourishes on the inside. With a sudden burst of power, I jolt out of bed and find myself standing on both feet! In disbelief, I shake one leg and then the other; I practice balancing on one limb with ease. Awestricken, I find myself bending, turning, and twisting my lower half into all sorts of contortions.

"Well, enough of that already!" Fandango cries. "You can play around later! Will ya just do me the favor of smashing that goddamned cup?"

Before his thought is completed, I snatch up the tea with a surge of otherworldly might and hurl it to the ground with every ounce of strength I can conjure. It shatters into hundreds of pieces and soaks in a puddle of its own steamy juice. Mr. Fandango commends me with a pat on the back and a wonderfully hearty laugh.

Amidst the mess I've made, a bruised and bloodied **Serpent** gasps desperately for its last breaths of air.

* * *

Mrs. Rory and Darren are engaged in quite an argument right outside my room. The ruckus they've created is likely to draw attention soon unless something is done. At this point, the distinction between their individual words has become nonexistent. When it seems their bickering has reached its zenith, Darren charges into my room, sweeps up his manuscript, and grabs me by the shoulder.

Frustrated, he demands: "You're coming with *me*."

Mrs. Rory tries to stop him, but Darren simply knocks her out of the way. He seizes me by the collar and drags me determinedly toward the exit. In spite of my illusionary paralysis, I find myself able to awkwardly—though successfully—keep up with his pace.

Rory shrieks with inhuman vigor and crumbles to the ground in defeat. The din of her high-pitched squeal is diminished once Darren and I make our way outside in a unified stride.

* * *

"Let them do as they please," he proclaims fearlessly. "If the two of us are to make any progress, then it is be now and *only* now."

So Mr. Fandango had spoken the truth.

Darren and I walk somewhat hastily around the recreational track among the other daily joggers. These patients give us strange looks, but I'm told to pay them no mind. He explains that the more attention we gather, quite obviously, the more suspicious we will seem. I'm not sure if it's just me, but something about this weather, scenery, and atmosphere just seems … *right*. Even the urgency of Darren's warning has become meaningless for just a moment; if at this very second I were forced to take my last breath and leave this terrible world, I would do so happily—I would be satisfied.

Darren spots an inviting bench along the track, so we park ourselves down and begin to talk.

Without haste, he pulls me in close to him, instinctually checks to make sure no one can hear what he says, and then whispers, "Have you at last figured out what this hellhole's all about? Have you at last made up your mind? Tell me, please tell me that you have!"

We are locked in a deep gaze for quite some time before I can get myself to answer him.

"*Yes.*"

A surging, emotional current erupts within Darren. He wraps his arms around me, and we engage in a brotherly man-to-man hug. The moment is utterly surreal—I feel like I've experienced this same scene before in the past, in a distant memory from long, long ago …

"We can discuss other matters in just a moment," he says anxiously, stumbling over his restless words, "but first, you must finish, you must finish the remainder of the story! Oh, there's not much left, not much left at all!

"If you haven't solved the puzzle yet on your own, allow me to connect the last few of its pieces—this is your story, *Ray. You* are its narrator. You wrote this with all your heart and all your soul, and now is the time to reckon its power! You wrote each passage with

The End in mind, with the idea that'd you'd never see the light of day again! That is why I'm here—to make sure that all your efforts and all you once loved and all you've ever believed in will not go to waste! Listen closely. I shall read its conclusion to you now."

He withdraws the crumbling stack of loosely bound pages and opens to where I've left off. He flips each page with remarkable gusto and passion, with determination to save whoever I really am, whoever I'm really supposed to be.

I shall announce this fact to the world loud and clear: my name is Raymond, Raymond James, and at one point in time, I had made a *difference*.

CHAPTER 6

If I had to trace the Cage Breakers' eventual demise back to the single event that jump-started our destruction, it is without doubt the time when D.J.'s mother (very, very literally!) tried to kill us. If you don't recall (you probably don't—I think I mentioned him once thus far), D.J. started off as one of us back in the day, but he eventually pulled himself out due to various emotional reasons; by the time we'd risen to infamy, he'd dug his own social grave. A little side story: D.J.'s mom had *always* hated us. We generally kept out of the way of most parents, but somehow our group always managed to cross paths with her ... and fight with her ... and cause trouble with her ... and obstinately fuck around with her ... so you can just imagine how much she *despised* us for (what she called) completely "ruining" her son. Even for a Dawsonite, she was out of control.

So anyway, like I said, she deliberately tried to *kill* us. We'd just been mindlessly roaming the streets one day, and all of a sudden she'd come out of nowhere with her big fucking jeep, trying to plow us down. It all happened in the blink of an eye.

And oh, this was *no* accident—if you'd seen that gleam in her eye, you'd know for sure how gung-ho that motherfucker was. She always told us (in that deep Middle Eastern accent of hers): "Joo all goin' da hell! I keel you, I keel you all in dee end!!" I suppose on that day she just decided to go forth with what she always promised to do; her intentions were forever quite clear.

To make a long story short, that incident led to a whole load of problems in the immediate future. The end result of her idiocy was a smashed fender and two ruined tires—we all were quick enough to get out of the way and scram from the scene. This caused a big public commotion, traffic jams, tie-ups, the arrival of cops, etc. She never learned any of our "real" names (each and every one of us was assigned his own derogatory Arabic curse word) and therefore we could not be directly reported the police. That, of course, made no difference: I'm sure you're aware of how quickly rumors spread. If all this trouble had not gone down on a public main street, perhaps we would have been able to avoid the impending disasters that would soon confront us, but what was to happen next was inevitable. We might as well have been caught red-handed.

Local loudmouths and gossip queens eventually twisted the story, morphing it so terribly to the point where the whole thing had become *our* faults entirely. (I think one legend even claims that we used sorcery to draw her off the road!) From thereon in, the shit starting hitting the fan. We became the center of attention in our town, and, quite obviously, that was a bad, bad thing.

The weeks following the car crash proved to be some of the Cage Breakers' most daunting struggles. Our supposed "cult" was put off for a short while in order to save our *own* skins, and that of course infuriated our phony-assed Disciples. There arose a demand for more parties, more drugs, and more mindless rebelling than there ever had been before—at this point in time, all of those things were quite impossible. Apparently, they all were blind to what was going on around them, blind to the sudden shift in our school system that directly intended to take them over; mid-year, things had begun to change. Big time.

Just when it seemed as though the presence of Dawson had taken a back seat in our lives, he resurfaced with more muscle and malice than ever before. The school began administering pseudo-philosophical pamphlets littered with the garbage that has always tainted our lives. Public speakers started coming in weekly to preach the Word, *his* Word; these ideals were further enforced by mandatory "social etiquette" classes that we all needed to take about halfway through the semester. This new unbelievable movement spread out into the town's politics, too—certainly, if the Cage Breakers were to make its affairs public, this was not the town to be in or the time to be doing it. There were threats hurled back and forth to those who chose to defy the Dawsonite code, the tunnel vision of "The Square." To our better judgments, we (the "Core") decided to hang low; our Disciples were highly advised to do the same.

But of course they wouldn't listen.

The culture we'd created began to backfire—those fools no longer wanted our advice, they no longer respected us as the brave forefathers we were; they just wanted to party and make trouble. I can assure you that more than half of them were no longer concerned with either following or defying the Dawsonites whatsoever: our Disciples were now rebelling simply for the sake of rebellion. It's a shame, but that's what the venerable Cage Breakers had become.

The world works in a way where the setting of trends and the passing of time equal normalcy; at the end of the day, the trendsetters themselves are forgotten and get left behind in the dust. Basically, all we ever stood for was disgraced. Even the Core's own parties and the Core's own sex and the Core's own drug use and the Core's own fun were all hindered by the stupidity these people associated us with.

After the school failed to convert its students back into submissive, docile robots, things just got worse. I began skipping school altogether because of the predictable mayhem that would always break out. All those bastards thought they were such hot shit, you know? Keeping them in line as a group was no longer possible. Things were just too far out of our hands. We had no other choice but to let go.

So we went from having three parties a week to not having a single one in more than a fucking month—you can just imagine how horribly that went over with our dim-witted Disciples. Ugh. Luckily, the Cage's location was still kept a secret, but rumors began to circulate that some mischievous gathering place had been established somewhere in the town. We were called in all the time and asked about it. I don't think the officials ever totally bought our lies, but because of our united persistence, there was really nothing that any of them could've done.

And then came the internal conflicts amongst us—the Core was constantly at odds with itself now. I never thought things would get this bad, but this, dear reader, is just the *beginning.*

Seth and Devin had the most trouble coping, I think; they were the most carefree of the lot, so this new style we were forced into didn't sit well with them at all. A whole load of other problems ensued, but for brevity's sake, I'll skip over them and allow you to fill in the missing blanks.

Thanks to the sudden rupture between its members, a new party was still yet to be held by what was formally known as the Cage Breakers. The spokesman for our new infuriated Disciples was none other than—!drum roll please!—*Cali.* You can refer back to the end of the last chapter if you've forgotten who he is. I *told* you not to let him slip your mind!

After constantly nagging us *every single day* for what seemed like all of eternity, Cali slowly began to fade away up until this point. Once this sudden change in our daily lives had taken place, however, that rat reared his ugly head yet again, this time more potentially dangerous than before.

Thanks to some ill-willed miracle, I suppose, he managed to round up our formal Disciples and turn them against us. We'd become "wimps," or so he preached, we'd become a bunch of *cowardly fools* who couldn't *stand up* for what we believed in. Of course, these things weren't at all the fucking case, but there was no point in arguing with Cali and his army—an army that not too long ago was our own. He claimed to be organizing a party night in the name of the Cage Breakers and demanded to take over its functions ... considering that we were doing such a "terrible" job. We seriously considered *killing* him, literally ganging up and beating every last breath out of him until he was dead, but that would've caused more problems than any of us needed, in *or* out of the Cage Breakers.

In retrospect, I think it was ever since Allie's exit from our lives that nothing really seemed the same; from that point on, we just became more and more awkward to ourselves. The things we did had gotten crazier since then, for sure, but the very essence of *who we were* seemed ... empty. Changed. *Forgotten.* This led to an inevitable communication breakdown in the very literal sense of the phrase—great distances grew between us, and we no longer felt as comfortable talking to one another.

All these things led to what we knew was likely to happen— an outright revolt against us. Not the Cage Breakers, but what had come to be known as its "Core"—*us.* Cali, of course, directed this whole extravaganza; if we didn't allow him to have a party at the Cage and rechristen him as either its new leader or simply allow him to function as one of us, he promised a living hell. Under any normal circumstances, we would never have let him get to us.

But we were hopeless.

As hard as it is to admit, we were weak enough and dumb enough and blind enough to let that motherfucking slimeball run our show.

In spite of our problems, we tried to remain as sane as we possibly could. It became obvious that Devin could never make up his mind: one day he was completely for us, one day completely against us ... he was the "flake" of the group. If we'd picked up on this characteristic earlier in the game, I'm sure he would've been kicked out of our inner clique long ago, but at this point, there was really no reason for more unnecessary troubles. The Core had been crushed, our friendship torn to shreds.

RAYMOND

It was during the third weekend of that May, I think, that Cali's brainchild was to be unleashed. We wondered whether or not it was worth it for us to go—we predicted the ridicule, we predicted the problems, but we refused to allow our initial creation to be disgraced with our absence; we'd already shamed ourselves with a forfeit, so we weren't about to give in *altogether.*

Allan, in particular, complained of bad vibes the night preceding this party, our *last* party, the only party that, in reality, wasn't even "our own." I couldn't disagree—Seth even refused to go unless he was readily equipped with a full set of homemade daggers for protection ... yes, out of nowhere, he'd developed an immense interest in crafting all sorts of his own weaponry. Don't ask. I haven't a clue why.

Though still technically united as the Core, we all felt alone. Our parents were out of our lives, the town despised us, the posse of phony followers we'd gathered turned against us, and among ourselves, there developed a lack of communication and total isolation.

Amidst this chaos, though, now that I look back on it, we had (in a very roundabout way) achieved *precisely* what we'd wanted—the return of "humanness" to our young and seemingly impenetrable peers. If only in our small town and our small town alone, we'd defeated the abominable might of Dr. Fucking Dawson. Our combined efforts were able to overthrow his morals, the morals that had an entire *country* in check.

If we hadn't met our demise in the disgraceful way that I'm about to tell you, I'd call our efforts an absolute success.

Darren—(who has been reading this aloud to me all the while)—puts the book down for a moment and asks me if I understand the power of what I've written.

"My" book, "my" words, "my" truths—it's all still very hard to grasp. It's hard for me to imagine myself participating in any of the events that the story describes. What went wrong? How did I *ever* wind up in unjust hands that seize me today?

"You will find out shortly," Darren says anxiously. He flips through the remainder of the book. "There's only one chapter left. You've made it this far, Ray, so there's no point in turning back."

Ray.

The way it sounds has a familiar ring to it, a ring that has been lost in time amidst an ocean of marauding chemicals.

Before beginning again, I notice something in the distance out of the corner of my eye: along with his troupe of fellow elves, Mr. Fandango's arms are outstretched to the sky in prayer.

CHAPTER 7

I suppose it's worth mentioning: we offered whatever compromises we could in effort to delay the party to a later date, but by the end of the week, it was obvious that there was no overcoming the irrationality Cali had drilled into our past followers. There was something new about him, something reborn from deep within—he adored the fact that we'd fallen into his scheme and that we had no other choice but to let him take over. I assumed that maybe he'd mature, you know, being that'd he'd already beaten us and taken things this far, but of course I was wrong, *completely* wrong; if anything, this whole fanfare skyrocketed his nasty little ego, and that bastard made damn sure we all knew about it. Forgive my repetition, but I've got to remind you just once more how terribly the Core's friendship had dissolved at this point. In truth, we were stranded in a game where the rules dictated every man for himself. We all knew that this was the end and that *something* terrible was waiting to ensue, but with all due respect to our dignities and our (admittedly dim-witted) "faith in things," we strode into the

RAYMOND

Cage's secret entrance at around 2 A.M. expecting the utter worst.

Recalling the night sequentially, it didn't start off so badly— for a short while, we actually believed that maybe we'd all been wrong, that we'd all let our own paranoid fears get the best of us. About an hour or so in, though, all that we'd anticipated (and then some!) exploded in a single furious eruption—the place had gone up in *flames*. Not in any metaphorical sense, either: The Cage was literally consumed in a blazing fire that nearly killed us all.

I'm not exactly sure how it started, but story has it that two over-smoked jerk-offs were engaged in a fistfight of sorts and had created a maddening riot ... *real bright idea*. They took their duel to the next level, I'm guessing, to the point where one of 'em snagged a can of Lysol (or some other flammable cleaning spray) and created a flamethrower with the aid of a few lighters. One ill-aimed shot set ablaze one of the many wooden planks that kept the joint boarded up, and then boom! Disaster. Silly? Yes. Somewhat remarkable (that people can be so *fucking* stupid)? Yes. But, however, that *IS* what happened, and that *IS* the final night that *ANY* of us would ever spend in our good ol' hometown.

Everyone went absolutely crazy, entirely nuts—just picture it: more than a hundred kids trapped in a relatively small building that's gone up in flames where, if you recall, all but one secret entrance is boarded up. If there was ever a sense of *true* unity among the Cage Breakers, it certainly was in that moment, that moment where everyone's shared thought was that they were going to fucking die, and I must admit to being a part of this communal fear. The Core sought out each other instinctually—with the exception of Devin, who was too fucking high to know what the hell was going on (and ejected out of our thoughts completely), the five of us pressed through this sea of fools trying to escape. People just lost all sanity—punching, kicking, shoving, biting, pummeling, just about whatever it took to get through that congested exit.

A full-blown squad of policemen and firefighters eventually

arrived, leaving those who'd escaped to an equally dreadful fate as those trapped inside. Following our breakout, we were met with an entirely predictable scene, that being dozens of half-assed cops busy imposing their half-assed power upon our half-assed followers. Having spent their whole lives as Dawsonites, our Disciples had no *real* balls, no *real* courage—they only had the guts that The Cage Breakers provided them with as an illusion. They were all scared *shitless* and immediately surrendered to authority.

As you might've guessed, we were not about to give up, or at least not yet, at least not *that* easily—it is thanks entirely to Seth that we weren't snatched up by the grimy hands of the policemen right then and there. I can't precisely explain to you what was going through his head when he brutally *stabbed* one of the cops to death, *stole* his gun, *shot* down two other policemen, *hijacked* a car, and *bolted* away, but I'm sure it was something along the lines of pure, unadulterated adrenaline.

In a blind fury, Seth—to our surprise—wielded one of his many homemade daggers against a cop who tried to cuff him up and take him away. Not just one stab, but a brutal onslaught of vicious blows. The other cops were awestricken, too amazed to even make a move. The initial shock of his spontaneous violence had everyone mesmerized. After that, Seth removed the fallen cop's gun from its holster and broke out in wild fire. At this point, the once overcome police were forced to retaliate; they began firing back as well, but by that time, we'd all found refuge through the open door of a latent police car. Seth caught a bullet in his shoulder, I think, but he managed to dive in and blast us away from the scene.

Yes, all of the aforementioned things are true. I'll stop for a moment and allow you to absorb the lunacy of it all before I go on, because this next part requires your utmost attention.

None of us spoke for about two whole days.

At around 3:30 A.M. on that same night, we successfully made our way out of town and onto a desolate highway, obliterating the vehicle's tracking device along the way. We got off the freeway as soon as we could, from there taking as many side streets as possible. After driving around aimlessly for about an hour, the gas had begun to deplete. With no other alternatives, we were forced to ditch the stolen car entirely.

It was kind of inevitable that we'd be caught eventually; there was no way we'd last very long living the way we did for those few days, anyway. Ha—we basically adapted to living without any resources in the middle of the woods. In just hours, we were devoured alive by all sorts of buzzing insects and had begun to feel sick. Our diet was reduced to dirty river water and weird berries, neither of which managed to satisfy. It was eventually a strange looking mammal of sorts that drove us out of the woods and into whatever town it was that bordered it.

It's safe to assume that word of our disastrous affair has spread through the local counties; a woman retrieving letters from her mailbox recognized us *instantly*. She literally screamed (as if we were monsters!), ran indoors, and placed in a call to the local police.

We basically knew that we were done for; there was no way out of this. We decided not to run, we decided not to hide. Instead, we parked ourselves down on a curb civilly and shared a cigarette together, the *last* cigarette we ever would. *Sigh*. The fact that we were soon likely to be taken away wasn't even half as troubling to me as the absence of my dear, beloved Allie. Presumably, she either A.] perished in the fire or B.] escaped and is facing some harsh penalty back home.

Somehow, I still feel like losing Allie is my life's greatest failure; we had great chemistry that could've worked and *should've* worked. But it didn't, and as I'm writing this, to my surprise, the fact that she's not here by my side hurts more than the fact that I'm here in the very first place. You know, all this has got me wondering if our efforts were ever worth anything to begin with.

In a way, we *did* disrupt the peace, now that I think of it from an outsider's perspective. In a way, we *did* cause problems in a time of none. But if we'd done otherwise, it would've felt *wrong*, blasphemous to our very selves—Godammit, everything had made such sense and had gone so well for so long!

Maybe our teachers and parents and the Dawsonites were right all along …

Does the world have a place for people like me? For people like Seth, Greg, Juan, Allan, or even Devin and Allie? Christ, if only I knew …

But that's all beside the point.

We put up no fight when the cops arrived. They shoved us around like animals, talked to us like animals, and spat upon us like animals. Since our escape from town, we'd still not yet spoken a word to each other—what developed between us was an instinctual, tacit form of telepathy.

It would have made sense for us to have been taken back home to the local police station for further questioning, but no—we were abducted and engaged in an hours-long drive to some top-secret headquarters. Soon after, we were forced onto a private plane and flown away to where I am now, to this icy cold cell where I presently write this memoir. They don't talk around here. I've managed to pen this story you're reading (if this in fact is being read at all) in under three days, 'cause I have a feeling that time is running out for me.

For all of us.

Since I can't tell you exactly where I've been taken (*'cause I myself don't even know where the hell I am*), I'll do my best to describe it. There are huge, white buildings everywhere, taller and more strangely designed than any I've ever seen in my life. Everything seems to be connected by a giant network of monorails, hovercrafts, and elevator-like shafts; I kid you not. It's as if I'm visiting a futuristic space camp! The people that seem to run this far-out city are cagey and reclusive. Everything's a big fucking secret. I know that this part of the story sounds absolutely ridiculous, but don't let me lose your interest now, reader—I'm just about to wrap things up.

Before we were taken away to separate cells, Allan and I exchanged a few last words. It was really emotional, of course— so emotional that I'm soaking in a stream of defeated tears as I write about it now. He thanked me endlessly for saving him, introducing him to his short-lived life of art, and opening up his eyes to who he was always supposed to be.

"Even if it's the last thing I ever do," he said to me, "I will be sure to keep my promise to you—in some way or another, I will repay you for all that you've done."

Allan was then torn away by some hulking security guard, and we've not seen each other since. That was sixteen days ago. Despite my usual optimism, I'm presently half-believing that all hope is lost.

I have a feeling that our torture won't end here, though. The widely believed truth is that we'd been found dead, or so says the main guy that's in charge here. Apparently, our whole fanfare has become a national news story—I'm nearly sure that what *really* happened is quite different than what's hit the air. Fuck it. Not that it matters at this point, anyway. I can no longer live out *there*, I can no longer live in *here*; I'm starting to believe that the only place suited for me is death.

Why the public lie, hmm? Why not the truth? I can only *imagine* what is to come of us. Perhaps we'll be skinned alive, sent through a shredder, and fed to the president's dog, packaged up nicely in a can of compressed mush or something.

Or maybe *that's* just wishful thinking.

Maybe our fate is something worse, way worse: I have a feeling it is.

I've still got my faith in things. It's what keeps me sane and prevents me from losing my mind *altogether*. Perhaps it's a bit foolish, but I've already broken the rules of convention so greatly already; going a little further is harmless.

There is one thing I've realized, and I feel so stupid for not having realized it earlier: I never needed the use of drugs. I never needed to be a part of the Cage Breakers' phenomenon. I never needed to initiate a revolution—all I *really* ever needed was the company of my friends. All *anyone* needs is the company of a few truly genuine friends …

If throughout my tale, dear reader, you've remained by my side and have seen eye to eye with me, then you are a comrade. If you are a compliant fool who succumbs to the power of conformity, then I fucking despise you. You are the

kind of person that got me into the mess that I'm in today.
You are the kind of person that destroyed my life.

-June, 2037

"So the story has at last reached an end," Darren concludes.

I am left awestricken by the marvels of my past. "This … this just c-can't be real!" I stammer, truly baffled at the story that's just been told. "There's no way that I was ever a part of all that! There's just no way I—"

"Don't fight what you know is to be true," he interrupts. I notice something different in Darren's face; his droopy flesh has been lifted and given a new sense of life. "You must believe that this account is totally factual, Ray—I know it is so! I was there when it all happened, I've been by your side since nearly the beginning! I'm the only one that Cohen hasn't gotten to yet.

"I'm the only one that can still save *you* the way that you once saved *me!*" Something about the shine in his bright blue eyes awakens an unexplainable emotion within me. "I was once your friend—no, *still* am your friend. Ha! What kind of façade is *'Darren'*? What kind of façade is a half-baked *college professor?*"

He laughs in relief and rejoices. A series of bright fireworks erupt into the sky, coupled with the celebrative dancing of Mr. Fandango and his gang. My world is glazed over with a sparkling glimmer for just a moment. The evil alterations of Dr. Cohen's chemicals do not stop me from experiencing this rapturous bliss. Darren does not need to further elaborate—I know who he really is. I know that every word he's spoken is true.

"Hello … *Allan.*" My declaration is surprisingly firm, surprisingly matter-of-fact.

Nearly in tears, he says, "It's been *far* too long."

He helps me up and suggests that we engage in another stroll around the track. As he tucks the manuscript away and initiates our circuit, I'm bombarded by a feeling a youthful intoxication.

Everything is distorted, but in a good way—a *great* way.

*   *   *

"Originally, my idea was to form a brand new relationship with you from the bottom up," Darren—err, *Allan*—says. (For reference's sake, I'll leave Darren's name as it is.) "The initial plan was for me to come in every day for a few weeks, have you get to know me on a more 'personal level', and then from there, I assumed that infusing bits and pieces of your past would be both more believable from your perspective and easier from mine; the manuscript was reserved for the big finale. Things obviously happened a bit less smoothly, but I think this disaster was in fact for the better. The dragged-out nature of the first method would have lost its steam quickly, anyhow. It would have been nice to have seen you rediscover your old values at a gradually increasing pace, but what's come to be has come to be ..."

A question that's never crossed my mind for dozens of years finally emerges. "Where exactly is ... *here*? I feel like ... like we're secluded in the middle of nowhere! And the government! What about the government? This can't be legal, it just can't be!" A series of puzzle pieces suddenly fall into place.

"Isn't it the government that sent you here in the first place?" Darren asks.

"So they *do* know?!"

"Well ... not *really*." He prepares himself for the unveiling of a wealth of secret information. "Let me explain everything I know:

"We're actually upon a California mountaintop called White Mountain. You can check it on any map—we're not in the middle of some mystery land or anything. It's a fairly typical peak and was actually a popular hike back about ... oh, I'd say seventy-five years ago, at the most. That was before this extraordinary facility was conceived." He waves his arms around, alluding to the prodigious towers that surround us.

"A bit of history: the government of California restricted its citizens from residing within a twenty-mile radius of the mountain. The reason for this sudden change was an allegedly dangerous gas that began tainting its geological makeup—that much is true. However, once the area was cleared out and the problem was taken care of, the government proposed something that it had in store for years: an *ultramodern science station* to deal with all aspects of the emerging 'biosocial' era that we currently live in today.

"At first, its construction was begun in secrecy, though it eventually became a part of mainstream public knowledge. It was portrayed as a *great American achievement* and deemed the 'gateway to the *future*'. Surprisingly, it was well received and did not garner much suspicion from those outside the project. By the time this magnificent work was complete, much of the hype around it died down—basically, it became old news. People with specialties in different scientific fields were recruited from around the world for this multi-purpose megalopolis. It literally became its own city, its own kind of *life*. To my understanding, its civilians, which in turn are its workers, rarely ever leave. It's not quite a utopia, but it certainly is an isolated world within the real world itself."

"And Dr. Cohen is one of those people?" I ask.

"Precisely. He runs—to your surprise, perhaps—one of the *genetics* departments. It's only a mask, though, a title he uses to fool those around him: being so well read in the field of science in general, he goes about with whatever he so chooses to do. Behind the scenes, he endlessly breaks the rules of the city. He follows the criteria he needs to, attends monthly meetings between the heads of departments, and sends out lab reports to the courts and other scientists around him. All of that is fine; it's the experiments he *doesn't* share with his peers that you are a victim of.

"My dear friend, you do *not* live on any mental ward and are *not* part of any institution. No, not at all: you live in the heart of what's known as the City of Biosocial Sciences.

"You are part of a *completely* legal operation."

"But how? I just don't understand! Is *torture* the sole purpose of the facility?" I shriek.

"No, and that's what I'm getting to. For the most part, this city is a good thing. It's most notably wielded an international cure for HIV and has improved cancer treatments."

"Then why am *I* in the situation that I'm in? How does Dr. Cohen continue to get away with all of his madness, his *bullshit?*"

"The reasons for those two things are simple. For one, you were sent here during the Center's very early beginnings, and *not* for the reasons you're probably thinking. Initially, we, the Core, were flown out here for intense psychological studies. Research of sorts." Suddenly, Darren arches his eyebrows and raises a finger in triumph. "You *do* know that Seth, Greg, and Juan have remained in your life ever since your preliminary captivity, right?"

"You mean ... my friends? From the *story?*"

Another relieving smile finds its way across Darren's face. "Do the names Gary, Butch, and Paulie ring a bell?"

As we round a bend for our first complete lap, I blurt out in astonishment: "So you're saying ... my friends from the lunch table are really ...?" I don't even need to complete my statement—Darren confirms that my realization is indeed true.

He continues on with his insightful tale. "How Dr. Cohen has managed to maintain his tactics for so long blows my mind, but the man is truly an evil genius. Obviously, a single person cannot run an entire facility—especially something on such a large scale as *this*. The few original workers that aided him all soon became victims of his wicked brilliance. He craftily disposed of them and now makes use of an endless supply of their clones. His entire staff is *exclusively* handmade, *exclusively* female, and *exclusively* programmable dupes. I can assume that Dr. Cohen's power reaches beyond this city and into the legal world on the 'Outside', as you call it. He's got false identifications and false degrees for each and every one of his sick creations. He's created a mini society all for himself, all *by* himself.

"You may ask yourself *why*; your guess is as good as mine. He's just a twisted man with a knack for science, deception, and obscure creativity."

For nearly all of my life (or at least what I can remember of it first-handedly), Dr. Cohen was my greatest hero. His kind, genuine ways, along with his especial interest in my wellbeing, were always immeasurably. All the falsities, all the lies ... all the sinful *evil*! To think that I was a part of it is simply unimaginable, though the fact of the matter is that it's all obviously very true. Each new thing Darren says brings up a new burning curiosity that's dying to be enlightened, though right now, there's only time for things of importance.

"What I don't get is why I have always been given so much more attention than the others. Why is the Doctor so ... *obsessed* with me?" I ask.

"It was your intelligence, my friend!" he exclaims. "It's because you were the only one that was brave enough to *write anything down*—you were curious, you challenged his supremacy, you seemed like the only thing in the world that could possibly get in his way! Your passions and ambitions sparked his obsession. I suppose he found something in you that he himself could relate to.

"His daily experiments eventually became habit—you became the center of his 'ward', the center attraction of his sick, fabricated world. The nurses he's built are trained to love you just as much as he 'loves' you ... loves to *torture* you is more like it.

"In order to mimic the social balance of the *real world*, he's brainwashed his 'patients' (which consist of countless experiments gone wrong plus biologically watered-down incarnations of Seth, Greg, and Juan) to *detest* you. Nearly half of the confines that make up his phony 'genetics department' have been morphed and rearranged to emulate a hospital, the very 'ward' that you're so familiar with. All this riffraff for you! To feed his disturbed fixation with *you*!

"Eventually, the nature of his obsessive works strayed away from the intents of the City of Biosocial Sciences altogether; because he's consistently maintained his cool and kept up with his regular work for so many years, his maddened little world has been able to secretly flourish with life."

Another lap around the track. He continues.

"I hadn't known of nearly half the things I'm telling you today until just a few weeks ago when Dr. Cohen and I got back in touch. He's a demented man, as you know, and takes great pride in babbling on about his horrible achievements. When I escaped, I couldn't imagine him getting any crazier than he already was, but thirty-something years later, I've obviously been proved wrong."

"Your escape!" I exclaim excitedly. Surely, this is to be most intriguing of all. "How in the world did you ever manage to get out of this terrible, terrible place?"

Just as Darren begins to explain, his words are interrupted by a hoarse cry.

Mrs. Rory comes bolting toward us from out of nowhere, looking like a total mess. Her eyes are red-rimmed and bulgy, her flesh is pale and sweaty, and her hair is muddled in ugly knots. She shakes uncontrollably as she delivers us a message. "Doctor Cohen needs to see the two of you right away!" she screeches. Darren and I exchange glances, particularly perplexed by the overly strained muscles in her neck.

"This should be interesting," he says.

Mrs. Rory robotically leads the way.

He looks back to me and puts his arm lovingly around my shoulder. "I've been waiting for this day for more than thirty years," Darren whispers into my ear, indeed genuinely grateful for the arrival of this day at last. He makes me feel loved, a special kind of love that was never offered here on what I've always known just as "the ward." As we approach the facility's entrance, the triumphant blasts of Mr. Fandango's fireworks return. "If there's one thing I promise you, it is the long-deserved answers to whatever questions you might have. If it's out of here that you want, then I'll be damn sure that it's out of here you *get*."

*   *   *

Guided by Mrs. Rory's (drug-deprived?) stride, we're led past familiar parameters and into some long, strange passageway that I've never been down before. There are huge windows that look out into this "city," and truly, it is astonishing. It's just as Darren said—this whole place is something of a high-tech metropolis! There is constant motion (bright, *whirring* motion!) carried out in the form of low, hovering spacecrafts and sky-bound power capsules. It seems that there is a great translucent dome that surrounds the vicinity.

"The passing of seasons and changes in weather are emulated through a built-in, computerized system that's operated regularly," Darren explains.

We eventually reach the end of the hall and proceed onward through another strange maze-like structure. I'm not sure if it's the loosened screws of my mind at work again … but are those *robots*? And what's with those strange, monster-faced creatures over there casually sharing a drink?

Our final stop is in front of large electronically operated door, adorned with a series of confusing locks and keypads. As Mrs. Rory turns away, I notice that she's shrunken and shriveled up into the shape of a dead Serpent. Equipped with a heavy scythe, Mr. Fandango materializes out of the foreground. With a single, swift blow, he slices the Serpent in half and ends Its pitiful life for good— that reminds me! I've totally forgotten to tell Darren all about Mr. Fandango and how much he's helped me through my struggles!

As I begin explaining my imaginary elf-of-a-friend to Darren, there is a great hissing sound that fills up the space around us; it exudes from a series of panels that line the enormous door before us. It is more than a deadly echo; it has *life*. Despite the liberation of my fear, it is a sound that's got me trembling like a newborn child. I close my eyes and am confronted with the face of an enormous creature, *scaled* and hideous, the face of Fear itself. It emits a deafening cry that hurls me backward into Darren's arms. At first he tries to pry out of me what's gone wrong, but soon realizes that I've temporarily been disconnected from all that is real. I conjure up the words of Mr. Fandango: *"There's no use in fighting battles you can't win, don't you know that much by now? You've got to learn to let things come and go. Ignore it …!"* All the strength I can possibly call upon chases the disgusting image out of my brain and away from me altogether. The hissing stops, the Serpent recedes, and reality easily returns.

Darren offers me comfort, but his words are overpowered by a sudden eruption of beeps and whirs from the massive door. Locks undo themselves, lights flash on and off, numbers disappear and reappear on various panels, and slowly, the door slides aside. Though the voice from behind is deep and commanding, it is filled with childish anticipation.

"Come in, come in, come *right on* in!"

And so Darren and I are finally confronted by the bloodthirsty gaze of Dr. Cohen. The monster grins, revealing a gargantuan set of impeccably white teeth. "So the time has come … where we all meet together *at last!*"

*   *   *

His domain is massive; it is sickeningly tidy, glossy, and overly obsessive. I am stuck in my tracks, hypnotized by the oddity of the realm I've just entered. Every corner is packed with strange devices that I've never seen before. The walls curve inward, making the room round and spherical. Everything is so starkly pale that I'm momentarily blinded upon entrance. In the center of this egg-shaped haven is Dr. Cohen's desk; with the exception of a test-tube rack and a few papers (covered in all sorts of obscene little sketches), it is spotless. For whatever unfathomable reason, there hangs a noose from the center of the ceiling. All kinds of fluid-filled tanks are placed strategically around the room in a decorative fashion; most contain dismembered or altered human body parts, though I spot a few packed tightly with the heads of strange hybrid-creatures not of this world. In amazement, Darren and I scan the scene and are faced with various killing machines, some so eccentric that I can't even describe them in words! What is this madness? What kind of mind could exploit such terrible tools?

"Are you fellows fans of my décor?" Dr. Cohen asks in the most riveting of inflections. "I've designed it all on my own. I'm quite an *artist*, if I may say so myself." His distasteful sarcasm is met with silence, a silence broken by his awfully sardonic laughter. "For such self-proclaimed imaginative fools, it seems you louts don't have any respect for *real* art!" Bubbling with energy, he hurriedly scurries over to a control panel, enters a series of codes, and barks into a voice-activated intercom. "L1-7 to the main office, please, L1-7 to the main office." Almost immediately, the doors to this sinister egg burst open, and a stout white robot wheels itself in.

"L1-7 has reported to the main office, sir," it utters in a digitalized voice.

"Excellent." Cohen strokes the manufactured head of this android as if it were a cat or dog. "Why don't you set up the hologram-projector while I brief our two little visitors on what they're about to see?" he says casually to his mechanical counterpart.

"At once, sir."

As if it were a fully conscious being, this little machine strolls over to a massive computer board and begins manipulating a series of wires and buttons.

He comes to us slowly, particularly scathingly, stroking the long red hairs of his thickly woven beard. If I've not told you what Dr. Cohen actually looks like, allow me to brief you: he is tall, *freakishly* tall, and defies all humanoid standards. His head is flawlessly shaven and always retains a robust luster. There's that beard of his, of course, which is something of a long, ginger rope that nearly reaches his naval. All four of his limbs are massively bulky—the Doctor's hands alone are so muscular that I'm sure he could crush me with a single, pressurized squeeze. Trust me, old man Cohen is *not* the kind of guy you want to mess around with. Ha—I should speak for *myself*!

Not long ago, I looked up to this man (both literally and figuratively) as if he were my father, my *God*. He'd embodied righteousness, he'd embodied perfection—every last word he spoke meant the world to me. The memories of our past together are so wonderful that, for a moment, I'm left questioning the malice that the Doctor could possibly impose upon me. There were times that he would pick me up, hold me in his arms, and rock me as if I were a little child. I *was* his child, or so he always used to say. I was his *life*, I was his everything, but alas, the truth is a terrible, terrible thing.

He pulls something out of the front pocket of his lab coat: it is small and rectangular, about three inches in both height and width. "Do either of you know what this little gadget is?" he asks condescendingly, already certain that we of course do not. "This here is a 'memory' card, a very *special* memory card—certainly not any kind that you'd be accustomed with, *Outsider*!" The Doctor sticks his finger in Darren's face derisively. "You, *Oizys* (he directs his attention to me)—this is virtually *your* memory. Anything you've ever seen, smelled, thought, heard, or tasted is recorded and preserved on this little piece of technology."

Darren and I exchange confused looks. Oizys? Who in the world is *Oizys*? And what kind of name is *that*?

Boastfully strutting in my face, the Doctor laughs maliciously; I am dwarfed by his immense stature. "You mean to tell me that you don't even know your role in my empire? Who you *are* and always *will* be to me? I suppose I've infiltrated your memory so badly that you've even managed to lose your true identity! So those dim-witted nurses of mine were right after all!" He grimaces with much disgust. "You are not Sid Tate, you are not Raymond James, you are not whomever my good-for-nothing nurses have confused you with! Oh *no, no, no!*" He takes a deep breath and pushes out his chest proudly. "You are none other than Oizys, the Greek goddess of pain and suffering!"

The mad Doctor enters a fit of hysterical laughter and loses touch with reality for a moment. By the look of that manic gleam in his eye, something tells me that he isn't being figurative; something tells me he actually *believes* that I am whatever strange-named "goddess" he speaks of. (*Goddess?* Am I not man enough to at least have been rechristened a *god?*)

Instantly, my throat dries up. I soon am immersed in a terrifying world of rotting skeletons, aimless flames, crumbling pillars, and stinking decay, all of which are frighteningly real. The Serpent rears its scaly head and shrieks a victorious cry. It slithers its way across the room, gliding up and down the walls hypnotically. "The hour I've awaited so long draws near, my boy," It hisses in a tongue only I can understand. "This is the day that my love runs out—this is the day that you are to be left alone to *die!*"

The whole room is swallowed in one fiery gulp; my vision is blurred by a great white light, but when it returns, the metaphoric hell disappears and the Doctor has re-emerged before me. I turn to find Darren equally puzzled. There is nothing that either of us can do—something tells me that in spite of his promise, he and I are going to die here together and going to die *soon.* Utterly helpless, we watch the Doctor's endless madness pour out.

He beckons the presence of his robotic servant. It takes the memory card and plugs it into some complex apparatus.

"Quite obviously, the technology that we use here in the city is *very* sophisticated. Some of the things our great scientific minds have formulated are yet *unthinkable* in your outside world.

"What you are about to witness is the unveiling of a great piece of equipment, something developed here about thirty years ago over at our neuro-technical center.

"Scientific advances are still controversial in your disgusting 'real world', so things such as these multi-purpose memory cards have been left unrevealed for quite some time." As if on cue, a blue beam is emitted from a projector mounted high above us. Something of a floating, translucent screen materializes, offering the still image of a young fetus. "Allow me to explain how such an incredible piece of vital technology works," the Doctor cackles, pacing aimlessly around the room in what seems like an anxious fit.

"Memories are a very complex thing. For years, top scientists have been trying to pinpoint the rudiments of such an amazing phenomenon, and of course, we've at last learned everything that we need to know. There is no singular cause behind the human capacity to remember things vividly on a completely intimate scale; there is a system that works together intellectually, combining the efforts of RNA, proteins, coherent molecules, and reacting chemicals that tactfully store and rearrange our perceptive data. Through means of molecular transportation, we have been able to isolate the very components of entire life-long memories and preserve them in artificial, cranial renditions. *In other words*, it is completely within my power right now to have any human brain digitally recreated in its entirety and stored elsewhere invariably.

"We've also acquired the ability to translate the stored data into electronic codes. By associating certain memories and memory-related functions with specific computerized scripts, it has become possible to recreate 'virtual memories' all within the confines of these synthetic storage systems. Most intriguing of all, however, is a more recent discovery. These codes have the ability to be manually altered back into the memories from which they've been derived.

With that said, when provided with the proper technology, it is possible to duplicate any given mind within the minds of *other arbitrary people*. These tools can be used to clone not only the physical body, but the abstract notion of 'the mind' as well … but of course I've begun to stray as I usually do!" He laughs and turns back to his massive screen.

"This gadget here visually emulates the inside of a person's mind; it acts as a portal into the memories stored in these cards. What you are about to see, my dear, *dear* Oizys, is your entire life flash before your eyes. Fifty years' worth of memories will all enter your consciousness in just moments. You might ask how such an extraordinary feat is possible, so allow me to explain.

"If you've been observant, you may have noticed those two large tanks settled on either side of that contraption over there (oh, that's just the control board to the hologram projector, if you're wondering). They contain two different gases—the one on the right is a highly advanced man-made substance able to translate the electronic codes from the memory storage system into a gaseous state. (Impressive, no?) When released and breathed in, they enter the brain through means of the bloodstream, thus uniting the gaseous memories and those immersed in it as one. The second tank to the left is filled with a mind altering drug, something that slows down the brain's perception of time in order to more readily absorb vast amounts of information at a rapid-fire pace; the change of life's momentum takes place in the mind and the mind alone. It also allows you to fully understand things without adhering to the 'standard' rudiments of comprehension.

"You are about to witness everything that has ever happened in your life in just a matter of minutes. The process will seem every bit as long as fifty years to you, but in the real world, only seconds will have passed.

"This distortion of time will drive you insane, Oizys. It will make you want to *die* on the inside. After what seems to have been a day, you will rather have had me kill you. After what seems what like ten years, you will wish you'd never been born at all. You will be tired but unable to sleep. You will grow antsy but unable move. In a matter of minutes, I will have emulated fifty endless years of being strapped down in hell.

"I know that such things are quite unimaginable to Outsiders such as yourself, but here in this grand, grand city, these wondrous achievements are passé, are nothing more than common knowledge! These tools shape our everyday lives!" The maddened Doctor prances around fanatically, leaping in glee like an amused infant. My stomach churns. I become dizzied to the point where reality begins fading in and out like a tease. Quickly, I try to call upon the presence of Mr. Fandango—he always saves me, *yes*, he always comes to my rescue. I try as hard as I can to deceive my mind with illusions, but my beloved elf is absent from this torture. Or *is* he?

He is trapped, I see, tied down and struggling for his life! I try to shriek in horror, but my mind is too perplexed by the tragedy before me—in an instant, Mr. Fandango's tiny head has been completely severed by a razor-sharp blade!

No-o-o …!

Time has transformed into an incomprehensible notion, a notion that instills fear into my bones … speeding heart, shaking limbs … world keeps on turning and turning … acidy taste of vomit in my throat … a stinging sensation on the surface of my brain …!

Eventually, my blurred nauseam recedes. I find that two metal chairs have arisen from the ground thanks to some code-working of Cohen's mechanical slave-machine. Darren expresses silent dismay through his wavering brow. I want to say something to him, I want to offer whatever kind of reassurance I can, but the computerized din of the Doctor's android insists that we take our seats. It speaks to us condescendingly, as if we are *indebted* to it or something! In what kind of world are humans downplayed by machines? In what kind of world are such life-like machines revered in the first place?!

As soon as we are strapped down, a bar slides into place that completely restricts our mobility. Metallic clamps snap down around our wrists, and with that, Darren and I both become inert. I glance over at him, but he seems lost—his gaze is distant, peering beyond this terrible world that has us trapped. Though our friendship is undeveloped and our fates are cursed with destruction, I would not have my life end in any other way; in these painful moments that are yet to seem completely real, I've faced the face of death and am somewhat sure I'm already dead. I will embrace whatever pain confronts me, because I know that I will soon be revived in a place far better than this. In his mind, I know that Darren thinks he has failed, but I want to let him know that he indeed has *not*; I want to exclaim his victory to the world! His goal was to save my life, but this enlightenment is better, better than any nonsensical *mortal* redemption! Ha—I am greater than flesh: I am of the spirit now. We've won, in fact we've defeated this abominable force *altogether*.

Though overcome both in this world and the last (first by Dawson and now by this mad, abhorrent genius), in truth, my friends and Darren and I never failed at all. We *cannot* fail. Something as strong and as pure and as beautiful as this unity that I speak of can never falter.

That's right.

We're indestructible.

The captivating blue screen that hovers above us surges mockingly, though I'm ready, ready for *anything*.

Just before Doctor Cohen demands our attention, he turns to me with a furious expression—in just a single instant, he understands my thoughts.

I just know it. I don't need to speak. I don't need to move a muscle. I have faith—just as I always *used* to—that he knows what I want to say to him. I am to die empowered; I am to die complete.

Once more, Cohen informs his robotic counterpart of a series of codified instructions. The procedures are soon taken care of, and the beast is ready to be unleashed. His burly hands take hold of a massive lever.

With that crazy gleam in his eye, he says, half to himself: "It's *movie-time*, boys."

*   *   *

But this, of course, is not just any movie. The gases are released, the journey begins.

Pale, blue smog fills up the room; my first instinct, of course, is to hold my breath and resist for as long as I can, though Darren's eventual surrender helps me realize the uselessness of my battle. Both aware and prepared for whatever my fate is going to be, I take an intentionally massive breath of the poisoned air I'm immersed in—it is thick and tasteless. The intoxication is not immediate (for a second I wonder if this whole ordeal is false, just some crazy creation inside of my head), but I am eventually transported to another dimension.

Before I have any time to make sense of the wild distortions around me (the walls are *soupy*, the ceiling is *melting*!), it suddenly feels as if I've been submerged in a giant tub of water. I turn to find either Darren or the Doctor, but they've both faded away into the scenery—the massive futuristic egg that this place once was transforms into something else, something *fleshy*, something that presently is being torn open from the outside. Light begins to pour in from the exterior. What follows is the bawling of a newborn infant. Doctors crowd all 'round me, buzzing in excitement. These images are simply hallucinatory, but their tangibility in my world is *remarkable*! It feels like they're passing me around now as if I were I newborn child.

In this instant, it occurs to me what's going on.

I have just relived my birth.

The very nature of what's happening sets in slowly—a powerful rush of adrenaline compels me. I shut my eyes to block out this terrible, terrible film, but I can't help but tune in to everything that's going on. The devastating alteration of time has not sunken in quite yet, but I will try not to let it drive me insane as quickly as the Madman foresees it will. If this is his idea of torture, then I suppose I've lucked out: I've got all the time in the world to waste, Cohen, so bring it on!

I become more relaxed within the metallic confinements of my chair; I sit back, anticipating this nonsense to be over in minutes.

Yet seventeen long and tiresome years later, I'm *still* here.

I have seen my childhood come and go, I have felt the pain of my adolescent struggles. The rise and fall of the Cage Breakers, the formation and destruction of my beloved friendships: I have now seen and experienced these things firsthand and understand them more intimately than ever. This, however, is all at the expense of my sanity—the fool that speaks to you now is merely a corpse dreadfully rotting away. Time has turned into a cynical enemy, perhaps the only enemy known to man that is completely unbeatable. There is no overcoming these endless hours, no strategic way to take this beast down. Monotony in the real world is one thing, but being forced into it like *this* is another. I find myself frequently roaring in horror, trying to shake my sorry self free of the chains that hold me down. My mouth is eternally parched, my skin forevermore withered—and to think I'm not even half way through this utter disaster! As I speak to you now, piecing together such thoughts as these is mind-blowing (it feels as if my head is about to explode!); I am reduced to fragmentary blurbs and disjointed ideas, due to both the obliteration of my patience and the anxiousness that has long ago begun to corrode me.

... head throbs in intense pain, muscles grow sore from such struggling ...

One event in particular catches my attention. The scene is that of an office, a huge futuristic room overlooking a great city of white. Everything moves busily outside, busy, busy, busy, zooming of rocket cars and magnificent spacecrafts. Darren and I and another named G. Duvall: tall, skinny, light blonde hair—young guy, about twenty-five years of age, refined in interesting, unexplainable way … leads legal department here in this city. Two of us taken to him, discuss politics of the city. Soft side to him; sympathizes with us. Feels our pain, relates to our sticky situation. Tries explaining the legality of our futures trapped here, gives up halfway through, admits the lies he is forced to feed us, shares sorrows.

G. Duvall: "In times like these, it is not *knowing* the law that counts—*being* the law itself is the only thing that can get you guys saved." Goes on, deeper, more emotionally. "I am the only person on the face of this earth who can save you, but unfortunately, there's no action I can take in favor of your cause. I know what they've done to you is wrong, but what's just or unjust is *not* my call to make. The world is ruled by political affairs, and this detached civilization that has captured you is no different. To be in a position such as my own is a terrible thing; power is a double-edged sword. Any network of government might as well be the bowels of hell itself. Morality, decency … such are nonexistent. If to be amoral is to maintain the 'flow' of things, then amorality is to be. It's just the way of the world. Society is made of people, and people are imperfect by nature. To emulate perfection on the outside, the faults and flaws of the inside must be kept a secret. This job here in the city is more than any old job—it's my *life*. In order to save any of you, I need to surrender myself … and that just doesn't seem like something I can do." G. Duvall is as genuinely troubled as us.

Spend hours together, talking, lamenting; offers whatever further help he can. Depart with a new emotional bond formed, with a dying wick of hope. The only sense of decency in this city thus far …

… back to isolation, back to the insanity. The screen begins to dissolve, overshadowed by the intense hallucinations formulated by my madness. Eventually, the images on the screen become less relevant than the strange sensations that have physically consumed me. I enter a dense whirling void and am carried away and out of this room. For an instant, every particle of my body disconnects and scatters like shattered glass. Each of these broken pieces has a mind of its own, sees the world for itself. Millions of separate reflections surround me, dancing around in mindlessness. A resurrected Mr. Fandango somersaults into my range of sight. "Endure!" he cries. "Persevere!" The fleshless construction of his figure is designed by a series of tiny, elfish bones.

The menacing hand of time no longer fazes me, for I am euphoric now; I've been ejected out of this world *completely*. The Doctor's evil machine still pumps out its artificial recollections, but the comprehension is through a means of which I cannot explain. Through the fusing of opposing realms, my madness and time itself have merged as one—I have come to embody my own destruction.

I float around in a blank, empty void, whirling gently in circles through my mid-air suspension. I am swallowed by wide-open space and digested in the belly of safety. The sweats, the cramps, the tireless insanity … all of these have vanished away. Another day goes by, and another, and another—the weeks and years and months just keep accumulating to no effect. (After so many long years, I wonder if Darren has escaped this torture as well. I'm almost for certain that Lunacy is the only savior … oh, how I do hope his mind is as far off as my own!)

In what seems like a single moment amidst this eternal madness, I am confronted by an onslaught of revelations all at once:

> … well the stone cold truth is that something's gone drastically wrong, and as of now, there's no way to cover it up …

> … precisely, and that's why we need to do something quick. If I understand correctly, the president will be flying

in shortly to set things straight—the president, Cohen, the president ...!

... in order to redeem ourselves, we'll need to put him through some rehabilitation process. Could you just imagine what the tabloids would say? 'New secluded science center performs unethical science experiments on innocent victim!'...

... bad enough we've still got the others here. What will become of them ...?

... I am unsure. I'm certain that *something* will work itself out eventually, but those other fools are not of our concerns ...

... but of course. Allan—was that his name? *He's* the one whose mind we nearly destroyed, *he's* the one that the government will make sure is corrected ...

... have you heard G. Duvall's proposals ...?

... G. Duvall? how has he gotten involved in all of this ...?

... he is in favor of sending the damaged subject back out ...

... back out? What could you possibly mean ...?

... back to the Outside. Back to the world from which he's come...

... oh, what nonsense! That's just suicide! Sooner or later, word will get out, for sure—do you not understand the seriousness of this, Cohen? One slip-up spells not only the end of you, but the end of this entire city, as well!

… that much is true, but I think G. Duvall knows what he's doing. I also think it's best, at least at *this* stage of the game, to do what he says. If there's one friend that everyone needs to maintain in this place, it's *him*. He may be young, but he certainly will be vital in keeping later endeavors a secret …

… I suppose you're right …

… we're worrying ourselves too much right now. Everything will work itself out. We repent, we send him away to whatever treatment is suggested, and then we ship him out with a new identity into the real world again. How hard can it be …?

… we will see in time. Yes, we will see in time …

As if it has been stored in my memories for years, the secretive plotting of this sick district lingers as a sour recollection. More shattering, however, is this next bit of secrecy that is revealed, a realization that kicks me out of this empty void and into total unconsciousness.

The Doctor towers over me in a scene from more than thirty years ago:

Virtually, Cohen's appearance has remained the same; his flaming beard and freakish stature are well preserved on the screen. Thanks to all sorts of genetic alterations, this Evil has been preserved for all of eternity—he has rendered himself immortal.

"How foolish can you be to rebel against something that doesn't even exist?" shrieks the **Serpent**. "Dawson, Dawson, Dawson—

what a joke! How on *earth* did you ever manage to conceive such a character? Face the truth, dear Oizys, face the truth: *Dawson is not real and has never existed.* He is merely a symbol of *monotony*; he represents your *dissatisfaction* with everyone else around you! I give you props for creativity, but that's about it, my friend. And how *crafty*, too! It is beyond me how any of you drugged-up fools could have ever garnered a *following*, but I applaud you for that as well. Tsk, tsk, tsk. Dr. Dawson … how incredibly absurd! How does an impudent shithead like you muster enough arrogance to believe he *could change the world*? Save such things, young one, for people like myself, your god *Kratos*.

"Oizys, you are both a wise, young man and a childish fool at the same time. Your duality is *astonishing*. I shall have fun with you, I'm sure, twisting and turning your brain in all sorts of ways.

"And the best part—or at least I so believe—is that you can never ever escape! You are doomed!"

… so the Doctor has proven himself right. I fade away slowly into a world of embarrassment, shame, and failure: this is the final hour.

*   *   *

I reawaken somewhere else, though to my surprise, I'm still *alive*. My head aches, but after a few moments of self-consoling, I'm able to withstand the pain. I lift myself up from the lab table I'm sprawled upon and scan my surroundings—I am unfamiliar with this particular laboratory. Aside from a few shelves and cabinets, the faces of these walls are starkly pale. Nothing in here is especially striking. The lighting is incredibly dim, so I can just about see past a few feet in front of my face. I pull myself up, stretch, and set my feet down upon the ground, anxious to fulfill my … *mission*.

I can sense His unwanted presence, I can smell His disgusting flesh; He's around here *somewhere*. This bloodthirsty barbarism cannot be quenched by anything but destruction and *will not* be quenched until my mission is complete. I've got a program to follow, you see, a program that's been *beaten* into my brain. There's no use in fighting this agenda, because I know the chemicals that inhibit me are far too strong. I am unconcerned with saving myself, I am unconcerned with saving anyone else: the only thoughts that pass through my mind now are explicit visions of death—*His* death.

So I bolt off of the lab bench and begin searching for whatever I can use as weapons. Mindlessly, I throw things around, smashing and trashing and bashing stuff just for the sake of obliteration. I find myself roaring in rage, stomping around the room like the very animal I've become. Here's a scalpel ... and here's a knife of sorts ... oh, and here's a mechanical drill (I of course can't help but rev it up and prance around the room hysterically). Joy of the strangest sort pumps through my veins. I open every cabinet and drawer only to ruthlessly hurl out its contents, stomping on whatever comes within reach. Don't you know that this is what I live for? *All* I've ever lived for?

After what seems like hours of my empty-headed demolition, I realize that my simple destructive bliss has distracted me from my original intentions. I pull myself together and resist turning back to wreak more havoc. I close my eyes in meditation, using my newly acquired sixth sense to scout out ... *The Enemy.*

He is not far; He lurks nearby. He is waiting for me, I think, to make the first move, but I will not degrade myself in such a way. Only a fool charges anxiously into battle, and I certainly am not of that caliber.

I decide to sit here in the open doorway of this lab (which leads out into an endless stretch of hallway) and wait. I cross my legs and enter a tranquil state. The various killing tools I've acquired sit beside me patiently, waiting to be put to good use. I close my eyes and enter a reclusive world of my own. I am ready for the Fool when he strikes; I am ready to take Him *down* ...

Hours pass by, though I have not budged an inch. I remain here silently, submerged deeply in my pool of thoughts.

After a long while, there is a twinge from deep within my brain, a sudden spasm that compels me into motion. My mind enters overdrive, a whirring display of graphic images.

I charge out of the room, only to find that my energetic sprint collides into that of another.

The Enemy and I are at last face-to-face. Luckily, he demonstrates no sign of remorse. This match shall be a fair one; the fight will be well fought.

Darren lurches toward me first, though I swiftly doge out of the way. We are both equipped with various forms of butchery, all of which are made use of. Blinded by sheer adrenaline, my mind ceases to compute pain as it normally would. The hall fills up with our dense war cries, an angry din of peril. The Enemy tries to end things once and for all with a furious slash of his blade, but I successfully dodge out of the way and score a powerful blow across his face. He is sent hurtling to the ground instantly, giving me just enough time to grab his legs and drag him back to the lab from which I've come. Ruthlessly, I stomp all over his face, wrecking his jaw and facial structure. The struggle that this vile slime exhibits glorifies me, fills me up with a feeling of total victory.

Once I have dragged Darren through the hall and to my destination, I slam the door shut behind us so he cannot escape. He's too beaten tired to get up and save himself. For sure I've won this fight, so I release a wailing cackle as I drive my foot directly into his gut. This causes him to cough up strange fluids and cry in total agony. I decide to tear the cabinets and shelves off the walls and fling them down into Darren's fidgeting body. *Crunch.* Some internal structure of his is shattered in half.

Once he's reduced to a whimpering heap of tattered flesh and broken bones, I crouch down (aided by a particularly sharp cutting knife that I've found) and begin slicing open his belly. At this point, I think, Darren is too tired to resist; he silently shuts his eyes in pain and allows me to go forth with my agenda.

I dispose of the thick layer of skin I've just removed with an agile thrust, peering maliciously into the window of internal organs I've just created. What am I to do next? Shall I attack the kidneys? Or the liver? Or the stomach, or even the *heart*? After a few moments of contemplation, I'm stormed by a brilliant idea.

I begin untangling all thirty-odd feet of his intestines, torturing my victim with occasional nicks here and there. My hands are drenched in human blood, but that does not stop my rigorous course of action. I don't doubt that Darren has already *died* by now, but just to make sure, I stretch out his intestines half way across the room and light the severed end on fire. Tens of feet away, his body lurches around until it can no longer quiver. The room is filled with the stench of burning flesh. Enchanted by an artistic vision, I take his unraveled innards and wrap them around his neck, forming something of a pink, fleshy noose. I pick up his demented body and hang him from a jagged structure that once kept a cabinet of sorts in place.

Squish, squish.

The expression fixed across Darren's face exhibits pure horror— quite a sight to behold. I step back to mull over the wreck I've created. Indeed, it is *beautiful.*

The sound of footsteps approaching from a long way down the hall catches my attention. It is the Doctor; aided by a sinister chuckle, he advances toward me slowly. "Good, my boy, very good." Surprised by the brutality I've demonstrated, he utters, "You've outdone yourself, by far!"

He hoots more loudly than before. The pleasure he seems to receive from the chaotic mayhem I've created fills my body with ecstasy. Once his musings are over with, he withdraws a pistol from his long laboratory coat.

Cohen hands it to me prophetically; the master needs

not to instruct, for I know what I am to do. I have fulfilled his preprogrammed mission, a mission issued unto me by God.

"And for the finale?" he asks, rubbing his hands together anxiously.

His face glows like a supercharged lantern. I bring the gun to my head and press forcefully down upon the trigger.

epilogue

The black of sleep slowly wanes away.

It's been five long years now since we've been free. I don't reflect on the matter very much anymore, but I've stumbled upon something that I haven't come across in ages.

I lift up my aging manuscript gingerly and skim through its pages, suddenly accompanied by the presence of a peculiar, nocturnal breeze. The others are sleeping, so I shouldn't bother to wake them up.

The time has come for me to ... *do it in*. That's right—there's no need for me to hang onto it any longer. It's served its purpose, that much is for sure. It has spoken to me in a dream and asked for a proper burial; all great things burn out rather than fade away. It'd be nice to revisit this old work of mine and add a formal conclusion, but I shall not fight intuition; I never readily have and never readily will.

I gently step into the obscure scene of shrubbery amongst which we live and am warmly greeted by the fading night's air. Sunrise is on its way, so I must get on with my intention before the coming of the new day.

Sometimes ... sometimes I feel as if there's always something *else* that surrounds me, that there's this omnipotent presence that simply *understands*. It is a massive force, I believe, one not to be toyed with or taken lightly. It is not the presence of God, or at least I don't think it is, but it certainly is something incomprehensible. There is indeed an ever-present consciousness that surveys humanity. Most of us are too caught up in this modern, pretentious nonsense to recognize it, and therefore it passes by unnoticed. I'm quite convinced that this power is the "faith" that I so passionately believed in when I was younger; I always knew something was there, but never was sure exactly what it *was*.

And I'm *still* not sure.

But as I clutch this manuscript tightly and behold the coherence of the microscopic particles that perform the spectacle of tangibility, I suddenly am convinced that some sort of mind possesses all that is lifeless as well. There are countless eyes and shrewd minds present in nature, and these are the judges that we can't help being naked before. They strip us down by virtue of their own will and sift through pretentiousness and passion. These are the judges that *know*. These are the judges that make the *real* decisions. They are lost and forgotten, but secretly and silently still persevere. It is because of this natural jury that I am blessed enough to ponder such things at all, for I had *died* and was brought back to life again. This is the jury that has watched over and understood me for my entire life.

I don't smoke much anymore, but something about this mystical atmosphere compels me to light a cigarette. I breathe in its polluted excretions and for a moment am transported back to the good ol' days. I indulge in these memories for quite some time before then striking five or six more matches, igniting my manuscript in flames.

In just minutes, it has irreversibly turned to ashes.

And now for how we—Seth, Greg, Juan, Allan, and I—managed to wind up where we are today.

The story is actually quite simple.

Months after my pre-programmed "suicide," Dr. Cohen made the great mistake of frequently over-purchasing large quantities of morphine. It was not before long that he and his so-called "nurses" had become metabolically dependent upon it. There arose suspicion from the stock companies, who then further brought the matter to the attention of the CIA. Representatives were sent in for investigation under a warrant of sorts, and of course this spelled disaster for old man Cohen. His schemes had seemed infallible, but his overt drug reliance helped destroy his obsessive, self-conceived empire. The brutality of his experiments leaked out into the mainstream media, and there arose a widespread fear and disgust of the science world in general. The government needed to do something, something *quick*, something that would coincide with the timing of Cohen's much hyped trial. That something, to my great fortune, I suppose, was the rebirth and rehabilitation of me and my friends.

The Doctor, over the course of many years, had established a virtual database that contained all of the Core's memories ... ah, now *there's* a phrase that I haven't used in years. (Allan's artificial memory bank was obviously the least extensive, but we've managed to catch him up on the times.) Anyway, "rebuilding" us was deemed a simple task by many of Cohen's scientific peers.

And so it was done.

There was heavy contemplation between authorities regarding whether or not our "reconstructions" should enter public knowledge, but thanks again to an informational leak, they did. Much controversy arose, most arguments claiming that such "rebirths" simply succumbed to the evils of our "biosocial" era. At the end of the day, though, the Core was rendered new once again. I know it's a foreign notion to comprehend, but things fell into place within a matter of days.

After a few minutes, my cigarette deteriorates to just a nasty butt, so I toss it away and light up another. Trapped between my lips, it gives birth to a swirling cloud of smoke. Again, I am shrouded in the nostalgia of my youth.

And then there was the so-called rehab center that we were sent to, something conceived as a publicity stunt on behalf of the government—their "public apology," their showing of mercy to our "poor, fucked up" souls. It's strange, *really strange*, now that I think about it: once we were up and running normally again, it was like only a single *day* had passed since the Core last met, as if only *hours* stood between our adolescence and the seemingly endless years of Dr. Cohen's torture. The love between us was restored, both untouched and unharmed.

At this point in our lives, we just wanted to be left alone. Here's a little quick life lesson: when things suck, people *rarely* ever want sympathy. People just want you to agree with them that indeed, things *really fucking suck*. It's that simple.

We still wanted what we always wanted, even in the years of adulthood: *freedom*. It was something we'd been deprived of all our lives, and certainly, none of us were ready to surrender the little time we had left to political compromises.

So we did what we'd done years before—we made a run for it.

We escaped the rehab center less than a week after we were transferred in. That's right. We broke the confines of that governmental cage, for we were and always *will* be the *Cage Breakers*. Now more than ever, our silly name makes perfect sense. Eventually, you realize that everything around you conspires in your favor; it's something that's been said before, but not something that's said *enough*.

Here, amidst this woody Californian vegetation (on the complete other side of the country from where we'd begun), the disconnection we've always sought finally has been achieved. The nonsense of society can no longer reach us here. It's just impossible. Our dues have been paid—excessively, at that—in the real world. No politics or laws or national affairs can affect us now; indeed, we've *won*.

It is arguable that fools like ourselves are the downfall of this "perfect" modern era, but who are we humans to try to make things perfect anyways? The *audacity*! We'd be crazy to ever go back out … *there*. I've learned more from this secluded forest than from anywhere (or any*one*) else. Nature is the most comforting classroom with the most patient teachers. The songs of twittering birds, the branches of prodigious trees, and the great shadows cast by whatever passes by have far more knowledge to offer than any pompous degree.

My second cigarette draws to an end. As I stomp it out, a sound from deep within the forest catches my attention. The sound repeats itself, this time closer in distance. It is unmistakably the low grumble of a bear.

The grizzly beast emerges slowly, materializing eventually out of a distant furry speck. I am not in fear of it—the creatures that inhibit this land share it peacefully with us, for they understand our situation perfectly, perhaps even *better* than other humans can. When we'd first retreated to this secluded haven, I terribly feared the hungry carnivorous predators that lurked among us. Allan then explained that no one relates to you better than the things—(both living and non-living)—that you're surrounded by every day. I'm reminded of a story that he once told me, one that parallels this present episode.

When he'd been "exiled" from Cohen's city, Allan was left emotionally destroyed. Fear, paranoia, loss, and failure all consumed his senses. Brainwashed that he was unable to report his dreadful circumstances back to the law, the rest of his life spent prior to my liberation were mindless years wasted away emptily in the woods. One morning, after a strange dream of which no details can be recalled, he'd encountered a bear wandering 'round just as meaninglessly as himself. The two then silently conversed in a language of sacred ambiguity. All sorts of realizations careened down upon him. It was in fact that very encounter that motivated him to reemerge in Cohen's world and save me. He was rejected a number of times, but persisted valiantly for years. In attempt to rid the world of the one remaining free man that was once part of the Cage Breakers, Cohen used some sort of bribery to convince the City's officials to allow Allan entry under the pseudonym of *Darren*.

If not for that courage inspired arbitrarily out in nature, I'd surely still be just a prop in the Doctor's gruesome puppet show.

There's a mutual bond between us and the animals here, something that's unspoken of and obviously incommunicable. Many times I catch them marveling at the simplicity of our living quarters— just a heap of well-constructed stones and wood. The animals here *respect* that; we're on the same wavelength as them. They don't understand that over-civilized wreck out there, and to be honest, neither do we (nor do we care to … that *crazy* world is a part of our past).

The bear looks down into the ashes of my burnt manuscript and then back up at me. I'm not sure if what my mind perceives is particularly accurate, but it seems to me that the bear is *smiling*. Its muscular body struts with a delighted sense of unity. Indeed, there is no doubting that it can read my mind. I've said it once and I'll say it again—people in the real world are too *blind* for this sort of stuff, and *that's* why I've always needed to get out of it. I *understand* the natural wonders this beautiful world wants to share. They're right in front of us, right at the very tips of our fingers.

The bear turns away with a sense of satisfaction. In just a single instant, I understand who this bear is and what it is a manifestation of. Here, in the flesh, is my life-long and ever-passionate faith. It represents all I've ever believed in. A wave of astounding happiness pours over me. I am told by a secret voice that I've now achieved all I've ever dreamed of—after sifting through the perils and nonsense of Life, I've reached that intimate realization that can only be understood by the beholder himself. This rapture is quite rare amongst people, especially nowadays, so this voice congratulates me on my very spectacular reward.

"Not many people achieve such a marvelous state of being," It states wisely. "You have indeed won the fight, child. Certainly, your fabricated world of Dr. Dawson and the Dawsonites is a rightful critique of this deteriorating modern era.

"The Enemy is dead. You've at last overcome the challenges that nature has burdened you with."

A gentle wind is summoned up, and the ashes of my past are swept away into eternity. I look up to face the bear once more, but it is gone. Instead, I catch the sight of an old friend—*a bald, bearded,*

and unusually short one—playfully running through the woods into
nevermore. I want to call out to him, but I stop myself.

His time has come and gone. I no longer need his assistance.

I turn back to our home of sticks and stones, satisfied.